It Came upon a Midnight Shear

A RIVERBANK KNITTING MYSTERY

ALLIE PLEITER

BERKLEY PRIME CRIME
New York

BERKLEY PRIME CRIME
Published by Berkley
An imprint of Penguin Random House LLC
penguinrandomhouse.com

Copyright © 2022 by Alyse Stanko Pleiter

Knitting pattern by Mitzi Thomas

ISBN: 9780593201824

First Edition: November 2022

Printed in the United States of America
1   3   5   7   9   10   8   6   4   2

Book design by George Towne

For Emily

It Came

upon a

Midnight

Shear

CHAPTER ONE

T hose eyes.
They were heart-stoppers. Large, brown, and soulful. I could stare at this guy's eyes for hours and not feel the time pass. As it was, I was barely aware of the Christmas carols playing on a loudspeaker. As much as I loved "It Came upon a Midnight Clear"—it was my favorite carol, after all—the melody's beauty couldn't match these eyes. Even the decorations behind him in the shop window, a joyful collection of green, white, red, and silver hand-knit stockings on a mock fireplace, weren't nearly as distracting. There was no street, no sound, no holiday rush. There was just me and him.

He blinked—a knowing sort of blink that let me know he was aware of my stare. I swallowed hard, transfixed. I'd seen pictures of him, videos even, but he was finally here, live, right in front of me. Talk about your yuletide treasures—any breathing woman would swoon.

He wasn't a brute; he was elegant and sophisticated. I watched him turn his head regally, as if to prove he didn't need to look at me like I needed to look at him. And then, after a moment of denying me his magnetic gaze, he looked at me again. Deeper this time, I swear. I've always been a goner for a great pair of eyes, but these were magnificent, framed with the kind of thick lashes women would die for.

I stepped a bit closer, feeling hopelessly drawn to him. I'm too old to fangirl anyone, but he was a celebrity. One of a kind. I'd probably never get the chance to be this close to him again in my lifetime. I was dying to touch him, to see if he'd feel as fantastic as I was certain he did. So I took one more daring step closer.

And then he spit on me.

After all, vicuña are a close relation to camels and alpacas, and both are notorious spitters.

I blinked and reared back, the shock of vicuña spit on my cheek blasting me out of my stupor.

"Pardon Zorro's bad manners," came a deep voice from behind me. A linen handkerchief held by a tanned hand floated into my field of vision. "He's not always a gentleman in new surroundings." Vincenzo Marani held up a chastising finger to his vicuña charge. "You should never spit on a woman like Libby Beckett. You should revere her." Still, a wry smile crept across his face as he turned back to me and wiped my cheek. "But I did tell you to take care if you got close."

He had indeed. I felt a flush of embarrassment at being too smitten to follow directions. "You did." I noticed the elegant *VM* embroidered on one corner of the brilliantly white linen square. "I'll wash this and get it back to you."

Vincenzo held up one hand. "Please, no. It can be yours. I have dozens—for obvious reasons. And I suspect you will need it again if the rest of Zorro's herd does not mind their manners." He shrugged. "I try to make up for them, but . . ."

Vincenzo Marani, otherwise known as the Gallant Herdsman, did a pretty good job of making up for his uncouth companions, if you ask me. The vicuña were intriguing and cute—rather like overgrown Bambis with wildly expensive coats—but I'd never use that word to describe Vincenzo. The man was stunningly handsome and suave. I'd spent the last three months researching his career and the small herd of vicuña he would bring here for his visit. Despite devouring a lot of articles and videos, I still hadn't figured out how he managed to pull off his beguiling aura of rough-hewn elegance. The man was as captivating as the animals he had brought—maybe even more so.

The sold-out tickets to his event at my yarn shop Y.A.R.N. the next afternoon were a testament to the man's charms. Vincenzo was somehow posh but not pompous, luxurious but still low-key. He could somehow live in the exclusive world of the Italian fashion design house his family ran and yet still dig into a great American cheeseburger. Charisma on a monumental scale.

All of which made his appearance the perfect event for my shop. Some attendees were drawn by the chance to experience the ultra-luxurious, ultra-exclusive fiber that came from vicuña. I had described the fiber to my friend Margo as "the knitter's Lamborghini." But probably just as many—if not more—were here for the Gallant Herdsman scheduled to demonstrate shearing them.

Y.A.R.N. stood to benefit either way, so as far as I was concerned, it didn't matter. This shop had been my dream for so long, and it thrilled me to think our second holiday season was set to brilliantly exceed our first.

"Will they be okay here?" I asked as Zorro's three companions, Agua, Pisco, and Rica, walked over from the other side of the small pen we'd set up in my shop's backyard. I was spending the next few days playing temporary landlord to a tiny herd of the world's most expensive fiber source. Well, that and Vincenzo's gleaming Airstream motor home, which now sported a small wreath on its door made of red and green balls of yarn with a pair of knitting needles tucked in one corner. One of my very artistic customers, Arlene, had made it for me to give to him as a welcome present. The trailer and pen took up so much of the backyard that we were going to have to set up chairs in the parking lot for the shearings. A great problem to have, in my opinion.

"They look very happy to me." Vincenzo's silky baritone somehow became silkier. "You are an excellent hostess." He actually took my hand and kissed it, like in the movies. "I am so glad to be here."

Normally, that sort of thing is met with a groan and an eye roll from me, but somehow the Gallant Herdsman made it look like the deepest of authentic compliments. The New England zoo from which his borrowed herd had come—you don't exactly just walk out of Peru with the national animal and most prized livestock—told me Vincenzo is the only non–zoo personnel the vicuña have ever accepted.

It wasn't hard to see why. The man had been in my yard all of six hours and I felt like Santa had brought me my heart's desire for Christmas. Honestly, Vincenzo could probably charm me—or anyone—into just about anything.

"I still can't believe we were able to make this happen." I tried not to sound breathless. "Vicuña can only be sheared once every three years, and you're going to shear four of them right here in Collinstown."

Vincenzo gave a small whistle, and the four animals

came right to him. No spitting involved. He looked at them with the same love I show my English bulldog, Hank. They looked at him with the devoutly loyal affection Hank shows me.

"They are magnificent animals," he declared. "I am happy to be able to show them to the world." Vincenzo gave me a wink and moved close enough that I could smell his expensive cologne. "But I will admit the very sizable donation the Marani family makes to the zoo on their behalf does help things along."

Many knitters knew the story of how the Marani family had championed the cause of Peruvian vicuña and the villagers who tended to them. House of Marani was internationally famous for its luxury clothing and textiles. I'd once drooled over a woven Marani vicuña shawl—until I saw the $2,600 price tag. Marani coats went for upward of $20,000. My very wealthy, very regrettable ex-husband was the only person I'd ever known to own anything from House of Marani. The rest of us couldn't ever hope to move in such seriously high-brow spheres.

And Vincenzo Marani was the epitome of high-brow. Everything about the man—his clothes, his manners, his gleaming top-of-the-mode transportation—spoke of vast wealth and impeccable style. I could easily believe his family had made a donation to the zoo large enough to make *anything* possible—including the ability to take these four animals on tour in the name of conservation and education. No one else had ever done such a thing.

And I'd convinced him to come here and shear the herd as the Christmas event for my shop. Vincenzo's arrival felt like my finest professional victory, and worth every minute of the complicated process of setting it up. I grinned. "Every business here in Collinstown has come up with some special offering for our holiday festival, but this? This is a whole different level of special."

Vincenzo stroked the neck of one of the vicuña, and I swear her big eyes fluttered in bliss. "A testament to Collinstown's Chamber of Commerce president, yes?"

I'm sure I blushed like a schoolgirl. "Well, the yarn helps."

"It is amazing, isn't it?" He continued stroking the animals with a loving reverence. "Did you like the skeins I sent over?"

Like? Vicuña yarn defies words. You think, "Nothing could be worth that kind of money" . . . until you touch it. "I haven't stopped touching it. I'm still trying to decide what pattern is worthy of it."

"I predict you will sell every one of your skeins by the time I am finished shearing. A fine holiday for your shop."

"I don't doubt it." I'd sold one already. Anytime someone balked at the $500 price of the fiber, I simply lifted the top of the lidded crystal bowl I kept them in and let them touch it. 'Nuff said.

Still, I'm not really doing this to sell yarn. I'm doing this for the sheer blissful experience of being close to something that luxurious. Not many things in life are perfect, but this comes close. Really, really close.

Vincenzo looked past me to the decorations now going up all over our main street, Collin Avenue. Only about a third of the wreaths, garland, and lights were up and the place already looked like a snow globe. "You know I am looking forward to spending this weekend here with you," he said in a voice that hinted at a dozen things. His features shifted, a wariness filling those dark, alluring eyes. "But I think you should know . . ."

"Marani!" came a shocking voice from behind me. "You devil, you! How do you manage not to age a bit?"

I was catapulted out of my bliss with the same force as Zorro's ill-mannered spit. That voice belonged to my aforementioned very regrettable ex-husband. And he was coming down the shop driveway.

CHAPTER TWO

"...Sterling is coming," Vincenzo finished needlessly. The Italian's expression told me he knew how big a bomb of bad news he'd just dropped—and how much I would not welcome the visitor coming down my driveway.

I wheeled around with none of the elegance of my companions, four-legged or otherwise. "Sterling!" It wasn't a greeting. More of an exclamation. Maybe even an expletive.

Sterling held up a not-quite-apologetic hand, a gesture of condescension I'd come to despise. "I should have called, I know."

"Yes," I said, trying very hard not to hiss. I'd been fending off most of his calls this month. He'd been making noises about renegotiating our divorce settlement, and I was having none of it. Evidently Sterling felt that the success of Y.A.R.N., something he annoyingly referred to as my "little project," changed the financial game plan.

To say that I did not agree was an understatement. I absolutely, wholeheartedly rejected the very idea.

"Why are you here?" It suddenly occurred to me that Vincenzo had known about Sterling's arrival. I wheeled back around to my guest. "How did you know he was coming? And why haven't you told me about it before just this minute?"

"Relax," Sterling cut in, walking right past me. "I called him about Adelaide, and we got to talking about his visit." I felt my jaw hang open as Sterling shook Vincenzo's hand. It was not an especially friendly shake. They'd been buddies in college, but I had gotten the distinct impression the men were no longer as friendly as Sterling used to boast they were.

In fact, Sterling seemed oblivious to the frost I was sensing from Vincenzo. "It's been years. You couldn't expect me to know Vin was so close and not meet up with him."

Yes, I could. Actually, I did. Sterling has never darkened the door of Y.A.R.N., and I've been just fine with that. Pleased, in fact. And I was rather annoyed that he'd picked *now* to show his face. I could have sworn the pine boughs gracing my front entrance were recoiling their needles in distaste. I certainly was.

I turned to look at Sterling. My ex-husband reeked of money and power as much as Vincenzo exuded elegance and luxury. Perfect hair, pressed and starched shirt, crisply pleated khakis atop high-end loafers—pick your upper-class trappings, and Sterling had them. I could just see the red fender of his Alfa Romeo parked on the opposite side of the street. There was a time when Sterling's affluence mesmerized me. Now, I'd seen enough of the man underneath to be mostly put off by it. These days, I preferred the heart of my handmade crafting to the boasting of Sterling's custom tailoring. When you get right down to it, maybe I always had.

What I hadn't yet noticed—but now saw Vincenzo staring at—was Sterling's belt. It was an oddly exotic choice for his usually classic old-school money taste: snakeskin.

Vincenzo raised a dark eyebrow, lips pressed tight while his eyes were still glued to the accessory. "Really?"

Sterling's hands went to the gleaming buckle. "It's my favorite new souvenir."

Even though I was pretty sure I didn't want to know, I asked, "Is that . . . real?"

"Yes," Sterling and Vincenzo said at the same time. Sterling said it with pride; Vincenzo said it with disdain.

Ick, I thought. As much of a souvenir as some taxidermy bounty from a safari. My ex-husband had changed a lot—and not in ways I liked.

"What's this about Adelaide?" I asked, mostly so we could stop talking about the garish belt Sterling seemed so proud of. At least it wasn't snakeskin cowboy boots—those would have been so far off Sterling's character I might have requested a psych evaluation.

Sterling took off his tortoiseshell sunglasses and pushed out a breath. "She's done her disappearing thing again."

Sterling's younger sister, Adelaide, was a dramatic, slightly flighty woman who still managed to be my favorite member of the Jefferson family. Granted, that's not saying much, but she at least had a touch of genuineness about her, which I could never seem to find in Sterling or his mother. The senior Mr. Jefferson—evidently a pillar of business wizardry who had amassed a sizable fortune—had passed away before I began dating Sterling.

Vincenzo's look changed to one of concern. "Still no word?"

"She and Mother are fighting. Again. I told her you'd be here for Libby's little thing and I thought maybe she'd get in touch."

Libby's little thing? The only live vicuña shearing on the Eastern seaboard—maybe the whole country—is *Libby's little thing??* I momentarily wondered if I could swing the large plastic candy cane sticking out of a planter to my left with sufficient aim. Or give in to my petty yearning for Zorro's spitting skills.

"She hasn't." Vincenzo tucked his hands in his pockets. "I'm not sure what I'd say if she did, to be honest."

I'd forgotten, until just that moment, that Vincenzo and Adelaide had been a thing. A brief, dramatic, not-happy-ending thing. Even I know dating your fraternity brother's little sister, no matter how smitten she is with you, is a dicey proposition at best. Sterling and Vincenzo had gotten into a massive fight over it, but as far as I knew, they'd smoothed things over.

But had they? There was never a shortage of drama with Sterling's family—something I was happy to leave behind. In all honesty, I think I would have liked to keep in touch with Adelaide. She always struck me as the only Jefferson who seemed to live in the same world as the rest of us. Sterling and his mother, the immutable Bitsy Jefferson, lived in a place far above the rest of us mere mortals—or so they would have you think.

Sterling forbade all family communication once I did him the tremendous dishonor of calling him out on his infidelities. That radio silence had suited me just fine, and until recently it had worked both ways. Now, though, I was forced to dodge relentless communication from both Sterling and his squadron of lawyers, armed with requests I had no intention of honoring. All talk of Adelaide aside, I was pretty sure this surprise appearance at Y.A.R.N. only meant he was upping the pressure campaign.

"Is there something you need, Sterling?" I hoped my words dripped with the impatience of a woman whose "little thing" was keeping her quite busy at the moment.

"I came to see Vin. And you. You haven't returned my calls."

Vincenzo clearly knew an igniting argument when he saw one. "Perhaps I should go see to the herd." With that, he walked back toward the trailer, leaving me to square off with my ex.

"I have attorneys for that sort of thing, Sterling."

My ex-husband applied a gleaming smile. On Vincenzo, it looked captivating. On Sterling, it felt glaring.

"Shop looks cute, by the way." He tossed the compliment to me in the same way I toss a dog treat to Hank. I did not share Hank's appetite for placation. "All that holly and ivy. And the little knitted things everywhere." Sterling shrugged and sighed. "Collinstown always did look great at the holidays."

I kept my gaze level, cold, and silent. All the "little knitted things" were impressive examples of gorgeous craftsmanship by myself and my talented customers. Charming crocheted ornaments and bright color-work scarves, cozy mittens and dramatic shawls filled the front window he had described as "cute." I gritted my teeth and told myself not to let his patronizing tone get under my skin.

"Come on, Lib," he went on. "It's Christmas. Be reasonable."

I have never liked Sterling's tendency to shorten everyone's name. As if most people weren't worth the energy it took to say multiple syllables. On our third date he made the mistake of calling me "Babe." The resulting look I gave him could have melted every icicle on the North Pole. He never did it again.

"Cut it out, Sterling. I'm not renegotiating." I had been reasonable. I'd been more than reasonable. More than one lawyer told me I could have taken Sterling to the cleaners. Still, I never had any interest in a slash-and-burn divorce. I just wanted enough funds to allow me to do what I was doing now: run a beautiful yarn shop and live a decent, happy life.

Momentarily thwarted, Sterling switched topics back to the shop. "You seem to have done pretty well for yourself."

He managed to sound just surprised enough to give the compliment a backhanded air. In a million subtle ways, Sterling had made it clear he was certain I couldn't succeed. He'd conveniently forgotten the rising career I'd had as a pharmaceutical sales rep when we'd met. I'm sure to him I had merely been an appropriate accessory to his stellar life.

"Yes, I have." I'd turned a colonial home into a charming retail shop, filled with places to gather, gorgeous fibers and supplies, and very good coffee. I had a strong and steadily growing customer base. I was now president of the Collinstown Chamber of Commerce and in charge of the holiday schedule of events about to launch in our little town. "Pretty well for myself" indeed.

Halfhearted compliment delivered, Sterling leaned in and got down to business. "So did you look at the papers my guy sent over?"

It was a telling detail that Sterling referred to any member of his staff at Sonesty Pharmaceuticals as "my guy." As if they were possessions rather than people. And, even more regrettably, he referred to all female staff as "my gal." It set my teeth on edge just thinking about how I'd inexplicably fallen for this man years ago. Only his owning the company could allow such an HR nightmare to continue—and even then I suspect it was a challenge.

"I had my attorney review them, yes."

Again the gleaming, inauthentic smile. "And . . . ?"

"The answer is still no."

I began to wonder if Sterling had really come to see Vincenzo or if he was simply using him as an excuse to wear me down face-to-face. Disgusted, I left Vincenzo tending his tiny herd and began walking toward the front of the shop.

Sterling hurried after me. "Let's go to dinner tonight, the three of us. For old times' sake. What do you say?"

I had already made reservations for Vincenzo and me to dine at the Blue Moon, the best Italian restaurant in Collinstown. I had no intention of including Sterling in my plans. "Absolutely not."

The man almost pouted. "We can do better at this. It doesn't have to be this way."

I would have liked Sterling to "do better" at marriage. I'll go to my grave wondering how all the graciousness and compassion he showed me while we were dating evaporated into thin air once we married. I didn't much care for Sterling's self-centered definition of "wife." It didn't give me much confidence he was capable of the complexities of a post-marriage friendship. Quite frankly, I didn't want one. I'd fought long and hard to craft my life beyond him. With no children or family ties to bind us, I saw little reason to go back on that now.

I tried a kinder approach before he irked my blood to a

boil. "I don't want to do this, Sterling. Please don't try to pressure me just because you've gotten some new idea into your head. Go live your life, and I'll go live mine."

"Well, I'm at the Riverside Inn tonight if you change your mind."

He was staying in town? For the night? When he lived only an hour away in DC? Why?

"I won't," I replied as firmly as I knew how. "Please believe that."

Sterling looked at me as if I was just some new account he still hadn't figured out how to land. "Well, maybe not *yet*."

Something was up with that man, but I was in no hurry to find out what.

CHAPTER THREE

I stomped back into the shop, annoyed that Sterling had managed to show up now, of all times. In ten minutes he had ruined my elation at Vincenzo's arrival and the gorgeous animals soon to wow my customers.

I walked past the display of plush red, green, and white knitted scarves, ignored the scents of peppermint coffee and gingerbread cookies from the shop table, and dismissed the cheery laundry line of holiday-themed mittens strung from the wall on my right. I was too peeved at how fast Sterling seemed able to steal my Christmas, a Grinch in Gucci loafers.

Sterling Jefferson is no longer in charge of your life. He can only disrupt what you allow him to disrupt. I made straight for the crystal punch bowl, lifted the lid, and fingered the precious skeins of yarn. I took a handful of deep, calming breaths. *Don't let him rile you. He can't take what you don't allow him to take.* So help me, that was going to be nothing.

"You okay?" My new shop employee, Shannon, looked up from attaching a silvery pom-pom to a bright green hat and fixed me with a look of concern. "Trouble with Mr. Marani?"

"No," I replied, replacing the lid. "He's wonderful, actually. I can't think of the last time I met someone I'd describe as 'debonair.'"

My deep breaths lured me to the solace of our coffee machine. Good coffee is essential to the Y.A.R.N. experience, so there is always a pot of something warm and soothing ready to pour for a customer. Or, in this case, me.

Shannon peered out the back shop window that looked out over the new encampment behind the shop. "Well, if he's as charming as he is handsome, that's not hard to believe." She lowered one eyebrow as she set down the hat. "But you still don't look okay."

I debated just how much to say. I had liked Shannon the minute she came for a beginners knitting class a month ago. She was smart, determined, and outgoing. She had that eager-to-learn adventurousness about her that made her take to knitting quickly and with a wonderful enthusiasm. So when I realized the store had been doing well enough to bring in a second employee for the holiday rush, she was the first person who came to mind. She'd mentioned she was looking for a "new start," and I certainly understand that feeling. I asked, and she started the next day. She'd been here for two weeks, had already managed to make two items for the church's hat-and-mitten drive, and had given me a reason every day to be glad I'd brought her on board.

That didn't mean she needed to hear my emotional baggage over Sterling's surprise appearance. The story of Sterling and me was a long soap opera I didn't want to dump on my new employee.

I settled for saying, "My ex just showed up," certain my tone of voice communicated just how I felt about his arrival.

"Oh." She assessed the sparkly pom-pom's position atop the hat before offering a timid, "Um . . . sorry?"

"Sorry indeed," I muttered as I dumped quite a lot of peppermint mocha creamer into my coffee. "He wants something. Well, something else other than the revisions to our settlement he's been pressing me for. I just don't know what it is yet." I certainly had no intention of giving him one minute more of my time and attention today. Vincenzo was here, and that was where my focus needed to be.

"If you get a call from a Sterling Jefferson, I am not available. Ever."

Shannon checked off an imaginary box with her finger in the air in front of her. "Gotcha. What if he comes in?"

"I don't think he will, or he'd be in here already." He'd clearly somehow decided I was doing well enough to be free of his support. He'd never been the kind of person who felt compelled to back up his assumptions with facts, so he wouldn't come in to do research. Sterling somehow simply decided the nature of the world he lived in, and more often than not, it manifested itself around him. It felt both a strange kind of admirable and decidedly unfair.

I gazed around the shop I'd just ignored while making my stomping entrance. *Look at this place*, I told myself. *Look at the success you've made*. Red and green holiday items were everywhere, but they were just part of the rainbow of sumptuous yarns around me. Blues, purples, creamy whites, and vibrant yellows spilled from cubbies and baskets and shelves all around me. Sparkly yarns celebrated the season while a host of soothing neutrals spoke of cozy winter evenings. An intricate Nordic holiday sweater stood next to adorable white fuzzy baby booties. A dozen scarves in a host of colors and patterns led customers to an endless choice of possibilities. Softness and creativity were everywhere. Creative people came here, and people became creative by coming here. What better definition of success is there?

A schedule of classes—my first full season of them—hung on the wall to my left. And to my right, what is perhaps my favorite detail of Y.A.R.N.: the blackboard. I had opened this shop as the fulfillment of a long-deferred dream. My biggest regret of my time with Sterling was how I'd ignored my own creativity. To me, Y.A.R.N. stood for "You're Absolutely Ready Now." I installed a large blackboard with the letters—and their meaning to me—painted at the top. Customers were invited to draw their own meanings on the board, and many had.

Yearnings Are Relevant Necessities

Youthful Attitudes Rouse Naughtiness

Yogurt Ain't Really Nutritious—no one said only truth could be written up there

Yardsticks Are "Ruley" Notions

Just this morning, someone had added **Yuletide Art Recalls the Nativity** and drawn a little Christmas Star next to the words.

The blackboard was one of the most wonderful, artful things about Y.A.R.N. I doubt someone like Sterling, however, would ever appreciate it. Vincenzo, on the other hand, had noticed it and loved it within minutes of first walking into the shop. I was hoping that sometime during his visit here he would add his own interpretation, and looked forward to whatever it would be.

The shop door opened and my best friend, Margo Payne, walked in from the Perfect Slice, the pie shop she owned across the street.

Her dubious look cut a sharp contrast to the cheery blue and white snowflake sweater she wore. She handed me a set of thick brown mittens. "One of my customers brought this in for the church drive. But first, please tell me that was *not* who I thought it was."

Margo has been my best friend for ages. She was my maid of honor when I married Sterling. She was also the person who picked me up off the floor and held my hand while I built my new life after my marriage went down in a blaze of infidelity.

I merely nodded as I handed the mittens off to Shannon. Okay, I probably added a dramatic moan—but wouldn't you?

"What is he doing here?"

I tossed my thick cream mohair wrap onto the chair beside me and let the moan fade into a long and weary exhale. "Trying to convince me I ought to accept his new settlement terms. Clearly my multiple no's over email and the unanswered phone calls didn't do the trick."

Margo planted a hand on one hip. "That's why God gave us lawyers." Shannon gave a small laugh at that and placed the mittens in the bag beside the counter, where we were collecting donations of hats, scarves, and mittens for the church to pass on to a local homeless shelter.

"Yes, well, Sterling has always given new meaning to the word 'persistent.' I used to think it was a virtue. I've revised my position . . . on that. Not on our much-litigated and agreed-upon divorce settlement."

Hank came trotting out of my office. He often sports knitwear, and today he was looking as debonair as Vincenzo in a red-and-white-striped sweater with green trim. Hank knew that Margo usually brought cookies, so he sauntered up to her in expectation of today's treat.

Margo leaned down to greet Hank with a thorough scratching behind his ears. "Oh, sorry, honey," she consoled. "I was in too much of a huff to remember your goodie. Next time, I promise." She straightened back up to look at me. "Why now? It's the holidays and you're in retail. Any idiot should know this is no time to sweep in and play hardball. Every business in town is busy. I guess the pharmaceutical business doesn't have a holiday rush."

"Oh, I don't know," Shannon offered with a wry smile. "All that holiday stress." She picked up the hat she'd just finished and added it to the bag beside the mittens Margo had brought. "I'd bet antidepressants and anxiety meds are flying off the shelves."

Given the current state of my blood pressure, that might be true. I knit when I'm stressed—or worried, or excited . . . or just breathing. I'd been doing a lot of knitting lately, despite the holiday rush Y.A.R.N. was enjoying. "He's using Vincenzo as an excuse. They went to college together, but that was before I knew Sterling. He tried to get the three of us to go out together for dinner tonight."

"Oh, I'd forgotten their history. Vincenzo came to your wedding, didn't he?" Margo motioned to the trailer pen behind the shop where Vincenzo was occupied stringing Christmas lights onto the awning of his trailer. "That was back before all this Gallant Herdsman stuff, wasn't it?"

I smirked. "Yes, back when he was just the lowly aristocratic son of an Italian clothing tycoon." They'd been fraternity brothers, and Sterling had often boasted of the friendship he had with someone who was so wealthy and influential. "Once Vincenzo veered away from high-end

Italian clothing and toward the less glamorous world of Peruvian livestock, Sterling lost interest. Or so I thought."

Margo peered out the window. "Doesn't look less glamorous to me. Looks like a bunch of Bambis and Prince Charming are glamping out in your backyard."

I managed a laugh at the description. It was a bit over-the-top, but still close to accurate. "Sterling won't ruin this." I straightened my shoulders. "I've created a one-of-a-kind experience for Collinstown and my customers for Christmas, and it will succeed. This shop is going to have a fabulous Christmas. So am I." For emphasis, I toasted Margo with my coffee.

"Joy to the world," Margo replied. "And God bless us, every one."

Hank stared at me as I buttoned up my coat and added a bright red feather-and-fan stitch scarf. "You're going to have to stay home tonight."

If anyone ever tells you dogs cannot sulk, don't believe it. The phrase "sad puppy eyes" didn't come out of nowhere. Despite his festive sweater, Hank looked positively heartbroken. I normally let him stay at the store when I am downtown on Collin Avenue for the evening, but not tonight.

"You wouldn't like the current guests in our backyard," I explained to assuage my guilt. "They'd bother you, and you'd bother them." Hank had somehow caught on to the fact that I was going to limit his access to Y.A.R.N. while the vicuña and Vincenzo were staying there, and he made sure I knew how he felt about it. He is normally a very well-behaved dog, but part of me was worried I'd come home to a chewed shoe. Or six.

I squatted down on my heels, giving him a big smooch

and a scratch behind the ears. "It's only for a few days. Then I promise Y.A.R.N.'ll be all yours again."

I grabbed my keys and handed him a compensatory shortbread circle from Margo's—his favorite treat. He took it, but with a reluctant expression that said, "Even this doesn't totally make up for you deserting me."

"I'll be back before you know it," I called as I headed out the door for the short walk to the Blue Moon restaurant, where I had arranged to meet Vincenzo.

Halfway there I found Collinstown's mayor, Gavin Maddock, in a very un-mayoral place. The man was perched up on a ladder, fiddling with a wreath attached to one of the historic light poles that dotted Collin Avenue.

"Gavin?" I called. "What are you doing up there?"

"It fell off," he said, grunting as he stretched to wrap a length of wire from the decoration around a hook. He looked like an updated version of the chimney sweeps from *Mary Poppins*, right down to the cheery scarf I knew his teenage daughter had knitted him for his birthday last year. Since I'd taught her how to knit, Jillian Maddock was one of my youngest—and most favorite—customers.

She was also one half of the two-person matchmaking team—the other half being my mother, Rhonda—bent on returning Gavin and me to our high school sweetheart status. We were resisting, mostly. But I'd be lying if I said there wasn't something of a slow-burn romance growing between us. Just a very slow burn.

"Don't you have people for that sort of thing?" I teased. "Public works? Streets and beautification?"

"Larry's wife went into labor." Gavin finished his duties and came down off the ladder, as if hanging wayward holiday decorations was on the "other duties as assigned" part of every mayor's job description.

Larry Bishop was, in fact, our town's one-man public works department. Despite being an hour from DC, Collinstown is as small-town as they come. It's one of the reasons I love the place.

"Ooh, a Christmas baby," I cooed, visions of candy cane–striped hand-knit baby booties dancing in my head.

Gavin leaned against the ladder and smiled. "I know that look. And Jillian beat you to it. She was looking up baby hat knitting patterns when I left." He pulled the work gloves from his hands. "I figured it'd be just as easy to take care of this myself as find someone else to do it." For all Vincenzo's highbrow suave, there was an authenticity to Gavin that I'd always found hard to resist. He stuffed the gloves into his pocket. "How's your goatherd? Settled in?"

"Herdsman," I corrected. "Vicuña are from the camel family."

Gavin's resulting expression told me he didn't see much of a distinction. I at least gave him points for not calling Vincenzo a shepherd—given how one of the local sheep farmers had sent a flock of spray-painted protest sheep down Collin Avenue this past spring, I'm not sure Gavin would have considered it a compliment.

"Besides," I went on, "it's not Vincenzo or the vicuña that are my current problem."

Gavin folded up the ladder as the red bow from the wreath began to flap cheerfully in the slight evening breeze. "What is?"

"Not what, who." I gave Gavin a frown to match Hank's. "Sterling. He's here."

Gavin's eyes went wide. Given our mutually disagreeable divorces, Gavin and I often traded war stories about inconsiderate ex-spouses. Usually it was Gavin's ex-wife,

Tasha, who took top billing, but tonight it was most definitely Sterling. "Sterling's here?"

"He says he's here to see Vincenzo—they went to college together—but I don't think even Vincenzo believes that." I checked my watch, not wanting to keep my guest waiting at the restaurant. "Sterling tried to horn in on my dinner with Vincenzo, but I said no. Repeatedly."

"Where's dinner?" Gavin didn't quite succeed in making his question totally casual.

My answer wouldn't help matters. "The Blue Moon." The place was both Gavin's favorite and mine. We'd had several not-quite-dates there. "It's our best Italian, after all," I added, feeling an uncomfortable need to explain my choice.

"Makes sense." Gavin's tone dipped a little toward a grumble. If we had "a place"—which we most certainly did not—the Blue Moon would be it. Just because it was nice doesn't mean it was romantic. I certainly couldn't have taken an important guest like Vincenzo to Tom's Riverside Diner for a cheeseburger, excellent as they were there. "Enjoy your dinner." His words didn't match the prickly look in his eyes.

"As long as Sterling keeps to his word and doesn't show up, I will."

The prickly look turned into a hint of playfulness. "Want me to call Frank? Maybe find a reason to tow Sterling's fancy car?"

While I was fortunate enough to call our chief of police, Frank Reynolds, a friend, that was pushing it. "Tempting, but it's still not illegal to be supremely annoying."

"Too bad," Gavin replied, hoisting the ladder over one shoulder with an athletic ease. "Otherwise we'd have been able to arrest King George years ago. He's still in a huff about how well all this is going." Gavin nodded toward the festive holiday decorations and the sign beside us announcing the special town-wide tree decorating ceremony scheduled to take place the night before Christmas Eve. All kinds of people and businesses were donating—and in Y.A.R.N.'s case, knitting—ornaments for the soon-to-arrive big tree. This holiday celebration was going to be the high point of my first term as Chamber of Commerce president, having beaten "King George" Barker for the position earlier this year.

Everyone was excited. Well, everyone except George. To no one's surprise, George had been a spectacularly poor loser, finding fault with this and almost everything I did. Gavin's stalwart support was one of the things that most kept me going, if I was honest. We made a good civic team, the mayor and I. The personal stuff? Well, we were still figuring that out.

"Have a good evening *with* your herdsman and *without* your ex-husband."

I tried to make sure my smile was warm and friendly. "Thanks. I'm sure I will."

As I continued my walk down Collin Avenue, the beauty of my hometown filled me with happiness and pride. Things *were* going well. The streetscape of shops looked like a postcard, with holly and ivy boughs dripping from every window and red bows and silver bells in all sorts of nooks and corners. The whole town looked ready for a Norman Rockwell snowfall to dust it with a silvery frost. Even the weather had gotten into the spirit, offering up sunny days that were crisp but not too cold, seasonable but not Siberian.

I indulged in the notion that my leadership in the Chamber of Commerce had convinced the shops to go the extra mile this year. Surely the windows that charmed every passerby with a nostalgic glow were more beautiful than in years past. More wreaths glinted in more doorways while an extra dose of white lights gave the streetscape a magical twinkle. Even the part of the Chester River that I could see seemed to boast a world-record sparkle from the creamy half-moon that peeked between clouds.

I wiggled my fingers in my thick woolen mittens and gave a satisfied sigh. This was Collinstown at Christmas. This was home. Sterling, in all his greedy Scrooge-iness, could never steal this from me. Certainly not this year. I had an amazing event, I had all the friends I could ever need, and I was about to share an exquisite meal with a very handsome and charismatic guest.

Life was very good indeed.

CHAPTER FOUR

Vincenzo gave a satisfied smile. "You're right; this is excellent."

Seeing as my guest appeared to be a man who often had the best of everything, I found that high praise for the chef's cooking. "I'll be sure to tell Tony the next time I see him. This place is my favorite."

"You brought me to your favorite." Vincenzo said that as if it meant a dozen things. He was clearly flirting with me, and I didn't know quite what to do with that. On the one hand, my failed marriage had given me an immunity of sorts to being swept off my feet with money and status.

On the other hand, Vincenzo's attentions were intense and, admittedly, flattering. Who wouldn't want a man like that—a man connected with the world's most luxurious yarn, to boot—paying you the kind of compliments Vincenzo had been paying me all evening?

I took another sip of wine as an elegant string quartet version of "Silent Night" wafted through the room. Leaning on one elbow, I asked, "How did you get into this?"

He cut his veal Parmesan with the precision of a surgeon. "The vicuña?"

"All of it." I had read his online biography and knew a bit about his life, but I wanted to hear him tell it.

He sat back, settling into the story with a lavish satisfaction. "The Marani family has been in the clothing business for four generations. Always the finest fibers, the best tailoring. A Marani garment is a work of art. 'A treasure to own, a pleasure to wear,' my father always said." He smiled—a dashing display of gleaming teeth that, while magazine-worthy, still managed to feel completely genuine. He raised one dark eyebrow. "It wasn't as if I could go off and become an accountant."

"Not you, no." I laughed at the vision of the man in front of me clocking hours behind some mundane corporate desk. It seemed impossible. Vincenzo Marani seemed to be born for great things—his exclusivity seemed to waft off him in irresistible waves. "But you did take a different tack than the rest of your family. You don't sell clothes."

Now he laughed and waved his hands in a grandiose manner. "A Marani does not *sell* clothes. A Marani *provides* you *fashion*." I got the impression he was mimicking his father. Then he gave me a grin and said, "It's just a pesky detail that a lot of money is involved."

"Pesky detail, hm?" I teased. I have often found that only really wealthy people can dismiss money in such a way.

"I wanted adventure," he went on. "The boutique or the warehouse was never for me." He leaned in. "Although I am an excellent salesman."

"Oh, I don't doubt that for a moment. But it's a long way from there to the mountains."

"When the vicuña fiber became hard to come by, my father became interested in the problems of the endangered animal. He admired the cloth above all others, and chose to see what our family could do about it. We made a trip to Peru to see the people and the dwindling herds. That trip changed my life. I could never go back after that."

"You and your family have made a huge difference." It was true. Many people attributed the Marani family with being the biggest source of private funding behind the rescue effort. An Italian family helping the Peruvian people save their national animal from extinction—it was a great story.

Vincenzo put a hand to his chest. "The vicuña are my passion. My life's work. I have had many advantages as a Marani, but my favorite is to be able to wield our family's money and influence to save them."

Despite the fact that I had banished Sterling from my thoughts for the evening, I couldn't help but recognize the distinction I was hearing. Sterling's family wielded their money and power only to serve themselves. The Jeffersons rarely gave to charity—only when I had asked them to or they found something that gave them some business advantage. Looking back on my time as Sterling's wife, I couldn't recall a single donation where higher motives like those Vincenzo spoke of came into play.

"Do you go to Peru often?"

I admit, the trip had crept its way up my list of dream vacations.

"I spend about a month there at least twice a year. The people of the mountain village are like a second family to me. And of course, I am always there for the shearing. Those years I end up staying closer to two months."

"I watched a documentary. It looks like an amazing thing." Since vicuña can only be sheared once every three years, the event of bringing them in and shearing the valuable coats is a full-community festival. Despite his current fancy attire, I could easily picture Vincenzo among the crowds driving the herd down the mountain to the waiting women and children, who would guide them into shearing pens. He was such a striking combination of elegant and rugged.

He nodded to the tiny sprigs of holly and frosted berries that were our table's centerpiece. "Not so far from what you are doing at Christmas, yes?"

What I had envisioned for Collinstown's community-wide holiday event felt a pale comparison to Vincenzo's description. "Well," I admitted, feeling a bit foolish, "it actually is what gave me the idea."

"I knew it," he said, looking pleased with himself. "It is part of the reason I said yes to your request." Vincenzo rested his chin in his hand and gazed at me. "Tell me about how you thought it up." He looked as if he'd be enthralled to know. I couldn't have resisted telling him even if it was a state secret.

"Six months ago, I stumbled across the footage while looking at some other fiber videos. You know, the one of women and children in the Andes holding hands and ropes to guide the vicuña herds into the pens."

"There is so much joy in that day," he commented. "So much hope."

"Exactly," I agreed. "I saw that and thought, 'That's just what Collinstown needs to feel.' Thirty minutes later I had the idea to pass the ornaments down the street hand to hand from the town hall to the tree by the river. Everyone can be involved. Instead of just gathering to watch it light up, we all take part in decorating it."

"Madam President," Vincenzo said with a dramatic formality that felt more teasing than mocking, "Collinstown is fortunate to have you."

"Chamber of Commerce president," I corrected. His tone made it sound like far more than it was.

"Good leaders lead however and wherever they are called. For you, it is yarn and businesses; for me, it is yarn and vicuña. We are rather alike, you and I."

I don't know that I'd agree with that. Vincenzo seemed to be in a different class of humanity, swishing through life with grace and style, while I was just sort of making it up as I went along.

I changed the subject off me. "However did you get the zoo to go along with your plans?"

"That was far from easy. I will admit, the hefty donation from my family supporting the zoo does help. But they need to be shorn, and this way it isn't just a matter of their care—it becomes a way to tell people about the animals. They know I take excellent care of them, and we donate a percentage of all our profits to their conservation." He grinned and spread his arms wide. "And I get to play hero."

I couldn't help but reply, "You're very good at it."

Vincenzo picked up his wineglass. "And I get to meet smart, wonderful women like you." He leaned closer. "How does Sterling not know what a fool he was to let you go? I would have come here even if he hadn't asked, you know."

I just about choked on my own wine. "Sterling *asked* you to come? How did he even find out about it?"

"Back when I did the first one of these, at the zoo rather

than out on the road, he mentioned how much you would like it. We had a conversation about Adelaide a while after you opened the shop. He made it sound like he would consider it a personal favor if I came to Y.A.R.N." He registered the look on my face and added, "I thought you knew. Actually, I thought perhaps you'd put him up to it."

The very thought made my blood boil. "I would never use Sterling. For anything. How very like him to think I'd need his help to pull something off." I glared at Vincenzo. "Please tell me you didn't do this as a favor to him." My pride in my self-sufficiency was bracing for a sizable hit.

"No. I did it as a favor to you. I had eleven shops request the event. Sterling was not the reason I chose yours. You were. But if you did choose to wield Sterling's influence, I would not hold it against you. I wield my influence for good. So do you. Sterling, not so much—as we both know."

I shouldn't have been surprised that Sterling had tried to insert himself in my victory. Vincenzo was right—it was squarely within his character to do something like that. My ex-husband liked to believe he was the catalyst for everything, but why this, and why now? Was he trying to make me believe I still needed him to succeed? That made no sense for someone pressing me to cut the financial support I received from him.

"He's up to something," I admitted.

Vincenzo's features tightened. "Sterling is *always* up to something."

I looked Margo squarely in the eye the next morning as I stopped in her shop to pick up some shortbread and pie for Y.A.R.N.'s big day. "Today's the day. Nobody gets to steal my joy today."

"That's the spirit," Margo said, wielding her pie server as if it were the famed Zorro's sword. Margo is such a loyal friend that I had no doubt she would defend me with any number of kitchen implements. I would brandish knitting needles with the same enthusiasm on her behalf without hesitation. "And if Sterling tries anything, you leave him to me. And Carl. That husband of mine will happily play bouncer for you. We'll keep that rat out."

I gazed out Margo's shop window at my own gorgeous display window, my wonderful carved wood shop sign, and the sheer perfection of my storefront. Green pine boughs framed the windows, with sprigs of holly and berries at the corners. From here you could see the row of red and white candy cane stockings hung across the mock fireplace in the window. Next to it, under a tree decorated with a yarn-ball garland, a cheery wealth of green and red hats, mittens, and scarves erupted out of shiny wrapped present boxes. Two small pines, decorated the same way, sprouted out of the planters on either side of my red door. The trees outside my shop even sported their own holiday sweaters, festively yarn-bombed last weekend at a Christmas craft party cooked up by my mother Rhonda and her gang of friends, who everyone called "the Gals."

My shop looked exactly like I'd pictured it, and that gave me no end of pleasure. "Actually," I declared with a magnanimous air, "I've decided I think Sterling *should* come. He should see what a success I'm having."

That caught Margo by surprise. "I thought you never wanted him to set foot in Y.A.R.N." She closed the lid on the second of the two boxes she was packing up for me. It was my personal law that all Y.A.R.N. events included refreshments from the Perfect Slice pie shop, today included.

"That was before Vincenzo told me Sterling felt he

needed to step in and lend his hand to help poor Libby secure the vicuña event."

Margo's eyebrows furrowed. "He didn't."

"He did. Vincenzo didn't fall for it, and he'd already made his mind up to give the event to Y.A.R.N. before Sterling decided to step in and try to play power broker. Unnecessary, unneeded, and unwanted power broker."

Margo slid the boxes across the counter to me. "I don't know. I don't think that man is capable of sitting back and letting you have the limelight today. Limelight you deserve."

"He *will* sit back," I declared with all the conviction I could muster. "And if he doesn't, I'll have a tall, dark Italian armed with a set of very sharp shears to back me up." I shoved my fingers through my hair in a shearing motion.

Margo giggled. "Sterling was always so proud of his perfect hair. I'd pay anything to watch Vincenzo shear it off."

I was just peeved enough to laugh at the cruel thought. "I'll keep that in mind." Still, Sterling was like any bully. The best way to defeat him was to ignore him.

"Have a great event this afternoon. But if you don't, Carl and I will be there just in case."

I scooped up the boxes, walked across the street, and pushed open the shop door to the surprising sound of an argument.

"You can't do it that way. It won't match the records," came the annoyed voice of Linda Franklin, my longtime assistant. Linda doesn't get riled easily, so this caught my attention. "That's probably how you lost it."

Shannon was standing behind the counter, hands planted on her hips, looking just as irritated as Linda. "I didn't lose it."

"What's going on?" I asked Jeanette, an exceptional sock knitter and one of the Gals, who was seated at the gathering table in the center of the shop. I moved a large pile of sparkly white yarn to make space for the treats on the table.

"They're fighting," she whispered, giving me a pained look from over the top of the snowman socks she was stitching.

Her whisper wasn't quite soft enough. "We're not fighting," Linda defended. "Shannon lost a skein. Of the vicuña."

"I did *not* lose it."

"Well, you didn't sell it, and it isn't here, so you lost it." Linda gaped angrily at me. "She's been here not even a month and she loses the most expensive, exclusive fiber we have to sell? Today?"

Shannon's chin tilted up. "This is exactly why I was saying you could use a better inventory system."

In all my excitement over being big enough to need two staff people, it never occurred to me that they might not get along.

"Our inventory system works just fine," Linda snapped.

Shannon looked at me. "Have you lost any stock to theft before?"

We had—any retail establishment does—but never enough to be a problem. My customers were as loyal as Margo. Tiny as Jeanette was, she or any other of my regulars would probably tackle anyone they found trying to walk out of the store with unpaid merchandise. I certainly was in no hurry to get all strict and accusatory about it. Y.A.R.N. was a welcoming place, and we assumed the best of the people who crossed our threshold. But something as expensive as the vicuña . . .

I was opening my mouth to offer that reply when Linda shot back, "*Some* loss, but not right under the nose of a clerk *and* the priciest thing we sell." Linda had large expressive eyes, but currently they were trained in a dark glare on Shannon. "That's *new*." Linda said "new," but it was clear she meant "you."

Poor Jeanette winced and looked like she couldn't get out of this conflict fast enough. "Maybe I should just go."

I couldn't have my employees scaring away my customers. "Oh, Jeanette, please don't." I held up a hand the way I'd seen Chief Reynolds do in confrontations. "Let's all take a breath here and not make assumptions. Are we sure the yarn isn't just somewhere else?" Expensive as it was, vicuña came in small balls about the size of an orange. I'd kept two of the dozen balls we had on display in a lidded crystal bowl, but the other nine were locked up in the stockroom. Now only one ball sat in the bowl. It was unlikely the other had been moved by an unsuspecting customer.

"Did you check to see if both were there before we closed the shop last night?" Shannon asked.

"No," I had to admit. "I was so thrown by Sterling's appearance that I don't think I did."

Linda's strawberry blond brows nearly shot to her hairline. "Sterling is here?" Yesterday had been her day off, but she'd been working at Y.A.R.N. long enough to know what a shocker that news was. "Why?"

I caught a hint of an exchange between Linda and Shannon at the mention of Sterling. Shannon looked understandably put out at the "You're too new to know why that's important" look Linda sent her way. How could I have missed the friction building between those two? They'd been fine when Shannon was a customer, and I always assumed knitters got along with one another. That evidently isn't true.

"I'm still trying to work that out," I replied. "But Sterling wasn't in here. And while he is a lot of things, I don't think 'yarn thief' is among them."

"I don't know," Linda muttered. "This is Sterling we're talking about." She had heard the worst of my stories, and I had told her about his latest campaign to change our divorce settlement on account of Y.A.R.N.'s success.

Jeanette hurriedly tucked the snowman sock into her knitting bag. "I really think I should go. It's . . . um . . . senior discount day at the grocery store." It made my stomach ache to think she was fishing for an excuse to get out of the shop. "I want to use my coupons before the shearing demonstration." Before I could stop her, she had scurried out the door.

Y.A.R.N. was supposed to be a creative haven, a safe space. I swallowed my frustration and said, "I'm sure it will turn up," with a confidence I did not feel. That was $500 worth of yarn we were talking about. I didn't want to start feeling like we needed to lock up all vicuña where nobody could see it. "Why don't I go out and check on Vincenzo and the herd?" I fought the urge to add, "If I can trust you two to stop bickering."

I walked out the back door to the yard behind the shop, refreshed by the pastoral little scene that greeted me. The four vicuña stood happily munching on feed, raising their heads to gaze at me with lush, doe-like eyes. The vicuñas' pen had a pine garland and wreath. The whole setup had taken on exactly the happy holiday glamping atmosphere I had hoped to achieve.

For all their tiny enclosure and decor, the vicuña looked

happy to meet me. "Good morning," I called to them in a cheery voice. "Today's the day. Which one of you goes first?"

Vincenzo came from behind the trailer, hauling a small platform with a V-shaped extension on one end. "You use a platform?" I asked. I'd seen something similar used to shear cashmere goats, but none of the videos I'd seen had used one with the vicuña.

"It's not the traditional way, but I've trained them to get used to it. And it makes for better visibility." He planted the heavy wooden platform on the ground with ease. "No one wants to watch me wrestle an animal to the ground, and that takes more than one person anyway."

Given Vincenzo's rather impressive build, I couldn't say I wouldn't find that entertaining, but I did appreciate his thinking. We were expecting a sizable crowd, and I wanted them to be able to see this amazing skill.

"In answer to your question, it's Rica I'm shearing today." He held up what looked like an overgrown set of barber's electric clippers, only with extra-long—and very sharp-looking—comb blades. I gave Rica an appreciative smile. I'd want to make sure whoever came at me with those had a lot of skill and all my trust. She walked up to Vincenzo and poked her nose at his stomach as if to reassure me this was true.

"Good thing we're not shearing all of them at once," Vincenzo said. "I'll need time to sharpen my shears in between animals, seeing as my other set's gone missing."

"Something's gone missing for you, too?" I wanted to gulp that admission back down the moment I said it. I wasn't in a hurry to admit we'd "misplaced" some of his exquisite yarn.

"My other set of clipping shears. Probably just my own mistake." He held up the implement. "I can get by with one—it won't be a problem. What is missing for you?"

"My nerves," I lied, trying to cover my tracks. "I can't seem to find all that clever confidence you spoke so highly of last night."

Vincenzo smiled. "All will be fine, *cara mia*. I guarantee a wonderful day."

CHAPTER FIVE

It was like watching a choreographed dance. Or a skilled sculptor creating a masterpiece. Every person in the audience Saturday morning was mesmerized by the way Vincenzo wielded his clippers. As he did, he offered a narration about the vicuña and the value of their fiber so that it wasn't just theater, it was a conservation education. Even with all I knew about the subject, I found myself just as fascinated as everyone else in the audience.

Police Chief Frank Reynolds, however, did not share my enthusiasm. In fact, he remained dumbfounded as he stood beside me watching the crowd applaud at the end of Vincenzo's demonstration. "I just don't get it." No matter how many times I praised the qualities of vicuña fiber, Frank just could not get his mind around the idea of that much money for *yarn.*

Vincenzo released the harness that held Rica steady and supported on the platform with a *"Finita!"* flourish. I swear she flaunted her new haircut as she happily leapt off the structure to join her companions. I know there are people who consider shearing an animal to be wrong, but Rica looked as pleased as anyone would be with a stylish new coiffure.

With a practiced skill, Vincenzo folded and tucked what had been sheared into a tidy roll and then walked among the audience. "Feel how soft it is even before we process it. And the color—like the finest caramel, yes?"

Sitting in the first row, my mother and the Gals were the first to reach out and touch the fiber. "Caramel's my favorite flavor," Mom said, even though I knew her to be a big fan of chocolate. She cooed as she and the other women ran their hands over the softness. "Who wouldn't want to knit with this?"

Mom had a habit of forgetting where she put things, so while she had free range of most of the shop stock, I admit I would hesitate to send her home with vicuña. It might end up in the compost bin or "safe" in some location she'd never remember. Besides, she's not really a luxury kind of woman. She'd be just as happy with a good angora.

"It's wonderful," Arlene, another of the Gals, said from her seat next to Mom. "If I had a scarf of this I'd never take it off."

Vincenzo touched the caramel-colored scarf he always wore. "Oh, I can assure you, that's true." He smiled in such a dashing way that I heard actual sighs come from the Gals—and a moan of exasperation from Frank.

"Oh, stop," I teased the chief. "You're just as romantic as he is when it comes to Angie." Earlier this year we'd finally convinced Frank to go public with the town's most adorable senior office romance: his courtship of police department receptionist Angie Goldman. Rumor had it they were getting "very serious," and most of Collinstown joined me in looking forward to the day Frank would work up the nerve to make it official.

"I trust you will all come back tomorrow when we shear Pisco and Agua," Vincenzo announced with the theatricality of a circus ringmaster. "Then, tomorrow night, Zorro will be the grand finale."

The cheer of the crowd told me Vincenzo was right: I had a hit on my hands. People had come from six different states to see the Gallant Herdsman do his thing. At my shop. Nothing could put a dent in that kind of satisfaction.

"Livestock. Again. Honestly, Libby, is there anything you won't stoop to in the name of publicity? Couldn't you do a *normal* Christmas promotion like the rest of us?"

George Barker's rant told me I might be wrong. Actually, *he* was in the wrong—in any number of ways. For starters, the flock of sheep that had sauntered down Collin Avenue to protest an event earlier this year hadn't been my doing. The second flock parade could have been called publicity, seeing as it had been in praise of Y.A.R.N., but that hadn't been my doing, either. This was simply George being George and grousing. Since the day I'd unseated him as Chamber of Commerce president, he couldn't find a way to forgive me for winning. Instead, George displayed an astounding talent for finding fault with everything I did.

I didn't even bother to address his grievance. "Merry Christmas, George. Would you like to meet the vicuña? They're very sweet." *Unlike you*, I snarked in the silence of my mind.

"I can see deer at the National Zoo in DC," George huffed. "And I have a groomer for my dog."

I simply rolled my eyes and walked away . . . right into a sight just as unpleasant: Sterling. Some days a yarn shop owner can't catch a break.

"Nicely done," Sterling said, although his expression didn't hold anything I'd call admiration. "Vincenzo did well for you."

I had had enough. "How dare you insert yourself into my dealings with Vincenzo!" I hissed, walking right up to him. "I didn't ask you to, I didn't want you to, and I resent that you did."

He shrugged. "Just trying to help."

"No, you were just trying to show off how important you could be. You know, I can't tell if you want me to fail so you can feel like I need you or if you want me to succeed so it will cost you less. Which is it, Sterling?" Mercy, but that man could push my buttons. The audience was staring as they streamed around us out of the event, but I didn't care. This was going to stop once and for all.

"I will not renegotiate," I declared, not caring who heard. "I will not let you out of our settlement. This is a free country, but if you get a craving to buy some yarn, I'll ask you to go somewhere else."

Mom and the Gals stared at my uncharacteristic outburst. She reached out to touch my arm, probably to calm me down, but I waved her off.

"You are no longer welcome here, Sterling. Not in the shop, not at any event. If you have anything to say, say it to my lawyer, but so help me, if you ever darken the door of this shop again, I will make sure you regret it."

Even George turned around at the shrill tone in that threat. I knew I was making a scene, but all the frustration of Sterling's recent annoyances had run off with my good sense.

I jabbed an angry finger at him. "You will regret it, and deeply. Am. I. Clear?"

I heard Vincenzo walk up behind me. "I think the lady means business."

"Oh, so now you're taking her side?" Sterling's eyes narrowed, insulted.

Vincenzo pulled himself taller. "That's just it, *mi amico*. I've always been on her side."

I couldn't believe it when Sterling lunged at him. How had this gotten so far out of hand? Vincenzo pushed him off with an ease that only infuriated Sterling. Had Frank not stepped in, I might have had an all-out brawl on my hands.

"Break it up, gentlemen," the chief commanded, stretching his hands between the two grumbling men. "Now."

"I always knew you were a fool about the things that mattered," Vincenzo muttered.

"And that was your problem, Marani," Sterling shot back, raising his voice enough that people all around us stared. "You never knew what really mattered."

I'd had enough of this nonsense. "Stop it, both of you!" If Sterling's raised voice hadn't caught their attention, I'm sure my shouts did. "Go back there and find something to do," I ordered Vincenzo, amazed at the command my frustration raised up in my tone.

Vincenzo looked a little shocked himself, but after shooting Sterling a dark glower, he turned toward the trailer and his herd. His exit knocked one of the Christmas bows off the pen, and he kicked it down the driveway with an angry grunt.

I wrestled my attitude under better control. "You are not welcome to come here and ruin my event." Sterling had never liked it when anyone issued him orders when we were married, and he certainly didn't take to my doing it now. Even though I knew I was irritating him, I couldn't seem to stop myself. "Stop making a scene in my shop."

He started walking down the drive as if my assertiveness wasn't worth his time. "I'm not in your shop. And you wouldn't even have this shop without me," he called with an infuriatingly dismissive air.

Oh, now that was a low blow. Yes, I had used the funds from our initial settlement to open Y.A.R.N., but Sterling did not enable my shop. I would have done it any way I could, with or without that man's—actually, *our*—money. No one would ever convince me Sterling's success hadn't been at least in part due to the support I gave him. Everyone else could see we had been a team, even if he would never admit it.

"Don't you ever make that statement again. I do not need you. While I deserve my share of our money, I do not need it." I stalked after him, suddenly determined that he hear my declaration of independence. "I can survive without it. I *would* survive without it if it means ousting you from my life. Honestly, Sterling, you're behaving like a child who can't get what he wants. Right now I don't think there is anything I wouldn't do to get you out of my life. Do you hear me?"

I stopped, suddenly aware we were out on the sidewalk in front of Y.A.R.N. I was dangerously close to ruining my own event, thanks to the edge Sterling was nearly pushing me over.

"Oh, I hear you," Sterling said with a mocking tone that made my blood boil. "I think they all hear you."

I was pulling in a breath to fire something back when I felt a hand on my arm. I turned to find Frank staring a silent warning at me, shaking his head. If that wasn't enough, the wide eyes of too many onlookers told me I'd gone far enough. I tamped down my anger with a deep breath, told myself I was better than this, and did my best impersonation of Calm Libby as I walked into the shop.

Tomorrow was a new day, and if there was any justice in the world, it would be a day without Sterling Jefferson in my life.

I had no idea how right I was as I was yanked out of my sleep by the sound of the front doorbell early the next morning. Yawning and annoyed, I padded to the front door in my bathrobe just as the sun was coming up. A small burst of shock ran through me when I noticed that the usual serene pastels of a Collinstown sunrise were disrupted by the sharp glare of flashing squad car lights.

My pretty little holly Christmas wreath rocked on its hanger as I pulled open the door to find our chief of police standing in the frosty morning air. He wore as dire an expression as I've ever seen on the man. "Frank?" I pulled my bathrobe tighter against the chill in the air and in his eyes.

"You need to get dressed and come to the shop."

Alarm iced my veins colder than the breath I could see in the air. "Why? What's happened?"

"May I come in?" Frank walked in, and my pulse skyrocketed as I realized he had Mom with him, looking like she'd seen a ghost.

"Mom, what's going on?"

She didn't reply, which meant something was really, really wrong. Mom had a comeback for everything.

Frank's voice was frighteningly official. "Have you been here all night? You went home after that scene with Sterling?"

"Sort of," I replied. "I took Hank for a long walk and

then came home to knit." Walking Hank had always been one of my favorite ways to calm down—next to knitting, of course. I knit to think, I knit to calm down, I knit to solve problems, and so I'd spent at least two hours last night making angry progress on a sparkly white cable-knit scarf. I'd finished nearly a third of the thing before the plush chunky fiber and the undulating cable design had calmed me enough to finally nod off. "Why?"

"Did anyone see you walking?"

That sounded like a very ominous question. "I suppose so. I don't know. Frank, why?"

"Sit down, Elizabeth." Mom's tone was tight and fearful.

Panic crept up my spine. "What? Why? Mom, why are you here? Will someone please tell me what is going on?"

Mom practically pushed me into the nearby living room chair while Frank took off his hat. In the spectrum of indicators of bad news, this was right up there. "Libby, I'm sorry to have to tell you that"—he wiped one hand nervously across his chin—"Sterling was found dead early this morning."

All the air fled the room in a single instant. I gripped the upholstery of the chair arm as the room tilted like a carnival ride. "What did you say?" I asked, even though I had heard Frank very clearly.

"Sterling has been attacked."

The words pushed through the room at me. My brain crashed the facts together in a strange slow motion until I gulped out, "Are you saying Sterling was . . . murdered?"

Frank's expression said "I'm so sorry" and "This is very serious" at the same time, both hitting me like a sucker punch.

"They found him out behind the shop, Elizabeth. On that thing Vincenzo used to shear the sheep."

"Vicuña," I corrected flatly, as if by remote control. "They're vicuña." I was both numb and feeling like I'd touched an electric wire. I looked up at Frank. "How?"

Frank was avoiding looking me in the eye, and I couldn't quite figure out what that meant. "A series of stab wounds along his carotid artery. Both sides. There's a mess over there right now, but we've got it tarped off so that no one can see it."

He crouched down in front of me. "Libby, I need to ask you again. Can anyone vouch for you being down at the river with Hank last night?"

It suddenly washed over me like ice water. "You . . . you think *I* did it?"

Mom's voice was beside me. "Honey, you made some awful threats to Sterling yesterday. People are talking. Frank's just doing his job; don't blame him."

I grabbed Frank's shoulder, which was probably not the smartest thing to do. "You think I killed my ex-husband? Me? Frank, you've got to be kidding me!"

"I'm afraid I have to treat you as a person of interest, yes."

The fact that I recognized Frank's "Let's all calm down" voice shot terror down my spine. "I did not! I didn't. Loads of people hated Sterling!"

"Well," said Mom, "loads of people did not declare they'd do whatever it took to get him out of their lives in the middle of Collin Avenue yesterday. It does complicate things."

I had certainly lost no love for the man in the last forty-eight hours, but I couldn't believe Frank would even for a moment consider me a suspect. "Frank, you don't really—"

"I need to follow procedure. It's not really up to me. I'll wait here while you go get dressed and I'll take you down to the shop."

Mom patted my hand. "I'll see to Hank and be down there in a bit."

I looked at Frank. "You called *Mom*?" I shouldn't have made it sound like such a drastic move, but I could think of several friends who would have been a better choice in a situation like this. My mother? I'm sure he was just trying to be kind, but my emotions were spinning all over the place.

"Please, Libby. Don't make this harder than it already is."

Hard? This was absurd. Impossible. Another murder was bad enough, but Sterling? This hit way too close to home.

Ten chaotic minutes later Frank opened the door of his squad car to let me out into a scene I could barely process. I pushed past the beautiful holiday decorations to find a small band of officers combing the drive and yard behind Y.A.R.N. Instead of twinkling Christmas lights, I watched the red and blue ambulance lights dance across a screen of white plastic. Just as Frank had said, a tarp had been erected around the space where the shearing platform had been. All yesterday's yuletide cheer had been swallowed up by a stark, ugly crime scene.

Another officer was talking to Vincenzo, who seemed to be trying to keep the agitated herd from jumping the pen fence. They were darting back and forth, making the shrill sound a video had told me was their alarm cry. I felt like one giant walking alarm cry myself.

When a gurney was wheeled out from behind the tarp completely covered by a white sheet, I thought I might keel over. Out of some strange impulse I started walking toward the gurney, but Frank stopped me. "Best not to."

At that moment Vincenzo's gaze caught mine over the wild scene, all his suave elegance gone. We were like frightened animals glaring at each other, total strangers to the two people who had enjoyed each other's company so much on Friday night. A primal, unstoppable surge of "Did you do it?" seemed to flash between us. After all, we'd both made a public display of our dislike for Sterling mere hours before.

I darted past the officers to push through the tarping. I thought I might somehow see something that would allow me to make sense of all this nonsense. What I found made me wish I hadn't. I lurched back out from the partitioned-off scene, leaning against the shop wall in an effort not to be sick.

"Libby, are you all right?" Vincenzo was suddenly beside me, despite an officer's attempt to keep us apart. He looked at Frank. "Is she all right?"

All right? I didn't think I'd be anything close to all right for a very long time. "I'm okay," I said, even though it was clear I wasn't.

Vincenzo made a small noise as an officer walked by with a set of clippers in a clear plastic evidence bag. "I'm telling you, those were in my trailer tool drawer the whole time," he insisted to the officer.

"And you're missing a second set of these. I heard you. But I'm still taking these in for examination based on the victim's wounds."

The clippers? "Were they . . . ?" I nearly whispered, unable to get the rest of the words out. I'd thought those things were sharp-looking before, but now the tool seemed downright sinister.

"We suspect so, based on the markings," Frank admitted. "The nine points match up, and they are sharp enough to do the job, if you know where to stab."

Stab. The word hit me hard. My ex-husband had been

stabbed with shearing clippers at my shop, perhaps by my VIP guest.

But as I looked around me at the faces of those nearby, one thing became frighteningly clear: several people thought perhaps by me.

CHAPTER SIX

I unlocked the shop door with fumbling fingers, overcome by a need to get away from peering eyes. Collinstown is charming, friendly, a bit quirky . . . but above all, it is nosy. Despite the early hour, I could be sure everyone would know about this fast—if they didn't already. I swear I could hear the buzz of texts and phone calls, as if a swarm of accusatory bees had descended upon me.

What now? I didn't know how to behave. A murder suspect? I couldn't think who to call or what to do. Hide? That would seem suspicious. Go about my business? That seemed impossible. My unfortunate experience with murders should have given me some insight, but being on this end of the investigation boggled my mind.

Who wanted Sterling dead? Lots of people didn't like Sterling. My ex-husband's talent for ticking people off was as stellar as his acumen for making profits. As such, I had no doubt there was a mile-long list of people who'd said mean things or hurled threats at him. My problem was I happened to be the most recent, the loudest, and the most public of them.

Still, it was a long way from threat to act, wasn't it?

I dashed to the shop bathroom and splashed cold water on my face—evidently people don't just do that in the movies. *Steady, Libby,* I told my pale reflection. *It only looks like you're a suspect. You're not. You did not do this. And you know how to find out who did. You've done it before; do it now.*

"Libby?" Vincenzo's voice came from the shop floor, reminding me that I was, in fact, not the only person in my position at the moment. "Libby, where are you?"

"In here," I called as I emerged from the washroom. It bothered my sense of vanity that even roused from bed and under investigation, Vincenzo still managed to look somewhat dashing. I, on the other hand, felt as if I looked like something that had washed up on the riverbank.

"Are you okay?"

Suddenly the requisite "I'm fine" didn't suit at all. "No," I said too loudly. "They just found Sterling dead in my backyard. I'm not fine *at all.*"

Vincenzo paced around the shop, letting out a long string of Italian that didn't really need a translation. "I can't believe it. Dead. Murdered." He paused right in front of the crystal bowl with the ball of vicuña yarn, then turned to me. "I didn't do it. I don't know who got those shears, but you heard me say a pair went missing. Tell me you believe I didn't do it."

Trouble was, part of me considered it possible. I could see how my hesitation wounded him. I managed to fumble out, "I don't think you're the kind of person capable of something like that," but the tone fell just short of confident.

"I did not kill Sterling," Vincenzo insisted, walking toward me.

I flinched. It made everything worse. "I don't know what to think about anything," I said. "I'm just . . . stunned. I'm upset." It wasn't much of an explanation.

Both of us startled as the air was again pierced by the high-pitched, brake-squealing sound of the vicuñas' distinctive alarm call. God or Mother Nature—pick whichever you think of as nature's creator—showed off incredible design skills on this bit of animal behavior. To me, it sounded like the animal kingdom's version of fingers on a chalkboard. I'd heard it three times already this morning, and it still made me jump.

Vincenzo peered out the back window toward the herd. "All this has them in a state. Even if I had any more clippers, or wanted to do it with manual shears, I don't think I could possibly do it now. I'm afraid we can't go ahead with things."

I hadn't even begun to think about what to do about the shop event. That seemed like a problem twenty steps ahead of the fog I was in now. "I suppose," I mumbled, unable to come up with anything more coherent.

"I should go take care of them. Probably call the zoo to come get them back. I don't think they should stay here, and your Chief Reynolds is telling me I can't leave until I have permission." His gaze bounced between the window and me. "But I would not leave you anyway right now. Not with what's happened."

He clearly was a suspect as much as I. But this tragedy had professional consequences for him as well—did that make him innocent? Set up by someone wanting him at the center of suspicion? Or just a very clever killer? "That's kind of you to say." Part of me was glad for the show of support. Another part of me recalled his words about enjoying playing hero. Really, how much did I know about this man, other than how very good he was at persuasion?

Vincenzo pressed his lips together and cast another look out the window. "There's something else."

I wasn't sure I had the stomach for anything else at the moment. "What?"

"I didn't tell Reynolds, because I wasn't sure. And I didn't think he'd believe me."

"What?"

He fixed me with an intense look and said, "I think I saw Adelaide."

"Adelaide?"

"Late last night," he went on. "I was doing a last check on the herd and I saw somebody—someone I thought could have been her—looking at the herd from the sidewalk. We had talked by phone a while ago, actually. I called after her, even started toward her, but she ran off."

"*Adelaide?* Really?"

"Sterling did say he thought she might turn up here. They were having a fight, those two. Well, another fight."

"Didn't you say you *hadn't* seen or talked to Adelaide?" *Lie number one.* My suspicious self had evidently started to keep score.

"Would *you* admit that to Sterling?"

He was right—we had been talking to Sterling at the time, and she never was a safe subject with Sterling. He and his sister had the rockiest of sibling relationships. "I suppose not."

Truth was, the basis of that friction was one of the reasons I liked Adelaide. She seemed to be the only Jefferson family member willing to stand up to Sterling. More than once she'd been my only ally in calling Sterling out on his many lapses in ethics. She'd supported me far more than her mother had when the highly unfortunate discovery that I couldn't have children came to light.

As far as Bitsy was concerned, I had committed the ultimate unpardonable sin: I failed to produce a full-blooded Jefferson family heir. You wouldn't think patriarchal sexism is still alive and well in affluent families, but you'd be wrong. For all Sterling's high-tech innovations, some days I wondered if the Jeffersons lived in the same century as the rest of us.

It didn't help that Adelaide had yet to settle down, find a suitable husband, and produce a "spare" to my nonexistent "heir." She seemed a bit of a lost soul, actually. Her family ties went in cycles from close neediness to defiant estrangement. She'd cling to Sterling for a stretch, then have it out with him over something and disappear for weeks at a time. This irritated Sterling—and Bitsy—to no end. Both of them often laid into her for her inability to "close ranks for the sake of the family."

Sterling and Bitsy—and probably his late father, although I had never met him—both believed having the Jefferson name was a sacred privilege. One that required you to blindly back even questionable Jefferson behavior. I was all the way through our separation before I realized that burden of "privilege" was one of the subconscious reasons I kept my last name when we married. You can imagine how Sterling and his mother both took that particular choice. Sterling eventually came to a begrudging acceptance, but I don't think Bitsy ever forgave me.

"What did Sterling and Adelaide fight about this time?"

As I said, the list of their brother-sister battles was a long one.

"I'm not really sure," Vincenzo replied, scratching his chin. "Adelaide was all vague and dramatic about it when we talked. You know how hard it is to pull things out of her when she gets all worked up." He looked at me. "But she did say something about Sterling pressuring their mother. Something about redoing her estate plan. Whatever it was, Bitsy thought it was 'unfair.'"

So I wasn't the only one—Sterling apparently had been planning to hoard resources. It didn't take much to connect the dots. "Maybe some arrangement where Sterling gets more power and Adelaide gets less?"

Vincenzo nodded. "Perhaps. Only Bitsy is still very much alive. Who knows if he succeeded in getting her to change the will?"

"And you can't change a will if you're dead. In fact, Adelaide gets more of Bitsy's money if Sterling is dead." I gave Vincenzo a direct look. "That's motive. You have to tell Frank. He can probably find her if she's here."

Vincenzo threw up his hands. "I can't prove it was her. He'll think I'm just making it up to throw off suspicion."

I wasn't going to admit to having the same thought. How would Adelaide know to find Sterling here anyway? Even I hadn't known he was coming. But Vincenzo evidently had.

"If she does show herself, and Frank finds out you kept this information from him, that will be a lot worse. Trust me, Vincenzo, I know way more about how this works than I ever wanted to."

He did not look convinced. "I don't know."

My eye caught the lidded crystal bowl over Vincenzo's shoulder. Swiping a ball of vicuña seemed just the kind of thing Adelaide would do. But also . . . "Could she have been the one to take your shears?"

Vincenzo ran a hand through his dark hair. "It's possible. But to do . . ." The hand dropped subconsciously to his neck. "Adelaide? I don't think she could."

The words I had too often heard from Chief Reynolds echoed in my memory. "You'd be amazed what people are capable of."

Mom stood staring at the scene in the shop backyard not thirty minutes later. "Well, this certainly isn't the Christmas you had in mind." Mom had a talent for understatement—or overstatement, depending on the circumstance.

"Not at all," I sighed, feeling as if my holiday success was evaporating in front of my eyes. Normally we'd be opening up the shop about this time on a Sunday morning, but I still hadn't sorted out my next move.

. . . Mostly because Y.A.R.N. was now a crime scene. Police were still milling about, and Vincenzo was doing what he'd been doing most of the morning—talking on his cell phone trying to make arrangements to get the herd home while also trying to keep them calm. Their screeching was getting on everyone's nerves. It didn't look like he was having much success on any front.

This was not an atmosphere conducive to holiday shopping. I tried to send up a silent prayer of thanksgiving that knitters weren't a last-minute holiday-shopping crowd. After all, you needed time to stitch up that perfect scarf you had in mind for Aunt Millie. Still, every knitter knew the misery of having "knitted off more than you could chew," and staring at a looming mound of not-yet-finished projects as the holidays drew near. More than one customer—and myself—could admit to boxing up a garment still on the needles with a promise to have it done in the new year.

Those were small holiday problems. I was not looking at a small holiday problem. I was looking at a murder. One that, if it remained unsolved, could spell big trouble for me.

Mom took my hand in a gesture so maternal and tender a lump rose in my throat. "How are you feeling?"

That seemed an unanswerable question. Ill, frightened, angry, worried, vulnerable—an endless list of unpleasant adjectives crowded my brain. "I don't know. It's . . . was . . . Sterling . . ." I moaned as if the man's name could somehow encompass all of what I was feeling.

Mom gave a small grunt. "I never really liked him, you know."

"Mom!"

I balked. Of the list of unhelpful comments, this topped my list. Whether it was true or not, now was hardly the time to voice that opinion. "He's *dead*. You're going to trash-talk my ex *now*?"

"Well, I know I said he grew on me, but he never really did." She crossed her hands over her chest. "You deserved better."

"So you said. Repeatedly." I stared at the spot where an official-looking person was trying to wash the blood off my grass. We often set up chairs in the backyard for people to sit out there in the summertime. I always loved to kick off my shoes and walk the lush green turf. Now I wondered if I'd ever have the stomach to do it again, knowing what had seeped into the ground.

I was surprised by the small spark of sadness that kindled in my chest. After all, I had been married to the man.

I'd been caught up in a deep and dramatic love affair with him. It had come crashing down with the same deep drama. Or maybe it had just dissolved so slowly I couldn't bring myself to notice.

When the divorce was final, I was so gratified and relieved that Sterling's ability to consume my life was over—but of course, now it wasn't at all, was it?

Mom squeezed my hand and looked at me with worried eyes. "How long do you think before Bitsy gets here?"

Bitsy Jefferson would be coming—that surely doused any spark of sorrow I was feeling. I was still in too much shock to have remembered that Sterling's demise meant her arrival. The specter of Adelaide sneaking around was one thing. Bitsy on the scene was a whole other level of red alert.

I covered my eyes with one hand and mentally calculated the driving distance. Bitsy wintered in a spectacular gulf-view condo in Naples, Florida.

"She's the one who won't fly, right?" Mom asked as if judging the distance from a lit fuse to the bomb ready to blow. It was a pretty apt metaphor.

I gulped. "Well, for this she'll probably charter a flight and stock the bar with every sedative Sonesty makes." Sterling's company had a large assortment of antianxiety drugs, so she'd have lots to choose from. What would happen to the company now? Sonesty was a privately held family company. Sterling had never been interested in who would augment or replace him—he considered himself indispensable.

The irony of that struck me hard. Could Sonesty survive the loss of its CEO? Did I need to care?

As if reading my thoughts, Mom whispered, "Who'd he leave the company to?"

There was a time when I had known that. Sterling had made a big tragic show of redoing our estate planning when we learned there would be no biological children in our lives. He and Bitsy would never consider adoption an option and were devastated at the thought of having no "blood heirs." My faulty biology had been the first of many blows to our doomed marriage.

"When we were married, the company went in equal thirds to me, Bitsy, and Adelaide." Bitsy was already a wealthy woman—something she never hesitated to remind her children and the world. "I don't know the setup now." And evidently Sterling had been looking to change it, if Vincenzo was right.

"So you might still benefit from his death."

I rolled my eyes at Mom. "Do you have to put it quite that way?" For self-defense, I added, "Some—that was part of the settlement, but we all treated it as only a theoretical detail. I don't have any reason to know what the percentages are anymore."

She shrugged. "Well, you know what they say on those television shows. People kill for love, greed, or revenge."

"So you're saying I tick two of the three boxes here?" Is that really how mothers are supposed to talk?

"Well, I can't think of anybody who loved Sterling, so it has to be greed or revenge. You and I both know there are a whole lot of people who might want what Sterling had or have a gripe with him." Mom looked over at Vincenzo, who was currently ranting a stream of Italian into his cell phone. "Him, for example. He's too perfect. It's hard to trust perfect people."

Mom could occasionally have a lopsided view of people, but her viewpoint made a certain sense. "Nobody's perfect, Mom."

"He was trying to charm you. Divert your attentions with those dashing good looks. You don't know—he might have said yes to coming here so he could kill Sterling."

"He didn't know Sterling was . . ." I stopped myself mid-sentence. Vincenzo *had* known Sterling was coming. And he claimed to have seen Adelaide and not mentioned it to the police.

Mom began walking toward the shop door. I noticed the knitting bag in her hands and realized she was planning a long stay today. I didn't have the energy to decide if that was good or bad.

"And he showed us all just how skilled he was with the murder weapon. I bet they'll find his prints are all over the thing."

"Who have you been talking to?"

Mom got an "I'll never tell" look on her face, but she and Angie from the police department were friends, and I wouldn't put it past Mom to grill Angie even though Frank had told her never to discuss police business with anyone—maybe even especially with Mom. "You've got to start thinking like a detective, Elizabeth."

And you've got to stop, I was thinking as a frowning Gavin met me at the shop door. The mayor of Collinstown was none too happy about having to deal with yet another murder. Some people have to surmount ordinary obstacles like history and emotional baggage when dealing with their past romances. Gavin and I kept finding ourselves dealing with murder. "Bev told me to tell you," he said, his frown deepening, "she just took a reservation from a Belinda Jefferson."

"Bitsy," Mom and I groaned in unison.

"Batten down the hatches," Mom said. "It's gonna get worse from here." She walked into the shop, leaving Gavin and me to stare at each other.

"Worse?"

"My ex-mother-in-law is on the way."

"Oh," said Gavin grimly. "That's definitely worse. What can I do?"

That was Gavin, always ready to stand by his friends and ask what could be done.

The problem was, there was only one answer I could give him. "Nothing. Except maybe get ready to do Christmas without me."

CHAPTER SEVEN

I went home, showered, and returned to the shop to open it up. Why, I'm not sure. Linda could have run it under the circumstances, especially with Mom or Shannon's help—if she and Shannon could stop bickering. I found I couldn't stay home. Hank's loyal companionship aside, I just bumbled around the house feeling scared and helpless. Y.A.R.N. is my second home, my safe space. Awkward as it was, this was the best place for me to be.

And, as I suspected, my best and loyal customers—known far and wide as "YARNies"—flocked to my aid.

"Don't talk like that," my customer Arlene, another one of the Gals, chastised me from beside the shop coffee machine when I moaned about not being able to have a Christmas. "Nobody is doing Christmas without you. If nothing else, there is no way I'm going to figure out this color-work beret without you looking over my shoulder." In fact, all of the Gals had shown up for moral support, camping out around our gathering table with various holiday knitting projects in tow. I was touched by their insistence that Y.A.R.N. could still be open for business despite what had happened.

"Thanks." I wish I hadn't sounded so fragile, but I was feeling as breakable as the crystal bowl of vicuña yarn on my counter. The loyalty and friendship of my customers is one of my favorite things about the shop. I love that knitters—and crocheters, and even a few needlepointers—come and sit for hours. Y.A.R.N. is about so much more than yarn. It's about how we're knit together as a community. Today, I needed that community more than ever. I hugged the lot of them. "You all are the best. I love every one of you."

Jeanette gave a happy squeak as I hugged her—she often mentioned what she missed most since her husband had passed was hugs, so I tried to hug her every time I saw her. "Can I touch the vicuña again?" she asked, wide-eyed as a child. "I'm sure I couldn't ever buy some, but it is lovely to be able to feel it."

"Me, too," chimed in Arlene, followed by Barb.

"Absolutely," I said, walking over to the bowl and grasping the lid's lovely silver handle. "But you could have just . . ." My hand stopped mid-lift when I spied only one ball in the bowl again. "Someone already bought one while I was gone?" I asked Linda, thinking she would have told me.

Linda frowned as she peered with me into the empty crystal punch bowl. "There were two in here. I swear."

"There isn't now. Another one's gone missing."

Linda looked horrified. Now a ball had gone missing on *her* watch. We could no longer pin lack of vicuña security on Shannon. Someone was targeting my shop, and this item in particular. This didn't do wonders for my stress level, as you can imagine. I'd always been grateful—and a bit boastful—that Y.A.R.N. never had much of a "shrinkage" problem of stock walking out the door unpaid.

"Someone is stealing yarn from Y.A.R.N.?" Mom made it sound like a more hideous crime than Sterling's murder.

"So it would seem," I replied.

"Someone very sneaky," Linda added. "I've been keeping my eye on that stuff."

"So we'd better not touch any of it now." Jeanette sounded so disappointed.

I didn't want any of this to change how I did business. I opened Y.A.R.N. to see and celebrate the best in people. I would not become one of those eagle-eyed shopkeepers who scowled at tourists and had a *Smile, You're on Camera* sign posted in their window. I plucked the remaining ball from the bowl and placed it in Jeanette's hands.

She sighed sweetly as she ran her fingers across the yarn. Out of sheer defiance, I went back into the stockroom and unlocked the file cabinet drawer where I'd hidden the other balls. I came back out with five of them, and within a minute every Gal, Linda, and I were stroking the balls of exquisite fiber like they were kittens. There was a stretch of surprising peace as we all touched and admired the sublime textures of vicuña. This is what I'd had in mind when I envisioned the event. A lot had gone wrong, but I'd still been able to give my YARNies the experience I wanted to—sort of.

"What? Wait, don't explain it. I feel like I walked into a petting zoo," came Gavin's voice from the shop door a minute later.

"I suppose you did," I replied, relieved to manage a small laugh.

"I'm not even going to try to understand that."

"Gavin, you need to call Frank," Mom declared. "Collinstown has a shoplifting problem."

"Don't let George hear you say that," Linda warned. Thanks to an unfortunate series of yarn-related murders, George was quick to pin me as the source of Collinstown's supposed rise in crime. I was infinitely grateful Frank had never agreed.

"Two of the vicuña yarn balls have gone missing," I explained.

"Before or after the murder?" he asked.

I took a moment to absorb the sheer absurdity of that question. I wouldn't put it past George to launch a recall vote by lunchtime, claiming no murder suspect should be allowed to preside over his beloved Chamber of Commerce.

"Both. I just saw you a few hours ago," I said wearily. "What brings you back?"

Gavin ran a hand through his hair. "Look, I know you don't really have time for this, but I need to talk to you about some chamber business."

Chamber business? Now? Life really does go on, whether you want it to or not. "Um . . . okay."

He cast his glance in the direction of the river. "It's about the tree. They just delivered it."

I'd totally forgotten that the twenty-foot tree was being delivered and installed in the little plaza at the bottom of Collin Avenue right next to the river. It would be the final destination of all these ornaments I'd imagined being passed from hand to hand down from town hall.

"Great. Glad at least that's going according to plan." The Chamber paid for and arranged for the tree as part of our holiday festivities.

Gavin's face went grim. "Well, not actually great."

My gut tightened. "*Why* not actually great?"

The mayor's hand brushed through his hair again. "Well, the guys were putting it up without Larry—he had a girl, by the way."

This brought coos from the Gals, all of whom were devoted grandmothers. Except for Mom, who took all her grandmotherly energies and focused them on her "adopted" grandchild, Gavin's daughter Jillian.

"They sort of . . ." Gavin continued with a reluctance that was almost comical were he not so serious, ". . . it seems they snapped the top off."

I felt my eyebrows slide up toward my hairline. My face was getting entirely too used to expressions of shock and horror. "Of the tree? They broke the Christmas tree?"

"You'd think that couldn't happen," he offered.

People in Collinstown got a little obsessive about the town Christmas Tree. How big it was, whether it was nicer than last year's, where it came from, that sort of thing. I was in no hurry to be the Chamber president who broke the Christmas tree. Of course, I already was, so there was really only one pertinent question.

"How much of the tree 'snapped' off?" It seemed to me that "snapped" implied the last foot or two. We could find a way to fix that. An extra large star or some creative trimming with some hedge shears, perhaps. Maybe even Vincenzo could lend his skills.

Gavin's pause was disconcerting. He wiped his hand down his face before nearly mumbling, "Half."

"*Half the tree?*" My voice took on a high-pitched squeak to rival the vicuña's alarm cry. And rightly so. I had visions of us hoisting the equivalent of an awkward shrub onto its podium in the park by the river. Businesses fighting for space for their ornaments on the much smaller tree. Or, worse, both halves set up like some odd twin topiary. This would go down in Collinstown legend. And not in a good way.

"Well, slightly more than half. I'd say we've got about twelve feet of usable tree. But it's funny-looking."

Mom peered out the shop window as if you could see the conifer carnage from here. "You showed me a picture of that tree, Elizabeth. It's huge. You'd have to back a truck into that tree to snap it off like that."

Gavin made a sound that was half-laugh, half-choke. "Funny you should say that."

I gave our mayor a pleading look. "Please tell me you didn't run over the Collinstown Christmas tree."

"No," he replied, "it was really more like backing into it. Ed Davis insisted he knew how to drive Larry's truck, but . . ."

My brain pictured the scene as if the massive crack of the trunk was in my ears right now. I fought the urge to bang my head on the shop counter. As distractions from murder go, this one was effective—and wildly exasperating.

"What do you need me to do?"

Gavin shrugged. "I'm not sure there is much to do. Lop off a few branches from the top half to make a trunk and put it up. A twelve-foot tree is still a respectable tree."

We weren't going for "respectable." I wanted splendor. Heartwarming, memory-making community splendor. Seeing as how that had pretty much gone out the window with a murder, I supposed we'd have to take whatever good vibes we could manage to scrape up. I had always prided myself on my ability to pivot to whatever "Plan B" was necessary, but this was pushing the limits of my adaptability. "I doubt it will hold all the ornaments, but we'll have to make do."

Gavin nodded. "What do we do with the other half?"

The tree was big. The bottom half would be biggest. I couldn't stomach the idea of the town's wood chipper running for hours to obliterate Ed's mistake.

Arlene saved us. "I know. I'll gather all the members of the garden club and we'll make wreaths. And garland. We can put it all around the base of the platform, and whatever ornaments can't fit on the tree can go there."

I raised an eyebrow at Gavin. "Works for me. It's better than letting all that pretty pine go to waste."

As solutions go, it was a surprisingly good one. Who wants a perfect Christmas, anyway?

After that bit of "cheery" news, I lost my nerve and hid in my office for the next few hours. I told people I had to manage the details of our canceled event, but I think nobody believed me. We all knew I wasn't doing any actual work. I mostly alternated between staring at the blinking cursor on my laptop screen or trying—unsuccessfully—to knit something to soothe my spirit.

I can count on the fingers of one hand the number of times I have been too emotional to knit. Oddly enough, one of them was the days after my marriage to Sterling dissolved. His death—his murder—unmoored me just as much, despite the affection long gone between us.

Usually, knitting is my comfort. It is both my coping mechanism and my thinking tool. I process anything—emotions, changes, challenges, problems—best with yarn between my fingers.

I'd taken all of the vicuña balls but one back into the office with me. I locked the others up, but kept one out and picked up a set of needles. If there was ever a time to let the softness of vicuña speak to my galloping pulse, this was it. I took a few deep breaths as I stroked the gorgeous, silky fibers. *Cast on*, my brain said through the clamor of worries. *Just start*.

We'd selected a cowl of intricate Celtic cables as the sample project for the yarn, a warm and elegant piece. I tried to muster up trust and patience as I mounted the two hundred or so stitches on my circular needles and worked the first row. The process gave me a tiny burst of accomplishment. Somehow, I was still Libby if I could still knit.

Odd questions pushed their way into my mind. Was I a widow if Sterling was my ex-husband? What had he done to provoke that level of violence? What would happen to his estate and his company? If he'd changed his will, would I know?

I was just thinking I ought to call my lawyer when my phone rang, showing *Kenneth Randall, Esq.* on the screen.

"Hello," I said, rather blandly for the circumstances.

"Have you given a statement to the police yet?" Ken's tone was equal parts concern and exasperation. The man was my attorney and had been all through my divorce proceedings. It probably would have been wise to call him earlier.

"No, that's tomorrow. Frank's taking Vincenzo Marani's statement first. I think he's putting off doing mine." I suspected that no matter how much Frank would do his best to be kind, even the biggest dose of compassion wouldn't be able to get around the fact that he'd be *interrogating* me. That can strain even the best of friendships.

I could almost hear Ken's efforts to frantically rearrange his Monday. Papers shuffled, and I heard his wife call to him on the other end of the line. "I'll get out there tomorrow. Do *not* do this without me. Do you understand, Libby? No statements without me present."

I'd known Frank for two decades, and suddenly I needed an attorney present to be in the same room with him. "I didn't do it, Ken." The urge to proclaim it tightened my throat. "I swear I didn't."

"I never for a moment thought you did," came Ken's reply. I hadn't realized how much I needed to hear him say that. "But things don't work that way."

"I don't have an alibi," I gulped out, my fingers clutching at the soft ball of yarn like one of those rubber stress balls they give out at trade shows. "I was home alone when they tell me it happened. But I said the most awful things to him just before. He was . . ."

"He was being Sterling," Ken replied. I remembered he had fielded his share of relentless phone calls from my ex in the past week. "The man had annoying down to an art form."

"Yep" was all I could manage. "I threatened him. In front of people. A lot of people."

Ken did not have a response to that. The silence in his pause made me start to wonder if my reputation—and the shop—could withstand what was coming. Would the fact that I was innocent even really matter?

"What do I do, Ken?" I was losing the battle to another bout of tears.

"You sit tight until I get there. Where are you now?"

"I'm at the shop. It's open." He knew me well enough to understand that's where I'd want to be at a time like this.

"Good. Stay there. Don't go home and hide." His unspoken "because guilty people go home and hide" came through loud and clear.

"Okay."

"Are Bitsy and Adelaide there yet?" Ken had endured a front-row seat to the kind of theatrics those two could create on the heels of a much smaller crisis.

"Vincenzo thinks Adelaide is here. Bitsy is on her way."

"What do you mean 'thinks'? Has Adelaide contacted him? Or you?"

"Vincenzo says he thinks he saw her, but that she ran off when he called out to her. Sterling said she'd disappeared again."

I could hear Ken scribbling down notes.

"If you see her, don't interact with her. In fact, I'd call the police. And as for Bitsy, just don't talk to her, period."

"Easier said than done." Bitsy Jefferson was a force of nature. You could no more put her off than waylay a hurricane. Things were sounding more dire by the minute.

"I was going to call you anyway, Libby. Before all this, I mean."

"With good news, I hope?" Silly, but worth a shot.

"Word on the street is Sonesty is over-leveraged. They were rounding up tons of capital for something. But it smacks of one of Sterling's Hail Marys, if you ask me."

That wasn't unusual for Sterling. He was an all-in, risk-it-all kind of man. His talent for pulling a spectacular success out from under the brink of failure had saved him multiple times. He'd dumped our entire savings into Sonesty for some life-changing new product more than once, only to build it back up even bigger. Life with that man was a wild ride I had honestly been glad to get off.

And now I was off for good.

"Until I get there," Ken said, his insistent tone pulling me back from my rising panic, "your job is to wrack your brain for anything that can establish your whereabouts.

Anything. Phone calls, doorbell cameras, someone you said hello to, or even emails you sent."

I was going to have to prove I hadn't killed Sterling. I knew that, but somehow it rang newly deep and dooming in my stomach at that moment.

"Okay," I said, my voice wobbling. I'd put in my best effort, but I feared I would be unable to conjure up any facts that would eliminate me as a suspect. Only Hank could vouch for my whereabouts when Sterling had died.

And he wasn't talking.

CHAPTER EIGHT

For the rest of the day, I made a genuine attempt to knit and to think of all the ways I could prove I had not been the one to send Sterling to his untimely death.

I failed at both.

Instead, I stared out the small window in my office at the scene that should have made me so happy. The small herd of doe-like creatures that had been blissfully wandering their pen in my backyard now huddled together in a somewhat nervous knot.

They looked like they just wanted to go home—and who could blame them? I couldn't help but worry they'd been traumatized by what they'd seen. And what *had* they seen? Like Hank, our star witnesses couldn't tell us what they knew.

Vincenzo sat on the steps of the trailer, looking exactly like I felt. Despite the festive wreaths and boughs that decorated his trailer, he appeared lost. Worried and withering—

just as I was—under the blinding glare of suspicion. He was also a suspect, yes, but he was also the only person in Collinstown who knew exactly how I was feeling. Unless he really was our killer.

Either way, the best course of action was to talk to him. I'd get either solace or more information—and either of those was a better choice than the half-sick, overanxious way I felt right now.

I filled two Christmas mugs with very strong coffee, dumped a load of peppermint creamer in mine, and walked out to the backyard.

Vincenzo noticed the wide circle I walked around the place where the platform had stood. One corner of his mouth turned up in a sad acknowledgment.

"I can't bring myself to walk there, either." He scooted over on the trailer's steps and accepted the bright red Santa mug I offered. "I'm sitting here wondering if I can ever pick up a set of clipping shears with a steady hand ever again."

Some little part of me recognized he might feel that way whether he was guilty or innocent. I hadn't forgotten the alarming fire in his eyes when he had shoved Sterling back.

We sipped the coffees for a moment, watching the vicuña. "They seem upset." I felt silly for stating the obvious.

"They are. I'd haul them back to the zoo this minute if I was permitted to leave town. They're sending someone with a truck to pull the trailer back, but there's a tangle of paperwork in transporting exotic animals across state lines. Heaven knows when they'll have it all sorted out."

My daydream of the vicuñas' charming stay on my property had popped like a balloon. I'd meant to showcase their unique beauty, and instead I'd put them in the cross-hairs of a killer. "It's gone so wrong. I want to go up and pet each one of them and tell them how sorry I am." I sighed. "But they'd probably only spit on me."

Vincenzo gave a weary laugh. "They would." He pushed out a long breath. "It's funny, but I can't help thinking they know what they saw. Vicuña have predators—other than the humans who practically hunted them to extinction, I mean. Animals recognize death. I believe they'd recognize murder."

My heart sank at the thought that I'd invited these precious animals to my shop, to my home, only to have them traumatized. The tightening knot of fear in my stomach began to harden into anger. I wanted to find who did this. Not only to clear my name, but to get justice. Ken's warnings to tread carefully and be sensible battled with a growing urge to go find the killer.

But who, exactly, was I looking for?

Any knitter knows there's often only one way to fix a knitting error—find the errant stitch and work your way back to it, row by row. "The whole thing seemed very . . . specific. I don't think anyone considers this random violence. Who'd want Sterling dead?"

Vincenzo had the same answer I'd given Frank. "Lots of people." Then, as if he felt it was necessary, he added, "I admit, I'd grown to dislike him. He'd become . . . different."

"How?" I wanted to hear if he'd seen the same transformation in Sterling I had in recent years. Was it obvious outside our marriage?

"He was always driven," Vincenzo replied. "I rather liked that about him at first. You just knew he'd be successful."

I nodded, wrapping my thick alpaca shawl more tightly around my shoulders. I pulled the steaming mug of coffee closer. The crispness of the air had turned sharp and cold for me, even though I don't think the thermometer had dropped.

"But he became a man willing to do anything to get ahead. He made choices that worried me. Choices that made enemies." Vincenzo looked at me. "Did he still carry a gun in his glove box?"

I nearly dropped my coffee mug. "Sterling kept a *gun* in his car?"

"He has for years. I thought you knew."

I glared at Vincenzo. "I most certainly did not know." It seemed crazy—and then again perfectly logical—that I hadn't known that. "I would have made him get rid of it."

"Which I'm sure is why he didn't tell you."

I grunted. "He didn't tell me lots of things." Funny how you think you know someone so well, only to discover you don't know them at all. I had married a carefully crafted version of Sterling. That was a very painful thing to figure out.

"I've actually worried Adelaide would sneak up on him one of these days and get herself shot." He glanced around the little yard. "She's here, Libby. I'm sure that was her. And you know her—she'll go crazy when she realizes what's happened. I half expected to find her screaming in the yard last night."

I had had the same thought. Adelaide was a high-volume, high-drama woman. She'd blow up like a hand grenade at a tragedy like this. "She must know about it if she's here. It's all over town. All anyone can talk about. She'd have to be in Ohio not to have heard someone say something." I gave Vincenzo a dubious look. "Are you *sure* it was her you saw?" Adelaide was a beauty, to be sure, but she wasn't a striking one. No blazing red hair or distinctive limp or anything that would enable Vincenzo to pick her out of a crowd with ease.

"As sure as I can be. And yes, I told your Chief Reynolds when I gave my statement." He made a sound that let me know that had been just as unpleasant an experience as I was expecting mine to be. "When the time came for me to ever hire a defense attorney, I confess I thought it would be for something more gallant than this."

"You are, after all, the Gallant Herdsman." I tried to laugh, but it fell short.

Vincenzo turned to face me, his eyes as intense as they had been during our earlier dinner. "But I am not the Gallant Murderer. Tell me you believe that."

I wanted to say yes. It would make things so much easier to have an ally here, one who knew Sterling and could help me put the facts together to solve this mystery. But I couldn't.

He shrank back, wounded by my hesitation. "You don't believe me."

"I don't know what to believe. I feel like I can't say anything for certain right now." That seemed cruel, but so did lying to him. "I'm sorry."

Vincenzo stood up. "So am I." He walked over to the herd, but stopped and turned back toward me before he got there. "You can trust me, Libby. You should trust me. And I will find a way to prove myself to you."

Frank looked as uncomfortable as I felt. We'd worked side by side to solve two mysteries, and we'd been friends for years. Never, in all that time, had we been on either side of an interrogation table.

At least I think that's what you called it. As a civilian, Frank had never let me in this room while he was questioning a suspect.

Since pushing through the door Monday afternoon, I'd

walked past two Christmas villages, a blue wreath, and a tree with a sheriff's badge for a star. Angie always went overboard in decorating the station for the holidays. The place looked like a law enforcement gift shop.

This room, by deliberate contrast I suppose, had no hint of yuletide joy. Small and bland, it was windowless, a bit claustrophobic, and very official-feeling. Intimidating.

Ken's very official-feeling presence beside me was a constant reminder that this wasn't just your garden-variety statement I was giving (if there was such a thing). This was supposed to be my shot at clearing my name. It didn't help that I was woefully short of facts and verifiable information, nor did it help that Ken kept shuffling papers with an attitude that seemed both defensive and agitated.

Frank turned on a tape recorder and opened his notepad. "State your full name, address, and your relationship to the deceased." Frank knew all of this, but I went through the process anyway.

"Okay, Ms. Beckett"—his use of the formality for the recording made my throat tighten—"walk me through the night of the incident. Every detail you can think of, even things that feel silly or insignificant."

Tell everything, I coached myself. *You don't have anything to fear.* "Vincenzo had just finished shearing the first vicuña, and the audience was touching the fiber. Sterling showed up just as things were ending. By the way," I said with an eerie matter-of-factness, "Vincenzo told me Sterling evidently keeps a gun in his car. Has for years, which I never knew."

Ken looked alarmed. Maybe bringing up lethal weapons wasn't the best choice in this circumstance.

"That's a little off topic, I know," I replied, feeling foolish and off-balance, "but you did ask for everything."

"We found it," Frank said. "We went over the car this afternoon for prints." The chief gave me a pointed look. "Forensics says it's been fired since its last cleaning, but there's no way to know how recently. He was licensed to carry it."

Sterling was licensed to carry a gun and had used it. It really was as if a whole different man had walked the earth than the one I had thought I married. As much as I had thought I knew that, this fact brought it home with shocking clarity.

"What happened after Mr. Jefferson arrived at the shop?"

This part wasn't fun to admit. "I yelled at him. Vincenzo had told me that Sterling had stepped into our dealings and tried to position himself as the person to make this event happen."

"And he wasn't?"

I know Frank was just doing his job, but I couldn't believe he had to question such a thing. "Absolutely not," I replied, still having to tamp down my annoyance at how Sterling had behaved. "And, well, that ticked me off. I made this event happen all on my own, on the strength of my store, not by any favors of Sterling's. And I told him so. Rather loudly," I added with reluctance.

"You made threats." He'd been there and heard them. His tone had an unsettling "I'm just sticking to the facts and not offering my opinion" quality to it that reminded me we were not exactly on the same side here. The steel band that had gripped my chest since yesterday morning tightened up further.

"I don't know that I'd call what Libby said a threat," Ken interjected.

At that point, a knock came on the door. Frank's annoyance at the intrusion doubled when Angie came in with a trio of Christmas mugs filled with coffee and a selection of holiday cookies.

"Angie," Frank grumbled, "this isn't a social call."

Angie gave Frank a sideways glance. "It's Libby, Frank. The least we can do is be nice." She smiled at Ken, who was looking understandably stumped. "Hello. Welcome to Collinstown."

"The least we can do is keep things *official*," the chief replied.

"Official isn't the opposite of nice." It seemed Angie had no beef with standing up to her boss—and beau. Ken and I looked at each other. On the one hand, I was desperate for something to take the seriousness out of the air. On the other hand, I wasn't sure an interrogation ought to come with *snacks*.

As if to settle the argument, Angie made a show of setting the tray in the middle of the table. Without another word, she set one of the mugs down in front of Frank—a Santa variety, no less—and left the room with nothing short of a "So there!" swagger.

I grabbed a mug and a cookie before Frank could change his mind. Ken sheepishly did the same. Frank grunted his disapproval but said nothing. We all covered the awkwardness with sips of coffee.

Finally, as if giving in to the absurdity of the situation, Frank cleared his voice and resumed his questioning. "Could you recount what you said to Sterling?" Frank asked with professional precision.

I swallowed hard. This was humbling to admit. "It was something along the lines of there being nothing I wouldn't do to get him out of my life."

As Frank was writing my words down I felt compelled

to add, "I didn't mean murder, Frank. I wouldn't. I was furious, but not homicidal. You have to know that."

"Let's just try and concern ourselves with the facts for now. He left after that . . . exchange?"

"Yes."

"Do you have any idea where he went? Did he get in touch with you at all after that?"

"No, but I'm assuming he went back to the Riverside Inn. He told me he was staying there. And his car wasn't out in front of the shop when I went out later."

"He drove back and forth from the inn to Y.A.R.N.?" Frank asked. "It's only a block or so."

"I expect he wanted to make sure everyone got a look at his sports car. He liked to show the Alfa Romeo off. A lot."

"And what did you do after that?"

"I was tired. It had been a long day, and Sterling's behavior wasn't making it any easier. I finished up at the shop. Vincenzo said he was tired and had to tend the herd, so we both agreed to make it a quiet night."

"So you'd been out together dining at the Blue Moon Friday night, but you weren't together Saturday night."

"What's that got to do with anything?" Ken asked.

Frank glared at him. "I'm trying to establish someone who can verify where Libby was Saturday night."

I wasn't sure what Frank was implying. "No, I was alone. And as far as I know, Vincenzo was in his trailer or seeing to the animals. That's what he told me."

"But you can't say for sure. You weren't at the shop, so he could have left the trailer or met up with Sterling or someone else and you wouldn't know."

I sat back in my chair. Those facts had been eating at me all day. "No, I can't say for sure." I began to wonder what Frank had learned from the statement Vincenzo had given him yesterday. I didn't think the chief would be sharing any of that with me anytime soon.

Frank continued. "So you went straight home on Saturday?"

"Well, yes and no."

"Meaning?"

"Like I told you earlier, I went home, but only to get Hank and take him for a long walk." Anticipating his next questions, I said, "We went down by the river all the way to the far docks. It was dark long before we got back, and I don't remember seeing anyone. I wasn't really paying attention, just stewing in my own thoughts, I suppose. Then I went home, ate an embarrassing amount of ice cream, got a few hours of angry knitting done, and finally went to bed. Next thing I knew you were pounding on my door."

"You didn't call anyone, send any emails, anything that would place you at home during those hours?"

Ken had nearly begged me to come up with something that would verify my whereabouts, but I hadn't been able to come up with a thing. Of all the nights I've stayed up late ordering yarn for the shop online, why hadn't I picked that night? "Unless my electric toothbrush has a time stamp, I've got nothing."

Frank gave me a look that let me know he was thinking exactly what I was thinking. Mom had been hounding me to get a videocam doorbell or one of those security systems for both my home and the shop. I had refused on both counts. As a result, I lacked one of the things that could have provided me with an alibi. Or, perhaps, recorded whatever had happened behind my shop.

I was now likely doomed to years of "I told you to do that" speeches—if I wasn't in jail for Sterling's murder, that is.

We finished the rest of my statement. It felt as if it accomplished nothing except tick off some procedural box. And make things more awkward between Frank and me—if that was possible.

The only bright spot was when Frank asked me, "Who do you think might have wanted to, or been able to, kill Sterling the way he died?"

I expect he was asking me if Vincenzo had the strength and skill to do what had been done to Sterling. He did, but Frank's wording knocked another memory loose. "You said it was the artery in his neck, right? A specific one?" Frank had told me that Sterling seemed to have bled out very quickly.

"That's true. His carotid. Both sides, multiple punctures from the clipping shear blades." He gave a small grimace, as if he'd rather not provide me such gruesome details.

"So, kind of a medically informed wound?" I asked.

"I suppose you could say that. Why?"

"Adelaide went to nursing school. Back when she had the idea to join the Peace Corps or Doctors Without Borders. She dropped out, of course, but she used to boast that anatomy was the only class she was good at. Vincenzo is sure she's here in town, Frank. I think we need to find her."

CHAPTER NINE

The next morning, I climbed the Riverside Inn's holly-wrapped stairs with a justified dread. No one faced Bitsy Jefferson without a certain degree of caution, even under the best of circumstances.

This hardly qualified as the best of circumstances. In fact, I was hard pressed to come up with anything that would qualify as worse circumstances.

I did not ask Frank or Ken if this was a good idea. I already knew what they'd say. And I did try and tell myself to stay away. But Bitsy would come find me anyway, I thought. She'd wait until she built up a good head of grief-and-anger steam and then launch into me without warning. I was better off facing her up front.

Besides, despite my current person-of-interest status, I decided I was going to behave the way an innocent person would. Because I *was* innocent. And I liked to think I was the kind of person who would visit my former mother-in-law in this time of grief, no matter how badly my marriage to her son had ended.

I confess, my hand shook a bit as I rapped gently on the door of her room. Bev Thomas, who ran the inn, had told me Bitsy had insisted on taking the room Sterling had used—which, of course, happened to be the inn's finest suite. Vincenzo wasn't the only one used to the best of everything. She'd been so demanding that Frank had to process the room's evidence as quickly as he could while Bitsy ordered gin and tonics at the inn bar with a daunting level of impatience. Frank was meticulous and rushed by no one, but Jeffersons had an exceptional talent for getting what they wanted no matter who stood in their way.

After a short pause, Bitsy pulled the door open as if she'd been expecting my visit. "Libby." She pronounced my name with a weary, tolerant tone. She didn't use my last name. She never did. It was her way of punishing me, I suppose, for my refusal to take the renowned Jefferson moniker.

For all her cold ferocity, Bitsy Jefferson was a beautiful woman. I'd never seen a woman wear neutral colors with such astounding power. And always in one color from head to toe—she'd somehow weaponized the monochromatic ensemble. The woman cut an intimidating figure wherever she went. I had more than once described Bitsy as "tailored within an inch of her life." It was still true today. She was in charcoal gray from head to toe, a nod to the current circumstances, I suppose.

I'd knit her several elegant lacework scarves and shawls in an attempt to win her acceptance over the years, but she'd never worn them. Today a single strand of perfect pearls graced her neck, while a diamond tennis bracelet sparkled from one slim wrist.

I'd always found it funny how far the pendulum had

swung with Adelaide, who always wore bold, bohemian colors. Adelaide dressed with a theatrical flair and moved through the world in a flurry of drama. But was Adelaide here? If Sterling's sister was going to show herself to anyone other than Vincenzo right now, it would be Bitsy. It was one of the things I'd hoped to find out with this visit.

"I'm so sorry, Bitsy," I began, feeling more than awkward. "I don't know what to say, what to do. It's just horrible." My voice caught on the last word. Death is sad. Murder is horrible.

She turned from the doorway and walked back into the room, leaving it open in a manner that felt more like an afterthought than an invitation to enter.

I walked in, shut the door behind me, and waited for her to speak next. With anyone else, I'd have attempted a hug. Not with Bitsy. I think I've hugged her twice in the whole time I've known her, and one of those times we'd both had far too much to drink.

She remained facing the tall banks of windows that let the bright December sunshine into the room. The day had been crisp and clear, too cheery for the fog of sorrow and suspicion I seemed to be walking around in lately.

After a pause so long it was making me twitch, she said, "My son was taken from me." It was a declaration to the world, not to me.

Then she did turn to me, and it was as if someone had flung those windows open and let a ghost enter in to chill the room. "Who did this?"

She didn't say, "Did you?" She didn't need to. In all my life, I'd never seen someone who could nail you to the wall with an unspoken accusation like she could. Sterling had the same talent, I admit, but he'd rarely used it on me. Bitsy, however, used it on me all the time.

I tried not to let it get to me the way it used to. "I know I said unkind things to him in our last—"

"You made threats," she cut in without raising her voice. "They told me."

"I came here to tell you to your face that I did not kill Sterling. He made me angry, I admit, and I'm not sure I expect you to believe me, but I didn't kill him."

I saw nothing in her face that made me believe my words had any impact. Even knowing her personality as I did, this cold reserve baffled me. She'd just lost her son. Where was the grief? The sorrow? The maternal agony? Perhaps she was in shock. Perhaps she was the kind of person—like her son—who loathed showing weakness of any kind.

"Did you finally agree?"

It took me a confused minute to realize what she was asking. "Are you talking about the settlement?" I saw no reason to edit the shock from my voice. After all, who talks about divorce proceedings at a time like this?

"Did you consent to Sterling's requests?"

You mean did I cave to his repeated demands? my brain shouted. I couldn't believe we were having this conversation. I was annoyed how my voice wavered when I said, "No." Needing to sound more confident, I cleared my throat and added, "I had no intention of doing so. Ever."

She laid her hand on the back of a chair with an eerie precision. "So the revised agreement was never signed. How fortunate for you, then, that he died when he did."

Bitsy believed I could kill Sterling in order to keep our current divorce settlement intact. Wow. It stung to know she thought of me that badly.

"There isn't a single *fortunate*"—I gave her accusatory word an emphasis—"thing about this. It's terrible. I never wished your son harm." I got brave and added, "A lot of people held ill feelings for Sterling, but I tried not to be one of them." Tried. I fell short more times than I'd care to admit to this woman at the moment.

Sensing this visit would soon be over, I got to my second point. "I came to say I'm sorry, but I also came to ask if you have heard from Adelaide? Sterling said she'd disappeared again, but Vincenzo told me he is sure he's seen her here."

"Vincenzo." In the opposite of Sterling's tendency to shorten people's names, Bitsy drew names out in long, unsettling ways.

"Yes, he is here for my event." I didn't really need to explain that, but Bitsy was making me nervous. She'd never once put me at ease, now that I think of it. Had all this not happened, I would have happily never seen her again.

"Adelaide is the one who called me with the terrible news."

"So she *is* here?"

With that, the door to the suite's bedroom opened and Adelaide Jefferson walked out.

"You're here!" I gasped, trying not to let my jaw hit the oriental carpet.

"My brother's been murdered," she rasped, and she took her mother's elbow in the crook of her arm. "Of course I'm here."

As I had guessed, Adelaide was the opposite of her mother's composure. Wild red eyes glared at me from underneath unruly hair—eyes that were so much like Sterling's it shook me a bit. I'd forgotten how much the siblings resembled each other.

"So Vincenzo did see you. Why didn't you turn around and say something? Why run?"

Adelaide looked at me as if I'd sprouted a third arm. "I just got here."

"So that wasn't you Vincenzo saw the night before Sterling was killed?"

"Of course not. I just said, I've only just arrived. I got here as fast as I could when they called me."

"But who called you?" I asked. "We've been looking for you since . . . since it happened."

She pulled herself up as if somehow it would allow her to look down her nose at me despite the handful of inches I had over her. "I don't have to explain myself to the likes of you."

We'd liked each other—or so I thought. This new Adelaide looked like the one I'd known, but she acted much more like her mother. I got the odd sensation the remaining Jeffersons—because really, that's what they were, with both Sterling and his father gone—really were closing ranks.

"I suppose you don't, but you will have to explain yourself to Chief Reynolds. Vincenzo is sure he saw you here in Collinstown while Sterling was still alive, and I expect you'll need to provide proof of wherever you were." Bitsy wasn't the only one flinging accusations in this room today.

Adelaide's eyes blazed. "Have you proven where *you* were when my brother was so brutally murdered?"

Bitsy flinched ever so slightly as Adelaide jabbed a finger at me. "I heard about what you said. They tell me a whole crowd heard it." Her eyes brimmed with angry tears. "I hope you've got a good lawyer, Libby. You and Vincenzo both."

I had wondered if the Jeffersons were going to declare war. I had my answer.

Of course, I went straight to Vincenzo with what I'd learned. "She *is* here!" he declared at my revelation, his hands flying wildly through the air as we stood outside his trailer. "I knew it! I was right all along."

"Well, not exactly," I cautioned. "Adelaide is here now. But that doesn't verify you saw her. She's not admitting to being here when Sterling was killed." The words still stumbled ugly and foreign off my tongue. It was hard enough to comprehend that Sterling was dead, but I hadn't quite found a way to get my head around the fact that he'd been *killed*. Rather brutally, if you ask me.

Vincenzo narrowed his eyes in defiance. "That was her. She can say what she likes, but that was her."

I won't say I hadn't had the same thought, but one question niggled at me. "Is she strong enough, though? I don't think Sterling got up onto that platform on his own. I couldn't have dragged him up there, so I don't see how she could have."

We both realized the line I was drawing toward his own strength at the same time. I hadn't meant it to imply him, but the truth was only someone of Vincenzo's size and power could have gotten Sterling onto that shearing platform.

"I didn't." His assertion was low and determined.

"I'm not saying you did." It was possible Vincenzo did it—he lacked an alibi as much as I did—but I didn't consider it probable. "Chief Reynolds says he thinks whoever did it knew enough anatomy to know exactly where to . . . stab . . . Sterling. For someone in the pharmaceutical field, that could point to a long list of Sterling's many enemies."

"All too true." Vincenzo chose to deal with that uncomfortable fact by changing the subject. "They've finally gotten the paperwork together, and the zoo is coming to pick up the vicuña on Thursday." He gazed at the herd, affection filling his features even now. "They're upset."

"The zoo or the vicuña?"

"Both. I could donate a bank full of money after this, but I expect these vicuña will never go on the road with me again. It won't matter that I'm innocent." He picked at a piece of pine bough stuck to the trailer awning and threw it bitterly to the ground. "It won't matter that this had nothing to do with them. Murder isn't good for public relations."

His aggravated sigh seemed to broadcast that he had wanted this event to go well just as much as I had. "There are no others in North America, you know," he went on. "Zorro and the rest are the only vicuña in captivity."

"I think it's rather amazing you've been able to bring them here at all. They're extraordinary animals."

Together we watched the herd for a moment. I've met a dozen species of fiber animals in my work with Y.A.R.N., but the vicuña seemed singularly beautiful. Rare and lovely. The knitter's equivalent of a priceless bottle of wine or a fine diamond. Now might be the only chance so many people would ever have to see them in person. It seemed such a waste for the event to have fallen apart the way it did.

We watched the herd in silence for a long while before Vincenzo asked quietly, "Can I tell you something I would never admit to Sterling?" I was surprised by his tone, lacking as it was in the drama of his earlier declarations.

"Of course."

"You're not the only one who needed this to go well."

I cocked my head in his direction, puzzled. I had always been under the impression that I needed Vincenzo's appearance far more than he needed my store's event. "Why?"

He walked over to the fence, holding out his hand for the vicuña to nuzzle like long-legged puppies. I know people project human behavior onto animals all the time—I ascribe all sorts of personality traits to Hank—but it seemed to me the vicuña genuinely liked and trusted Vincenzo. Maybe he really did see their traumatization as a violation of that trust.

"I have always thought my father was one hundred percent behind what I did." Vincenzo's voice sounded far away, perhaps back in Italy. "I thought he had accepted how I'd veered off the family path."

I was surprised to hear his doubt. All that money to the zoo, to the Peruvian community—wasn't that an endorsement from the Marani family? "He isn't?"

"Papa can roust up a high level of tolerance for anything that generates big profits. Or big promotion. He is not as high-minded as I make him out to be once the balance sheets don't line up the way he likes." Vincenzo gave me a small smirk. "He is more like Sterling than I would admit to anyone. Except you."

"Meaning what?"

"Meaning if I had not been able to make a massive success out of touring with these animals, the donations would stop. I thought he liked the idea, but as it turns out, Papa was just humoring me." His shoulders stiffened, and I was surprised to see the vicuña react as well. "I am a man who likes to be taken seriously."

"And here I thought you just liked to be admired." I don't know what made me crack a joke. Maybe I just felt we were getting a bit too serious. Or I was getting a bit smitten. Even under suspicion, Vincenzo was what many of my friends would call "swoon-worthy."

As if to prove my point, he gave me that brilliant heartthrob of a smile. "I do like to be admired. Rather a lot. But they are sort of the same thing, are they not?"

"I suppose." *Don't like him so much*, I lectured myself. *Don't let yourself like him so much. You don't really know him, even if he makes you feel like you do.*

"Which is why I feel almost silly asking you something."

I couldn't imagine Vincenzo feeling silly about anything. The man could look swoon-worthy flossing his teeth. "Ask me what?"

He actually blushed. The look on his face was startlingly charming. "Would you . . . I mean while I'm here, which I'll need to be for a while . . . could you teach me to . . ." He mimed knitting with his hands as if he didn't even dare say it out loud.

I couldn't have been more shocked. "You don't know how?" I blurted out. Feeling ungracious, I quickly added, "I mean, you of all people . . . I'd have thought you knew how."

Vincenzo looked around and stuffed his hands into his pockets as if I'd just outed some enormous secret. "I understand the concept. And my nonna did try to teach me when I was a boy." He touched the toffee-colored scarf that never left his neck. "She made me this. I wanted to make one for Papa. I was disastrous at it, of course."

This made no sense to me, but I realized Vincenzo was serious. "You really want to learn? Now?"

He shrugged, again looking elegantly sheepish. Like a duke who'd wandered into Costco and couldn't work out where they kept the caviar. "I find myself with a lot of free time on my hands. I've worked with this yarn for the last six years, and I realized I've never actually made anything from it. You won't trust me until we truly get to know each other, and I can't think of a better way for that to happen than for you to teach me to knit." Again with the gleaming smile. "They tell me you're very good at it."

Now, this was dirty pool. Most knitters on the planet can't resist the chance to share their love of yarn and needles with someone else. I would teach anyone—even someone I didn't like—to knit if they asked. I've even tried to teach people who didn't ask.

But to have someone like Vincenzo Marani ask me to teach him to knit? That was the exact definition of "an irresistible invitation."

And he was right about one thing—if I wanted to get a true sense of who this man was, how much of him was authentic and how much was facade—this would do it.

"I will learn how to knit, and I will prove to you that you can trust me." He declared it as if there couldn't possibly be a reason for me to refuse.

He was right.

"I don't see why I couldn't—"

The vicuña cut me off by making a loud, instant chorus of their screeching alarm. A dark brown blur of legs, tail, and ears rushed up to the fence and slammed into it with a clumsy thrill.

"Mocha!" Margo yelled as she dashed down my driveway with a leash and collar in her hand.

Vincenzo leapt to get the herd under control while I threw my arms around what I realized was a puppy. An adorable, wild Labrador puppy with sweet eyes and oversized paws looked up at me and covered me with licks.

"I'm so sorry, Libby. I thought I had him. I should have named him Houdini."

Vincenzo moved the herd to the far side of the pen while Margo and I wrestled the harness and leash onto her frantic brown companion.

"You got a puppy??" I asked, still fending off multiple licks. It was better than being spit on by a vicuña, I'll give you that. "I didn't know you were getting a puppy."

Margo looked at me with a rather helpless expression.

"Neither did I. Carl told me not to go to the shelter fund-raiser without him. I just . . . well, look at him."

Mocha looked up at Margo with the same "You are my universe" gaze that had won my heart when Hank was a puppy. I could no more have gone home without Hank that day than I could have gone without breathing.

"I was going to tell you, but with everything going on . . ."

Mocha sat down, panting and goofy-grinned, a pink tongue hanging out of one side of his mouth. He was, without a doubt, that chaotic sort of adorable that captures every dog owner's heart. The kind of sweet "I didn't mean to" face that keeps you from getting too angry when they chew your favorite shoes.

"You've always said you were going to get one some-day." Margo had mentioned getting a dog several times in recent years, but her husband, Carl, always seemed to talk her out of it. I wasn't entirely surprised, just a little startled. Margo is more of a planner—this seemed a bit out of character for her.

"I'm going to need dog mom lessons," she said, holding out a hand to Mocha. He responded by bounding up on to her and sniffing loudly into her ears. She laughed, and I couldn't help but be caught up in her happiness. "Lots of them."

"You've had so much practice with Hank, I have no doubt you'll do just fine."

"He can't come to the shop with me the way Hank comes with you. We're going to need doggy day care, at least for a while. Can you recommend anyone?"

"Sure. Come on into the shop and I'll give you a name or two." Mom—or Margo—usually watched Hank on the rare occasion that I needed someone, but I did have a short list of dog walkers and boarders that I could share.

We started toward the shop's front door, but Mocha suddenly pulled on the leash. He slipped out of Margo's grasp again and bounded toward the vicuña pen until one of them offered a screech. Startled, he then dashed across the yard, then back toward us to sniff wildly at the spot where the platform and Sterling's body had been. Vincenzo, Margo, and I all tried catching up with him, but he ran speedy circles around a tree, started digging a hole by my stone wall, then decided my bushes needed investigation.

"Probably a lot of weird smells here," Margo panted as we continued to race after the exuberant puppy. "Let's go, boy."

Mocha wasn't listening. He was in a frenzy of sniffing all over my property, starting to dig a hole and then finding something more interesting to run toward before we caught up to him.

Mocha's wild racing came to a halt as he began digging in earnest under the patch of rhododendron at one end of my property. Something had very clearly caught the pup's attention at that spot. He dug more, then tried to push his way through the leaves and branches, barking and lunging.

As Margo caught up to snag hold of Mocha's leash, I got down on my hands and knees to see what had caught his frenzied attention.

"Well, what do you know?" Even I was surprised at what lay close to the base of the plant, half covered with leaves and pine needles. I grabbed one end of the black electrical cord and began tugging. "Your pup's got some serious skills, Margo." I motioned for her to lean over and see what I saw, even as Mocha continued barking.

Two more hefty pulls yanked a pair of shearing clippers

into view. And not just any clippers—a pair with big, sharp blades, just like the one the police had taken from Vincenzo's trailer.

"My missing shears!" Vincenzo cried out. Only his happiness died shortly after the words, when he saw what we all saw: the nine sharp tips of these blades were stained with dried blood.

CHAPTER TEN

I watched Frank carefully deposit the second set of shears into a plastic evidence bag. If the blood sample matched— and no one doubted that it would—we had our murder weapon. The sight of the fateful shears was both satisfying and slightly sickening. I couldn't help but feel the weight of staring at the thing that had killed Sterling. I tried to imagine someone with enough strength or rage to jam that into someone's neck and couldn't. It seemed such an unlikely, specific way to stab someone.

"So," I began, reaching for the easy conversation that used to be how Frank and I talked. We both were trying to regain the sense of partnership we normally had, but it seemed beyond our reach. "What did it feel like to write 'stabbed by shearing clippers' in the blank marked 'cause of death'?"

The lame attempt at humor fell way short of the mark. "I don't do that, actually," he replied gruffly. "The coroner fills out the death report."

"But you must fill out the part about the murder weapon."
Frank had told me that first day that the wounds on Sterling's neck matched the spikes in the clipper blades exactly.
And now he had blood to test and match with Sterling's. It was beginning to look very bad for our Gallant Herdsman.

Or not. After all, past experience had told me that sometimes using the very obvious weapon choice is a pretty good way to frame someone. Or divert suspicion. Still, vicuña clipping shears? My list of yarn-related items that couldn't be weaponized seemed to grow shorter with each year in Collinstown. Who would have ever thought I'd have reason to be thankful that no one had ever attempted assault with knitting needles in all the time Y.A.R.N. had been open? That shouldn't even be a thing, right?

"Well, I do fill that out, but it's not as clear as you might think in this case."

I stared at the brownish-red tinge on the shear blades.
"What do you mean, 'not as clear'?"

"I need you to tell me what you know about Sterling's health."

I wasn't expecting that question. "Sterling was obsessed with his health and fitness. For a guy who made his fortune in pharmaceuticals, he prided himself on never taking anything. I used to have to fight him to take an aspirin."

"And now? Recently, I mean?"

"We didn't discuss his health. These days I tried not to talk to him at all, actually. He never mentioned any problems."

"Just that he wanted you to alter your divorce settlement. Reduce your alimony."

I'd already given Frank an extensive statement. "Frank, what are you getting at?"

Frank waited until the officer was out of earshot. "What

kind of access do you have to the drugs Sterling's company makes?"

I frowned at Frank. "None. Come on, Frank, what kind of question is that? What's going on?"

"Sonesty makes a drug called Hypandin. Blood thinner."

I'd been a sales rep for the company when Sterling and I met. I had a rudimentary knowledge of the company's catalogue, but that was years ago. "I remember it, sort of. A common drug, one we sold a lot of, as I remember. Why?"

Frank cleared his throat. "Can you explain why we found it—a lot of it—in his system?"

Sterling? On blood thinners? "I suppose it's possible. But I didn't know about it. That doesn't sound like something you take a lot of."

"Exactly. The bruising we found indicates this wasn't a regular dose. And we found an injection site. Two, actually."

"Can you murder someone with a blood thinner?" I knew the answer almost as fast as the words left my mouth.

"If you stab them, it certainly ups your chances of success, yes."

I leaned back against the wall, daunted by the news. This was a premeditated, well-planned murder.

"There's more," Frank said. "There seems to be another drug in his system. It's not a known substance. But we do know it acted as a coagulant. A blood thickener, if you will."

I glared at Frank. "A thickener *and* a thinner?"

"Like I said," Frank answered, "the coroner is asking questions. There's no medical reason to have both those drugs in his system at the same time."

"But there could be a criminal reason." I followed his train of thought.

"This is going to sound like an odd question, but did Sterling keep snakes?"

"Snakes?" I laughed—until I remembered the belt he'd been wearing.

"The mystery drug seems to have some trace elements of snake venom," Frank explained.

"Sterling didn't do pets. One of the best things about splitting with him was that I could finally get Hank. Snakes? No. But . . . there was the belt."

"What belt?"

"The first day he was here, Sterling was wearing a snakeskin belt. He boasted that it was real—Vincenzo goaded him about it—and that it was a souvenir from a recent trip." Another fact from my sales rep days surfaced. "Sonesty makes diabetes drugs, and several of them are derived from snake venom. It's not one of those?"

"My guy's pretty sure this isn't a diabetes drug. And there's no evidence of Sterling having diabetes. This kind of drug would be for someone with a blood disorder. A clotting issue."

"You mean like a hemophiliac. Someone whose blood won't clot, so they're in danger when they've cut themselves."

Frank nodded. "Could be. Was Sterling one of those?"

"No. I'm sure I'd know if he was. I think it's a genetic thing you have from birth. Besides, wouldn't your medical guy have been able to see that?"

"Who knows? I'm in way over my head here."

Facts were clicking into connections in my brain. "Sterling was murdered with his own drugs. Or might have been. That sounds like a crime of hatred or revenge. And I'm afraid lots of people had gripes with Sterling." I felt like

I had to repeat it. "But, Frank, I'm not one of them. I didn't do this. I'm not even sure I would know how to do this."

It sent ice down my spine to see the lack of certainty in Frank's eyes. "We've got a lot to work out yet. We should be able to get Sterling's records from his doctor and pharmacist and confirm if any doctor had him on either of those drugs."

"I can't believe he was on either of them." Then again, what did I know?

"Was he scheduled for some kind of surgery? Anything that would demand a high level of either drug? Who's got his medical power of attorney? Do you know?"

"Not me. Anymore, that is. I did once, but I don't know who's on his emergency contact list now. It'd have to be Bitsy, I think. I don't think he'd trust Adelaide for that."

Frank's eyebrows lowered into a reprimanding glower. "You talked to them."

"I gave them my sympathy," I explained, even though we both knew that was only half of it. "They lost a son and a brother."

"I asked you to stay away from the situation." Yes, definitely a reprimand.

I changed the subject. "Are you going to induct Mocha into the police auxiliary?" After all, we'd never have found the murder weapon without that little dog's insistent nose.

Frank's only response was a darker look. Our friendship was on rocky ground. I wondered if things would ever get right between us after this.

"Frank," I called as he started to go, "I can still come to your birthday party, can't I?" Angie was throwing a get-together for Frank in a few days. It stung that I felt I had to ask if I was still invited.

"Of course you can, Libby."

The consolation in his tone didn't quite reach his eyes.

Much as part of me wanted to go home and wave a white flag, life and Christmas kept coming. And so it was that despite having found the murder weapon—or, perhaps, only the stabbing weapon in a rather complicated murder—I stood in the town hall reception room later with Gavin ticking off holiday tasks.

"The tree's not so bad," I offered to Gavin's grim face. We'd just come back from a "make the best of it" inspection of the half-tree now standing at the bottom of the avenue. "Shorter than our usual tree, but the wreathes and garland make up for it. Almost."

Arlene, Mom, and the rest of the Collinstown garden club had, in fact, risen to the occasion. They'd done an admirable job of making the stumpy little tree look something close to deliberate.

Gavin huffed as he held up a little felted Christmas tree Linda had made. "It'll be summer before Ed Davis lives down his driving on that one." The mayor lowered his voice. "And speaking of driving, Jillian is signing up for driver's ed next semester."

I suddenly felt ancient. "How can your daughter be getting old enough to learn to drive?" I know, on a factual level, that Gavin's daughter Jillian was indeed old enough to begin that process. I had enough parent friends to know that could be at least part of the reason why he looked so weary.

I tried to lighten his mood. "So tell me, is it harder to raise a teenage girl or run a nosy small town?"

At least that managed to return a small spark to the man's eyes. "Pretty much a toss-up, depending on the hour."

"She's a smart girl. Sensible—well, as sensible as they come at that age."

"Which isn't very," he cut in, as he peered again into the large box where the town's ornament collection was steadily growing.

Gavin would be a patient, if stern, driving teacher. Not much of a risk-taker, our mayor. The kind of guy who checks the position of his rearview mirror every time he gets into the car, even if he's the only one who drives it. In the few times that I have hosted Gavin as a passenger in my car, I pretended not to notice that he checked the clearance before I changed lanes. Life didn't hand single fathers a bigger challenge than a teenage daughter behind the wheel, I suppose.

I dared to put a hand on Gavin's arm as I leaned over to inspect the ornaments as well. I picked up one that Deborah from the flower shop had contributed to the cause, a beautiful bright red poinsettia. "I predict she'll do great, even if you do lose a lot of sleep from here on in." I put that one back and found a tiny knit stocking that looked to be Jeanette's work. "Half the fun of passing these from hand to hand down the street is going to be getting to see so many of them up close. We're a very talented bunch, us Collinstown merchants."

"Talk like that has you ending up as president of the Chamber of Commerce." Gavin reached in to find a miniature *Barker Real Estate* sign with a plastic candy cane hastily hot-glued to one corner. "Now who do you suppose contributed these?"

I laughed. "I'm no longer as popular as you think. Next

to Mom, I think you, Margo, and Linda are the only people who treat me like they used to. I feel suspicious eyes all over the place."

"It's your imagination," Gavin replied as he tossed the blatantly advertising ornament back into the bin. With a twinge I noticed there were at least ten more in there.

"I wish I could say that, but I overheard some people at the coffee shop yesterday when they didn't know I was standing nearby. They were theorizing that Vincenzo and I plotted to kill Sterling to free ourselves for our desperate love affair."

That was not the thing to say to Gavin. "That's absurd. Sterling didn't stand in the way of . . . what you two . . . aren't anyway . . ." He stopped himself, perhaps remembering that Vincenzo and I had been seen in deep conversation at Collinstown's most romantic spot. "Some people watch too much TV."

I was grateful this gave me an easy change of subject. "Or listen to too many true crime podcasts. Jillian helped Mom download a dozen episodes of one of them onto her phone. Now Mom thinks she's a trained detective." Mom had been spouting an endless number of theories as to how and why Adelaide and Bitsy could have killed Sterling. I'm ashamed to say I found them ridiculously entertaining.

"Mom's latest is that Sterling's company had discovered a youth serum. He kept it secret from Bitsy, of course, so that he could inherit the family money more quickly. Bitsy found out and killed him out of spite and the unquenchable desire to live forever."

This was as outlandish as any of Mom's other theories. Bitsy's medical knowledge didn't extend beyond med-spa treatments, and she wasn't strong enough to haul Sterling's body around the way we believed it had been. And, perhaps most compelling of all, Bitsy hated all things messy—and Sterling's murder had been a most messy business. Adelaide, on the other hand, fell neatly into too many of those categories with ease.

I was pulled from my thoughts by Gavin's grimace. "About Rhonda . . ."

Far too many doses of worrisome news in my life started with the phrases "About Rhonda" or "About your mother." I braced myself. "What about Mom?"

"I was trying to keep it from reaching her, but the Newmans are putting their place up for sale."

Here was the ultimate "good news, bad news" scenario. The good news was that Mom was looking at places to live back here in Collinstown that were not my house. She'd come to regret moving to a townhouse across the river, and she wanted to return back to town. I'd only narrowly escaped her idea of "moving back to town" becoming "moving in with Libby." So in my view, any place that wasn't mine was worth considering.

. . . Except for the fact that the Newmans were Gavin's next-door neighbors. And they owned a tiny colonial house much like mine. One that Mom had always adored.

Rhonda Beckett is my own dear mother, but I would not wish her as a next-door neighbor on someone I disliked, much less someone I liked as much as Gavin. The man's "I'm getting it from all sides" expression made total sense now.

"Oh," I said in a rather dread-filled tone. "We can't have that."

"No," he said with equal fear, "we can't." He pinched the bridge of his nose. "We have to come up with something. She's already called Mark Newman. Twice."

I hated asking, because I already knew the answer. "Who's their broker?"

Gavin merely glanced down at the Barker Real Estate signs.

"George wouldn't do that to me, would he?"

We both knew George would take *anyone's* money. He'd probably even encourage it, knowing that Mom would need to put her own townhome on the market. Mom would never use George as a selling broker, but she'd have no control over who the Newmans used. The thought of my mother giving George Barker business—even indirect business—made me queasy. I suspect it made George practically glow.

"We ought to put the brakes on that. For any number of reasons." That felt safer than saying "I like you too much to have you involved—or even near—the drama this is sure to be."

Gavin's brows knit in war strategy. "There may not be a way."

The number of problems swirling around my life was making me claustrophobic. "And here I thought the hardest challenge of the week would be teaching Vincenzo how to knit."

I tossed it off as a casual remark, but it seemed to hit Gavin like a cannonball. "You're what?" he nearly shouted, his words echoing in the large, empty hall.

"He asked me if I would teach him." When his eyes narrowed, I added, "I am rather good at it." I was. Half the knitters in Collinstown learned from me. I taught Gavin's own daughter, although he looked as if that fact escaped him at the moment.

"He's got to be lying. He has to already know how." Suspicious disbelief dripped from Gavin's tone.

"Well, you'd think, but evidently not. His grandmother tried to teach him, but it didn't work out. I actually think it's kind of sweet that he asked."

Oh, that was the wrong way to put it. Gavin paced a small circle before coming back to glare at me. "He's playing you, Libby. The vicuña, the Blue Moon, Sterling, and now this?"

At least he'd used the correct name for the animals. "The Blue Moon was my idea. So were the vicuña."

Gavin looked almost wounded that I'd have dinner at the Blue Moon with anyone other than him. I'll admit, as enjoyable as my evening at the place with Vincenzo had been, some part of me had felt as if I was cheating. On a man who is *not* my boyfriend. To be honest, I'm not really sure what Gavin is to me, but his current territorial glare wasn't doing his prospects any favors.

"He's"—Gavin searched for a sufficiently evil word— "schmoozing you. Everyone knows how much you like teaching anyone to knit."

I couldn't help myself. "*You've* never asked."

"I don't want to learn," he barked back. Then, when he seemed to realize how that sounded, Gavin softened his expression. "I mean," he bumbled, "you know . . . it's Jillian's thing. She'd probably want to teach me if I ever wanted to learn."

"Nice save," I admitted reluctantly. And I knew he'd never want to learn. While I could very easily picture Vincenzo working yarn and needles, I could not conjure up an image of Gavin doing the same. I knew many men who knit—some of them with spectacular skill—but I'd never expect to count Gavin among them.

"Seriously, Libby, don't you think it's a bit . . . opportune? He's trying to get on your good side."

A part of me knew that. But I agreed for the same reason that Vincenzo had asked—it is a very good way to learn a lot about someone.

I gave Gavin an "Oh, grow up" look, even though I did take a small enjoyment in his envious reaction. No one likes to be taken for granted, and it did feel good for Gavin to realize that another man appeared to find me attractive. But I had no intentions of having any wool—vicuña or otherwise—pulled over my eyes. "I've not forgotten that Vincenzo is a suspect in all this. There's a lot of history between him and Sterling that I don't know. This is my chance to ask questions."

That seemed to calm our mayor down a bit. "Just . . . be careful. I don't trust the guy. When's your first lesson?" He gave the word "lesson" a sarcastic tone, as if he believed it was never intended to be a lesson at all.

"Tomorrow. Why, do you want to join in the fun?"

The mayor practically ground his reply of "No" out through his teeth.

CHAPTER ELEVEN

We opened the shop with a bit more ease on Wednesday. I had survived three days as a murder suspect, and while things weren't anywhere close to normal, they did feel slightly less catastrophic. I actually felt I had enough mental clarity to try and tackle the prickly topic of where Mom wanted to live. We needed a solid plan for diverting her away from the Newman house, even though Gavin and I currently had no idea how.

The opportunity presented itself when Mom came into the shop that afternoon. I looked up from helping a customer put the finishing touches on a Christmas present of hat and mittens for her niece to see Mom carrying two large plates covered in tin foil. This was a welcome cue that she was in a good mood. Mom is not a stress baker. Mom bakes to spread joy. That's always good news for us in the shop, because while Mom is as skilled a knitter as I am, her baking far exceeds mine. And just because Margo has goodies galore across the street doesn't mean we don't always welcome more.

"Look what I made," Mom boasted. She peeled back the foil over one of the plates, revealing what looked like a couple of dozen reindeer cookies with holiday touches. Their scent took me back to dunking gingerbread men in a tall glass of milk after school in my childhood.

"Oh, wow, these look amazing, Rhonda. Thank you." Shannon gushed, coming out from behind the sales counter to admire the collection.

It took me a minute to realize what I was looking at.

"Gingerbread vicuña?" Even I was impressed. Mom had taken what I guessed to be a reindeer cookie, nipped off the antlers, frosted them in a butterscotch-looking vicuña-colored frosting, and then given each a little holiday wreath collar.

She grinned. "What do you think?"

Mom may have her moments of confusion and senior sensibilities, but there were days she flat-out amazed me. "You should save a few for Vincenzo. He'd love these."

"Oh, that second plate is for him."

"You should take these over right away." I imagined our Gallant Herdsman lavishing Mom with compliments.

"Well, I was going to," Mom replied, "but he had company. Some very official-looking man who mentioned Sterling's name. It didn't look like a pleasant conversation, so I came in here first." Mom leaned in. "The guy looked government. Do you think the FBI may be on the case?"

My ex-husband had been an important man, but I don't think he rated FBI attention. "I doubt it." I peered out the window to see Vincenzo stomping into his trailer and slamming the door loud enough to make the herd jump. Those animals were growing more skittish by the day—why on earth couldn't the zoo get someone down here faster to transport them back? If a vicuña got sick on my watch, I don't know what I'd do.

I watched the serious-looking man in a dark suit and somber tie as he came up the side walkway toward the shop's front door. Mom wasn't wrong—he did look "government." Had he interrogated Vincenzo? Was I next?

Seconds later, he pushed through the front door with an expression that confirmed he was not here for worsted wool. In fact, he took the whole shop in with a bit of a sneer.

Mom opted to spring into action. "Hello again. Would you like a gingerbread vicuña?"

Granted, that's not a question you hear every day, but the guy could have been nicer about the grimace he gave Mom.

"I'm VP of R and D Kevin Webster." He spoke all those initials as if they ought to mean something to me. Given the shop name, I suppose that wasn't much of a stretch, but I was still clueless.

"Hello, Mr. Webster. What can I do for you?"

Mom extended the plate of cookies again with a gratuitous smile.

He ignored Mom. "I'm from Sonesty."

Mom immediately withdrew the cookies. She was no fan of Sterling's company since our split. As a matter of fact, she made her doctor check all of her prescriptions, and if they were Sonesty products, she insisted on something else.

I couldn't think of a reason why a Sonesty executive would need to talk to me. For that matter, I found it far more interesting that a Sonesty executive wanted to talk to Vincenzo.

Opting for the high ground, I extended a hand to Webster. "I'm Libby Beckett. I'm sorry for the loss of your

CEO. This must be a difficult time for everyone at the company."

Webster was unmoved by my attempt at a welcome. "I know who you are."

Mom set the plate of cookies down away from Webster and crossed her arms over her chest. "Then you know you are talking to Sterling's widow, I assume."

Again, I wondered if the term "widow" applied here. While I was playing a host of different roles in this scenario, grieving widow wasn't really one of them.

Webster ignored Mom's chiding. "Is there somewhere we can talk?" He threw Mom, Shannon, and the other customers annoyed glares before adding, "Privately?"

I was in no hurry to squeeze into the tiny confines of my office with this man. "I'm afraid there's only the stockroom. Perhaps that will do?"

When he nodded, I led Mr. Webster into the crowded forest of boxes and shelves that is our stockroom. It was overloaded with holiday yarns and kits at the moment, but I managed to clean off two boxes and set them facing each other. "I'm surprised to see you here," I offered. "I don't have any dealings with Sonesty."

Webster opened a folder and scanned some papers. "But you still own a sizable portion of stock. One that provides an income for you." He named the amount of my last dividend check, which I found nosy and intrusive.

"That's true." *Although I don't see how that's any of your business*, I thought.

Webster closed the folder and closed his hands on it as if it was a conference room table. The position looked absurd with him perched on a box of baby alpaca skeins with a rainbow of superwash merino about to spill off the shelf behind him. He cleared his throat. "I'd like to think that makes you an interested party in keeping Sonesty viable and operating."

"I'm afraid I don't place much stake in the health of my ex-husband's company."

"But you profit from it," he insisted. "Nicely."

I didn't like where this was heading. "I negotiated an appropriate settlement with Sterling upon our divorce, yes." I leaned in. "Mr. Webster, why are you here talking to both me and my guest?"

Webster lifted his chin with an air of superiority that tagged him as a clear colleague of Sterling's. "Why I might be talking to Mr. Marani is no concern of yours."

Sonesty's C-suite was nervous about something, that was clear. I wasn't a major shareholder, nor did I stand to become one upon Sterling's death, as far as I knew. To my knowledge, that benefit went to Bitsy and Adelaide. "Am I allowed to ask if you've made this same visit to Sterling's mother and sister while they're here in town?"

"Of course I am in constant communication with them." Webster cleared his throat again. "Am I correct in my assumption that you no longer have medical power of attorney over Mr. Jefferson's affairs?"

If he knew the size of my dividend check, I suspect he already knew the answer to this. "Not since our divorce. Although I'm not sure why everyone is asking me that. In fact, I have a few questions about Sterling's health, given the nature of his death. Perhaps you can fill me in?"

I didn't expect him to say yes, but I didn't expect the dark look Webster threw me at that question, either. But he clearly knew something, so I pressed on. "For example, why blood thinners were found in his system? Along with an unidentifiable drug? Would you know anything about that?"

Another startled look. My wild guess apparently hit a nerve. Sterling's flustered and frantic attitude made a certain sense now—devoted to strength and perfection as he was, I could think of few things that would bother Sterling more than a health issue.

But what issue? And how was Vincenzo connected to all this? Trouble was, I needed answers, and I only seemed to be gathering more questions.

Webster stood up, knocking a package of bright pink skeins down in the process. "I'm sure you understand I'm not at liberty to discuss anything like that with you at this time." His formal pronouncement jarred with the cascade of yarn around him.

"But there is something to discuss," I pressed, sure of it now. "Sterling was being treated for something; you just won't tell me what."

Webster did not reply, only handed me one of the skeins and pulled the stockroom door open with an efficient yank. His exit out the door was just as expedient.

"What was that all about?" Mom asked, munching on a cookie.

"You know," I said, "I'm not sure. But I intend to find out." I grabbed a cookie myself. "Good thing it's time for Vincenzo's first knitting lesson."

"You're teaching the Gallant Herdsman how to knit?" Mom balked. "He doesn't already know?"

"It's more about what *I* don't already know," I replied. "The Gallant Herdsman has some explaining to do."

I grabbed the plate of Mom's cookies and snatched up the pattern and needles I'd set aside earlier. It was time for a little investigation of my own.

* * *

It wouldn't do to barge in there ticked off, so I stood outside the shop for a moment before heading around back to Vincenzo's motor home. The day was beautiful; no snowfall yet, but the sort of sparkling December morning that proclaimed the joys of the season. I looked up and down Collin Avenue, pulling in a cleansing breath. The crisp, refreshing air held the hint of the river that was such a bone-deep sensory memory for me.

Cheery wreaths hung from each of the antique lampposts that dotted our main street. Across from me, I could see Margo's gorgeous window all done up as if the Nutcracker's Sugar Plum Fairy had taken up residence there. Down the block, I could see Angie's award-winning efforts to decorate the police department. There was a good reason the police station had taken the town holiday decor award more years than any other building.

"Christmas is still coming," I declared to the clear blue sky. Yes, the tragedy of Sterling's murder had dampened the holiday for me—and for many people—but it hadn't taken it all away. For a few moments, I embodied the Grinch's wonder that Christmas had come no matter what. That was surely something to take joy in, right?

Bolstered, I turned toward the little encampment still set in my backyard. It made me happy that the four vicuña looked up at me with pleasant eyes. It was silly, but I wanted them to like me as much as I liked them. There was something soothing in how they meandered about, delicate hooves pawing at my grass and wide eyes taking in the world. I thought of the gingerbread versions in my hand and managed the first smile I'd felt in too long.

There. My heart felt restored to the right place to teach

knitting. I prefer to avoid "angry knitting"—for spiritual reasons as well as the truth that it rarely produces good results—I certainly didn't want to do this particular teaching session angry, either.

Curious? Yes. With a slight investigative agenda? Yes. But angry, no.

My reverie was broken by a steady stream of intense Italian coming from inside the motor home. Vincenzo did seem to have a lot of intense conversations in his native tongue. I had a strong hunch that the connection between him and Sterling went beyond myself and the vicuña visit. Frank once said, "When clues feel connected, they usually are." I just hadn't figured out *how* these clues were connected.

One thing was sure, I would get much further if Vincenzo felt I was on his side. I didn't really believe anything dubious about our Gallant Herdsman. Still, I was listening to the nagging little voice in the back of my head insisting I might not have the whole picture.

I applied my helpful face—perfected from months of Y.A.R.N. customer service—and rapped on the door.

The high-speed Italian stopped and Vincenzo pulled the door open. His face changed from a grimace to a pleased expression, and when I held out the plate, he added that heartthrob smile. "Aren't you a welcome sight," he said, pocketing his cell phone.

"Mom made you gingerbread vicuña."

His eyebrows furrowed at the unlikely announcement. But when he pulled back the tin foil, he erupted in a cascade of Italian much different in tone than what I'd heard a moment ago. "Incredible."

"And very edible," I added. "Mom's a good baker. So it seems your lesson comes with snacks."

Vincenzo pulled the door farther open and motioned me inside. "Who can resist a beautiful woman bearing yarn and cookies?"

Don't fall for it, I told myself, even as a little bit of me fell for it.

The motor home was exactly as I expected—sleek, luxurious, and as neat as if a maid came in every morning. One of those old-school espresso pots, the kind that go straight on the stove, sat on a burner next to a small china cup. "Would you like some?" he asked. "I make mine very strong, but I could ease up on that for you."

"I get the feeling I'd be up until New Year's if I drank what you do," I said. "I'm fine for now."

"But you will have a cookie." He said it as if he'd be personally offended if I didn't.

No one had to twist my arm, despite the two I'd already eaten in the shop. "Of course."

"Come and sit." He patted a place on the plush couch right next to him. "This will be lovely."

I thought about saying something about the very unlovely visitor we'd both just had, but opted to put that off until a bit later.

"You know," I said as I showed him how to cast on the stitches. "You're only the third man I've ever taught to knit. And certainly the first person I've ever taught with yarn this luxurious." I thought that a better choice of word than "expensive." One look around these mobile lodgings told me Vincenzo was used to expensive things. The other night I'd looked up the cost of trailer homes like this, and the price tag was four times the price of my current car.

"I am a most fortunate man," Vincenzo replied.

"Are you sure you wouldn't rather learn on a more basic fiber?" I didn't want to imply that his first attempt at knitting might not live up to the standards of vicuña yarn, but most knitters make rather a mess of things at first.

He looked at me as if I'd suggested he knit with barbed wire. "Why would I knit with anything other than vicuña? It will be the only yarn I use. It should be the first as well."

The man was persuasive. What he said made an odd sort of sense, but honestly, he could have suggested something absurd in that voice with those eyes and I'd likely have agreed.

I needn't have worried. Vincenzo took to the complicated cast on so fast, a part of me wondered if he was lying about not knowing how to knit. Then again, Gavin's daughter Jillian had taken to it just as fast. Despite Gavin's refusal to ever knit, something felt a little . . . I don't know . . . sneaky about knitting with Vincenzo. As if I was somehow cheating on Gavin, which I most certainly was not. This was an investigative knitting lesson, not a flirtatious one. Well, mostly.

After the cast on, I took the yarn and needles from him to show him the basic knit stitch. Vincenzo leaned in as if I was showing him the most interesting thing in the world. He looked utterly fascinated. And not just with knitting. I began to doubt there was a woman on the planet immune to this man's charms. The trailer began to feel a bit warm.

"Now you try it." His hands may have lingered against mine just a bit as I put the yarn and needles back into his hands. "Take it slow, each part in order—in, over, through, and out."

I watched him go through the motion, repeating the four parts of the knit stitch. There is a rhyme many people use to learn—"*In through the front door, Go around the back, Out through the window, And off jumps Jack*"—but I couldn't bring myself to use it with someone as sophisticated as Vincenzo. I'd recently discovered another one: "*Stab the pirate, Strangle the pirate, Pull him through, And off the plank!*" but you can likely see why I opted against that one as well. Even as it was, the man somehow made "in, over, through, and out" simmer like a passage from a romance novel.

I began to wonder if Gavin hadn't been right. I was being wooed. Stitched off my feet instead of swept.

Remember why you're here, I reminded my slightly smitten brain. *He knows something.*

"It is so soothing," Vincenzo remarked in a silky tone. Now, I'm a good teacher, but even I know I'm not that good. No novice knitter ever finds knitting soothing in the first hour of learning. That zen quality comes, but not for a little while.

"It can be wonderfully soothing," I agreed. "Especially with something like vicuña." Determined to stick to my knitting espionage, I added, "Especially after a visitor like you and I just had."

Vincenzo's stitches stopped. "You saw him."

"Well, Mom saw him, but he came into the shop and grilled me just after he talked to you." I dared a steady look into those arresting brown eyes. "I know why Webster is talking to me, but I can't work out why someone from Sonesty is talking to you."

Vincenzo gave a dismissive shrug. "There isn't a reason, really. Webster thinks I know something, but I don't."

I wasn't entirely sure I believed him. I backed off, returning to guiding him through more of the stitches. I fixed the several errors he made along the short rows of the simple scarf pattern I'd chosen. The simple shape of scarves makes them a good first project, and Vincenzo's ever-present vicuña scarf would gain a sibling when he was done.

After a handful of rows, I tried again. "You and Sterling kept up over the years since college?"

"Sterling viewed me as important. Well-connected." His mouth thinned out before he added, "Rich." After a pause, he continued, "And we both know those are . . . *were* some of Sterling's favorite things." His gaze traveled out to the stretch of grass where the shearing platform had been.

"I liked him," Vincenzo went on. "Used to. We had some grand times together. But a friendship with Sterling always felt . . . transactional. I believe friendship should be a gift, you know? An embellishment to life."

"Funny you should use that word," I admitted. "Things got to the point between Sterling and me where all I felt like was an embellishment. A decoration added to his important life."

Vincenzo turned up the—sorry, there isn't another word for it—smolder in his eyes. "You should never be an add-on. A man should make the woman he loves the center of his life. The thing he prizes above all else."

"Well," I replied, more breathless than I would have liked, "that certainly wasn't Sterling." I looked down at the knitting. "Two more stitches on this row and then I think you're ready to learn how to purl."

Vincenzo looked down as if he was surprised to discover the amount of stitches he'd accomplished. "Look at that. You are an excellent teacher. Nonna would be proud—and a bit jealous."

I attempted to steer the conversation back to my original purpose. "Webster seemed to think I knew something medical about Sterling. An issue. Sterling had never mentioned anything to me. Had he said something to you?"

"Medical? Sterling would never admit something like that to me. Or anyone."

"They found two drugs in Sterling's system. One was a Sonesty blood thinner. The other they can't identify. Did Sterling mention anything about a new Sonesty drug to you?"

Vincenzo dropped a stitch. Chief Reynolds had told me once that a careful observer can tell whether someone's reaction to something is surprised or startled. "Surprised" means they didn't know whatever you just told them; "startled" means they're rattled to know you know it. I had learned to spot the difference.

Vincenzo was startled.

CHAPTER TWELVE

So that is what killed him?" Vincenzo asked after a telling pause. "Not the . . ." He raised his hand to his neck. I knew the impulse—I did everything I could to avoid using the violent word "stabbing."

"They don't know. Given that I'm still 'a person of interest,' Chief Reynolds isn't doing a lot of sharing about the case."

Vincenzo put down the knitting and gave a pained sigh. "I am 'a person of interest' as well. It's disturbing, isn't it, to think people consider you capable of such a thing?"

I didn't know how to answer that. Vincenzo was by all accounts an intense man, and Sterling's death seemed an intense act. Was that connection, or coincidence? "We need to find out who did this. For everyone's sake. So, do you know anything about what Sterling was up to at Sonesty?

Anything, perhaps, to do with the remark you made about Sterling's snakeskin belt?"

Oh, that hit home. Vincenzo rose to walk about the cabin. He was tall enough that I kept waiting for his head to knock against the ceiling. He was an imposing figure in any space, but the confines of the motor home made him seem even larger. "All I know is that Sterling would stoop to just about anything to put Sonesty ahead. But I am not telling you anything you don't already know."

"And the belt?" It seemed so out of character for Sterling's taste in clothes that it had to mean something.

"I hate snakes. I'm sure he wore it just to irritate me."

I didn't believe that. "Like Indiana Jones, huh?" The tension in the air made the joke fall flat.

Vincenzo ignored my remark, choosing instead to change the subject. "I hate that my shears have become a murder weapon," he said darkly. "Even if they are not what killed Sterling, it makes me sick to think they were used in that way."

"I agree." I would have felt the same way if we'd found Sterling impaled with knitting needles. In fact, a visiting designer had been strangled with yarn a while back, and I shared Vincenzo's disgust at something I love being used as a weapon like that.

"I want to find who did this," he declared with a theatrical air. "I want them brought to justice. I may not have liked Sterling much anymore, but even he deserves to rest in peace."

The pronouncement sounded more like something I'd expect from Adelaide. Experience had sadly taught me to be wary of such declarations. Could he be overcompensating to hide something? After all, if I had learned nothing else on this little reconnaissance knitting lesson, I was now pretty sure this man was hiding something.

A knock on the motor home door prevented me from pursuing any further espionage. Vincenzo opened the door to find Mom.

"Well, look at you two all cozy in here." I did not care for her tone one bit. She grinned at Vincenzo. "Did you like my cookies?"

Vincenzo struggled to answer. "They were delicious, Rhonda. Thank you."

"Well, fun's over," Mom declared. "You need to get back to the shop, Elizabeth. More vicuña's gone missing."

"Someone's stealing the vicuña?" Vincenzo's voice rose in alarm. I'd been trying to keep that from him to avoid just this kind of reaction.

Mom either missed or ignored the glare I gave her. "Two more skeins," she said. "That's four total. We've got a serial yarn thief on our hands."

"That's two thousand dollars of yarn," Vincenzo said.

"Grand theft larceny," Mom replied. "I've been listening to a podcast that—"

"Let's get back to the shop and sort this out," I cut in before Mom went into any further crime theory detail.

Vincenzo unfortunately took the "we" literally and attempted to follow my exit out of the motor home. "What?" he said when I held up a hand to halt him. "This is Marani vicuña being taken."

"This is a shop problem that I will solve as the shop owner. We've never had this kind of trouble before, so I'm sure we'll get to the bottom of it."

Vincenzo Marani did not like being told to stay put. "So I am to just sit here while someone steals my yarn from you? I am to just stand by while this happens?"

I was definitely getting a front-row seat to Marani intensity. "Well," I tried to reply with a calm smile, "you can always knit."

The look Vincenzo gave me as he slammed the motor home door shut was as sharp as the man's clipping shears.

B y the way," Mom asked as we walked back toward the shop, "when did those two start fighting?"

My brain was so busy whirring through possible yarn bandits that I barely heard her. "Who?"

"Linda and Sheila. They're shouting at each other, each sure the other one is to blame. When did that start?"

"Her name is Shannon, Mom." Mom hadn't gotten her name right once in the few weeks she'd been working for me. At first it was amusing, but it wore thin pretty quick. "And I don't know. They got along great when Shannon was a customer. I can't figure out what's so different now."

Mom stopped. "Really, Elizabeth? It's so obvious."

I threw her a sideways look. "Not to me. I didn't see this coming at all." Nor murder in my shop yard or now grand theft vicuña.

"That's because I raised such a nice girl. Linda feels threatened. She's been your loyal partner since the beginning, and now there's someone else. It's territorial, like those wolves on the documentary I watched last night."

That made no sense to me. "Linda is my right hand. I adore her. She has no reason to feel threatened by my bringing Shannon on. In fact, Linda is the one who suggested we get someone else in here so we had some help covering the holiday hours."

Mom put her hand on my arm and gave me one of those "Bless your heart—you really don't get it" looks. "These things aren't supposed to make sense. Emotions aren't logical."

I spread my hands in a wide arc of frustration. "I can't have this nonsense. Y.A.R.N. needs to run smoothly right now." Instead, I felt like those letters on my chalkboard stood for "Yikes! Alarm! Ridiculous Nonsense!"

Mom pulled open the shop door. "So go in there and play alpha dog to your wolf pack."

I had no idea what that meant. But I was going to have to do something.

The air in the shop was so tense I felt like I practically had to machete my way to the counter, where Shannon appeared to be on the verge of tears. Linda stood over by the coffee maker, fuming. I was amazed there were still customers in the store. I would have turned around and left the building rather than try to buy yarn in this battleground.

I summoned up my quietest "leadership skills" voice and stood in between them. "Ladies, this has to stop."

"We've never had a theft problem until she arrived," Linda accused.

"We've never had much of a theft problem *at all* before this," I countered. "But we've also never carried something with that kind of price tag. Maybe we can't leave it out the way we have."

"Not with *her* behind the counter." Linda's sharp tone was so unlike her. She was usually the coolest head in the room, even with our prickliest customers. It took a lot to get under her skin, and I had never expected Shannon to be the one to do it.

"Maybe we're being targeted by animal rights activists," Mom chimed in. "They could have followed Vincenzo here. I heard they do things like this."

I turned to my dear, aggravating mother. "*Not help-ing*, Mom."

"I didn't do this." Shannon still looked on the verge of tears. "I don't know how that yarn is disappearing, but I swear to you, it's nothing I've done."

"No," countered Linda, "it's what you've *not* done. As in watch our stock."

I needed to separate these two, and fast. "I'm convinced this isn't about Y.A.R.N. This is about the vicuña." Maybe I'd overstepped in my excitement to bring in something so exclusive. Maybe this was about Vincenzo. Whatever it was, I was reasonably certain this wasn't about Linda or Shannon. I checked my watch. It was just before noon, but the day was feeling endless already. "Mom, can you help Shannon with the shop while Linda and I go take a walk and sort this out?"

"Sure," Mom said. Mom had her challenges, but she was still helpful as a last-minute shop staff. "Come have another cookie and calm down, dear. No one thinks this is your fault."

Linda shot me a sideways glance that let me know she didn't agree. I pointed to the hook where her coat hung and gave her a "Do as you're told" glare that Margo would have admired. Alpha dog indeed.

We weren't out of the shop ten seconds before Linda turned to me. "I don't like her."

That much was clear. "Linda, I don't get this. Shannon's been in the shop dozens of times as a customer. You get along with everyone. What's going on?"

I was surprised to see Linda swallow hard before she replied, "She doesn't care." She didn't say, "Not like we do," but I heard it loud and clear. "It's just a job to her."

I began walking in the direction of the riverbank and the pretty little gazebo that was my favorite place to think. There was more to this than Linda's dislike of a new employee.

"I don't think that's true. But even if it was, that's not a reason to go on the attack. She's been a good employee so far." Another thought struck me. "And if she didn't care, why is she making suggestions on how to improve our inventory system?"

I was glad to see that make Linda think. She always set her jaw in a certain way when she puzzled something out— be it how the row of ribbing got messed up or why the Wi-Fi suddenly went down. "It's different," I continued. "I get that. It's different for me, too. But I'm not so sure it's bad."

Linda gave me a mumbled, begrudging, "Maybe."

We turned off Collin Avenue and onto the little path that led down to the riverbank. "I love our partnership," I went on. "I couldn't make Y.A.R.N. work without you. I'm not sure I could make *life* work without you. But we have to figure this out. I'm under enough stress as it is without having to referee squabbles between employees."

"I know you didn't do it." Linda gave the declaration the weight of the fierce loyalty I'd always loved about her. "No matter how awful Sterling got, you wouldn't. You couldn't."

"It feels good to hear you say that. All this is really getting to me."

We sat down at the gazebo and let the silence and the flow of the river smooth out the kinks in ourselves and the world. "I'm sorry," she said softly after a long while.

Her apology sounded wide and heavy—as if this was about more than Y.A.R.N. It led me to ask, "Are you okay? Outside the shop, I mean. Is everything all right?"

Linda's eyes welled up. I have never seen this woman cry. Suddenly my memory recalled a dozen tiny details that should have clued me in to the fact that Linda was barely holding it all together. She was always so steadfast, I think I forgot she could lose it like the rest of us mere mortals.

Her "No" was heartbreaking. For a minute or two she let a few small sobs escape her, her strawberry blond curls bobbing with the shaking of her shoulders.

I took her hand and squeezed it tight. "What is it?" I asked gently. "What's wrong?"

Fear and worry filled her big green eyes along with the tears she wiped away with one hand. "We might have to move."

Linda loved Collinstown. She made some comment about how much she adored our little town almost every day. This was devastating news for her. "How? Why?"

She sniffed and pulled in one of those big "I'm trying not to cry" breaths. "Jason's company is getting bought."

A corporate merger had ended Linda's finance job a few months before I opened Y.A.R.N. We used to jokingly toast that merger for releasing her to my shop, where she continually told me she was so much happier.

"He doesn't think he'll survive the merger, so he started looking for a new position. Out of state."

It all made sense now. Change at Y.A.R.N. would be hard enough to swallow, but to think about leaving the shop and being replaced by someone else must be a bitter pill to choke down.

She gave me a wet, wobbly attempt at a smile. "So I may have been taking a bit of that out on Shannon." Her eyes filled again. "I don't want to leave."

I pulled her into a giant hug. "I don't want you to. Ever."

I let her cry it out, thankful to now know what was going

on in Linda's life. She was a dear friend, not just an employee. When she straightened back up, looking a bit more like the unflappable Linda I knew and loved, I asked, "Is it a sure thing that you have to leave? Could Jason still find a position here?"

"He's trying hard. He doesn't want to leave, either. But you know how these things go. It may not be up to us."

"When does the sale go through?"

"First quarter next year. So at least we'll get the holidays here. But I don't want them to be our last." Linda's voice broke a bit on the final word.

I tried to swallow the lump in my throat. "Me neither." We stared at the water moving slowly past us, feeling the chill of the day finally overcome the bright sunshine. "I'm glad you told me." I raised one eyebrow at her. "It explains a lot."

Linda lifted her shoulders, then let them fall again with a bit of a sigh. "I haven't exactly been my usual self, have I?"

"Well, no. You could go a bit easier on Shannon. It'd help things." When she gave me one of her classic Linda looks, I added, "I don't think we're dealing with a regular old brand of shoplifter here. It's not fair to blame Shannon." I gently reminded her, "Skeins have gone missing while both of you were in the shop."

She pressed her lips together before admitting, "I'll try to lighten up."

I stood up. "Go on home for the day. We've got it covered. You probably could use a little time to yourself."

"Maybe. You sure you'll be all right?"

I wasn't at all sure. The thought of losing Linda was like losing a limb—I wasn't sure I could function without her.

But if there's one thing my months at Y.A.R.N. had taught me, it's that life goes on whether you're ready or not.

"We'll be fine. Mom's at the store today."

Linda's eyebrow raised again. "Are you sure that's help?"

"Mostly." Sometimes you take the help you can get.

CHAPTER THIRTEEN

The house door felt twice as heavy when I finally pushed it open at the end of that long day. Most days, Hank's excitement is a welcome greeting, but today I was doubly grateful for his big eyes and happy licks. If there's one thing dogs are truly wonderful at, it's making you feel welcome when you come home. As if they've spent the whole day just waiting for the moment when you come into view.

"Hello, boy," I cooed as I hunched down and let him love me in all those messy wonderful doggy ways. You'd think I had been gone a year by the way he greeted me. After the day I'd had, it really did feel like a year had passed. And as near as I could tell, we were nowhere nearer to the solution of Sterling's death. How much longer would this go on?

I fished one of Mom's gingerbread vicuña out of my bag. "I know you hate being kept away from the shop. But I brought you a goodie to make up for it."

After a brief sniff at the unusual treat, Hank pronounced it good and promptly polished it off in two bites.

"You should be grateful you got to stay away from all the drama at the shop today, boy. Christmas is definitely not feeling like the—"

I stopped short as I caught sight of my living room. "Hank!"

Living alone, I don't go especially all-out in the holiday decor department. The shop window gets most of my decorative attention, although I had been rather proud of myself for getting up a small tree this year and a lovely collection of red and green Christmas throw pillows to adorn my couch and armchairs.

All of which were now scattered about my living room. In various states of destruction. With an avalanche of white pillow stuffing cascading over everything.

"I ought to reach in there and take that cookie right back. How could you? You've never done something like this!"

Hank hadn't. With the exception of one misbegotten shoe, Hank had never chewed on anything but his vast collection of dog toys. Then again, he'd never been kept away from the shop for as many days as the vicuña herd had required.

I picked up a gorgeous needlepoint Father Christmas pillow, irritated to note that Father Christmas was no longer in possession of his left arm. A flurry of shredded yarn and backing edged a large hole in the now-empty pillow. Two feet over, a tapestry Christmas tree had met a chomped-in-half fate worthy of the tree downtown. On another day, I might have been able to laugh at that. Not today.

I stomped to the kitchen door, yanked it open, and proceeded to dismiss a sulking Hank to the small fenced-in yard that backed my colonial cottage. "Outside until I clean this up. And go think about what you've done." Useless, I know, but it felt good to say it.

I'd gathered up the last of the batting snowstorm into a trash bag and was contemplating how much of the leftover Alfredo to heat up for dinner when Hank began barking. When he added a very territorial growl, I set down the bag and opened the door.

Adelaide stood on the far side of the fence, staring in toward my house and my "guard dog."

Adelaide? I would not have expected a visit from her. Either she had opted to spy on me, or something had spurred her into the 180-degree turn of a voluntary visit to me.

"Does he bite?" Adelaide practically squeaked.

"Only if you're a throw pillow," I sighed, wondering if my dinner would now have to wait. I was rather hungry, and an argument with Adelaide could tip that over into hangry pretty quick.

"Huh?"

Adelaide never did possess much of a sense of humor. "Meet Hank, demolisher of decorative pillows."

She managed a half-hearted laugh—more to be polite than anything else, I expect.

"Ziggy used to eat socks. Well, more like find them, hide them, and chew them. I don't think he ever actually ate one. He liked Sterling's best of all. Drove Mom nuts."

Sterling had been so against us ever getting a dog that I had completely forgotten he'd ever owned one. Lots of people thought I got Hank to get over Sterling. The truth was that separating from Sterling enabled me to bring Hank into my life. Hank wasn't so much a coping mechanism as he was reward. And he'd been rewarding me in so many ways ever since.

"I can't believe he's gone," Adelaide moaned. "Can you?" All of the fight I'd seen in her the other day seemed to have evaporated. I was glad to see a bit of the intriguing young woman—dramatic, but intriguing—I'd known while married to her brother.

"No." I walked over and opened the gate, inviting her into my little backyard and now-dormant garden. Hank, bless him, came to my side, ever ready to defend me. She hesitated to come through the gate. "Did you do it?"

While that felt a tad direct, it was better than the "You did it!" of our last meeting.

I met Adelaide's eyes with the most direct look I could. "No. Your brother and I no longer got along, but I didn't kill him. Nor did I wish him dead."

She still didn't cross over into the yard. "Mother thinks you did it."

Bitsy had made that abundantly clear. I didn't quite know what to say to that except, "Do you think I did it?" I'll admit, half of me wanted to say, "Did *you* do it?"

"I did at first. But, no, I don't."

I thought about asking why, but decided to leave well enough alone. She looked rather lost and lonely as she worked up the nerve to come through the gate. "Do you want to come inside?"

She hesitated, looking around before offering a shrug and an "Okay."

"Who called you to come here?" I ventured since she'd finally come into the yard. "Before Sterling's death, I mean. Vincenzo says he saw you Friday night, before everything happened."

"He called me."

"Vincenzo called you to tell you Sterling was going to be here?" He had acted surprised to see Adelaide here. And he'd said nothing when Sterling had asked if he'd seen her. And yet he had been the one to invite her here? Clearly it wasn't to watch him shear vicuña. When Adelaide nodded, I asked, "Why?"

"He wanted to see if I could smooth the way between him and Sterling. They were fighting." She didn't hesitate when I pulled the back door open and we walked into my house, but kept talking. "Mad at each other. And a bit scared of each other, I think. Each waiting for the other to do something—only nobody was telling me what."

I knew that feeling too well. "So it went both ways, whatever it was." I led her into the kitchen. "Did Sterling ask you to smooth things over with Vincenzo, too?"

"No. I sort of went off the family radar after Vincenzo asked. I didn't want to get involved. But Vincenzo said it had something to do with those poor people in Peru, so I . . . well . . . I felt like I had to, you know?"

"The community he visits? The ones who tend the vicuña?" Adelaide was proving to be full of interesting information today.

She leaned up against the counter, looking more like a teenager than her twentysomething self. She'd never struck me as the kind to grow up on schedule—"adulting" seemed to be too much work to her, and Bitsy's steady flow of money made her listless, nomadic lifestyle too easy. "Yeah, them. Something about them needing to be protected. He made it sound like Sterling was going to do something to them, but that doesn't make any sense, does it?"

Very little about this made any sense. But it wasn't hard to envision Sterling considering a tiny Peruvian community as inconsequential if they stood in the way of something he wanted. "Has Sterling been to South America recently?"

"He made a couple of visits to the Amazon. Some weird

stuff about snakes. So I don't think he went where Vincenzo goes."

I tried to picture Sterling whacking his way through an Amazonian rain forest and almost laughed. The snakeskin belt was more likely a purchase from an upscale Brazilian boutique than any kind of hunting trophy. Still, this proved that Vincenzo and Sterling were in more contact than our Gallant Herdsman was ready to admit. I was pondering the implications of that when Adelaide turned to me and blurted, "It's Vincenzo. He did it."

I'd always thought Adelaide still firmly smitten with Vincenzo. Now she was accusing him of her brother's murder. "What makes you think that?"

"They were ticked off at each other. And c'mon, the clippers? It had to be someone big like him to do it, don't you think? Oh, no thanks."

I hadn't even realized I'd gotten the teapot down—it was the subconscious "company's here, put the kettle on" Mom had ingrained in me. I put the pot back up into the cupboard and filled Hank's kibble bowl instead. "I had the same thought—whoever did . . . what happened to Sterling . . . would need to have a lot of strength." Seeing as Adelaide was feeling so chatty, I ventured, "Chief Reynolds asked me if I knew of any health issues Sterling was facing."

"Yeah, he asked me that, too. He's—*was*—super-healthy, you know that. Sterling only makes drugs; he doesn't need them."

"He might not admit taking something to most people," I replied. "But I thought he might tell you, seeing as you went to nursing school. If you know anything, this isn't a secret you should keep, Adelaide." She wasn't off my suspect list. Adelaide had more than a common understanding of anatomy—like exactly where to puncture an artery if you wanted to make sure you got all the family inheritance. Or maybe how to inject a lethal dose of blood thinners—if such a thing existed.

"Sterling didn't take anything," she declared sharply. "I'm not keeping secrets from anyone." She straightened up and began walking to the door. "You know, I came here to try and be nice. Now I see Mom was right. This was a waste of time."

I'd pushed too far. "Adelaide . . ."

"You and Vincenzo can have each other, as far as I'm concerned. Who knows? Maybe you both did it. Maybe you both can have a merry Christmas together in jail." With that, she yanked my back door opened and exited into the night.

I looked at Hank. "What just happened?"

Hank only stared at me for a second, then started in on his kibble.

Thursday morning, I planted myself in Chief Reynolds' office doorway with all the confidence I could summon. "I'm here to report a crime."

I'd been racking my brain trying to come up with a way to get Frank to talk with me. Not *to* me like a suspect, but *with* me like a friend. Or, if not a friend, at least not an adversary. This whole business had strained that friendship. We didn't know quite how to treat each other.

In the middle of the night last night, I'd sat straight up in bed practically slapping my forehead with the fact that I'd had a way under my nose the whole time.

He looked up from his paperwork. "Murder wasn't enough?"

I knew he was trying to make a joke, but it fell short.

"Theft, actually. Felony theft, if Mom's true-crime podcast education is accurate."

"Which it isn't," he grumbled, then added something about the cursed nature of podcasters. "Suddenly everybody thinks they can do my job."

There was a tiny bit of the old Frank in that crack, and I welcomed it. "Well, I don't think I can do your job. Which is why I'm here. Someone has stolen yarn from the shop. Very expensive yarn, and a fair amount of it."

"That vick . . . veye . . ." His eyebrows scrunched up with the effort to remember the name.

"Vicuña. Two thousand dollars' worth of it has gone missing, in multiple thefts."

I have never been so pleased to see Frank Reynolds click his pen. It was my signal he was taking the case seriously, despite being in the middle of a murder investigation. "Seems a bit specific for your run-of-the-mill shoplifter."

"That's what I thought." It felt oddly comforting to be mulling over clues and theories with the chief. "Either they're making a point, or they know how much the stuff is worth."

"Something is only worth what you can get someone to pay for it. Who else would pay the kind of money you say that yarn is worth? Marjorie knits, and she told me she'd never shell out that kind of cash for yarn."

Frank's daughter Marjorie was indeed a very good knitter. She'd made her dad a splendid sweater last year. "Most knitters won't. I didn't expect to sell as much as I did. But I didn't expect anyone to come in and steal it right from under our noses, either."

Frank sighed. "This would be a lot easier with security camera footage, Libby."

I glared at him. "Not you, too. I'm sure this is an isolated incident. Not a reason to treat Y.A.R.N. customers like criminals."

"We are a tourist town, Libby. People come in here from all over. I'm as sure as you are that no Collinstown resident is stealing from you. You advertised the event, didn't you?"

I could see his point. "Quite a bit."

"Used words like 'luxurious' and 'exclusive,' I bet?"

"A lot," I had to admit.

"So any hooligan with a smartphone could look up how much this stuff is worth and how small the ball of yarn is"—he mimed putting something in his pocket—"and hatch a plan to make a quick buck."

That made about as much sense to me as putting a Picasso out at a yard sale. "I don't think so. Any knitter with enough sense to pay the retail price would know it was illegal. It practically takes an act of Congress to get that stuff into the country. I mean, Vincenzo's having a terrible time just getting the paperwork in order to get the herd back across state lines ahead of schedule."

Frank leaned back and patted the tall filing cabinet behind his desk. "I got a lot of paperwork in here filled with people who don't care something was illegal. People's ethics go south pretty fast if they think they can get away with it."

"I don't want them to get away with it." My whining tone sounded too much like Adelaide. "That's why I'm here."

"Libby, I can't put an APB out for balls of yarn."

I knew that. But I couldn't bring myself to add the stolen vicuña to the pile of injustices that had been done. "Can't we do something?" After a second I added, "Other than put up a camera, I mean."

"A camera doesn't mean you don't trust your customers."

I rolled my eyes. "Then what does it mean?"

"It means you value your customers enough to do what's

necessary to reduce theft and keep your prices where they belong. Come on, Madam Chamber of Commerce President, you know that shoplifting drives up prices for small businesses. Your customers end up paying for the crime committed in your store."

Yeah, well, who ends up paying for the murder committed in my backyard? my weary brain complained. At least I knew enough not to voice that toddler-tantrum of a thought to the chief.

"I don't want to put up a camera." I'll admit, my words did have a stick-my-tongue-out-at-you tone. "There has to be something else."

Frank pinched the bridge of his nose. "You said this stuff is highly regulated, right? Permits and such?"

"Quite a lot of them. Right now there's only a handful of shops in the entire country that have the ability to sell vicuña." I had been so proud of being able to pull off that distinction—until the whole thing became tainted by murder.

"What about customs? I suppose I could try getting them involved as an illegal international trade issue."

I'd come here to get Frank's cooperation, not launch an international incident. Could you launch an international incident over yarn? Even vicuña? Visions of seriously dressed government agents laughing in my face danced in front of my eyes.

My expression must have shown my desolate thoughts, because Frank leaned over his desk and gave me one of his grandfatherly looks. "Get a camera, Libby. Put it up. Now. Set out some dummy yarn—wrap a bunch of regular yarn in a thin covering of this expensive stuff—and turn it on. That's the best advice I can give you if you want to catch whoever's doing this."

It killed me that he was right. I felt like I was going back on everything I'd set out to do in opening Y.A.R.N. We did not spy on our customers. YARNies were loyal, loving people.

But Frank was right: YARNies weren't the ones doing this, and in order to protect our own, we needed to find out who was.

CHAPTER FOURTEEN

I've been telling you to do this since you opened," Gavin said Friday morning as he tightened the last screw on the highly unwelcome camera now installed in a corner of my shop.

I could have done without the "I told you so" in his voice. Being talked into doing this thing I swore I would never do wasn't helping my grumpy demeanor. Or perhaps I should say "Grinch factor." Irrational as it sounded, I did feel like someone had stolen my Christmas. Arlene had needlepointed an artful little sign that read, *Smile, you're on camera*, but I confess it made me frown every time I looked at it.

Gavin came down off the ladder. "I know you're upset. But this is the right thing to do. I'm glad Frank convinced you if I couldn't." There was just a hint of hurt in his voice, as if he felt I valued Frank's advice over his. That wasn't true, but Gavin seemed to be feeling jealous about a lot of things in my life lately.

As if to make my point, Gavin inclined his head out my window toward Vincenzo's motor home and the vicuña still milling about their tiny pen. "When are they leaving?"

I could tell he wasn't just talking about the animals. The vicuña had calmed down and actually appeared happy. I'd caught myself gazing out the window at them, peacefully trotting about and looking generally elegant and adorable.

Vincenzo, not so much. He was a man of action, and sitting around waiting for the man from the zoo, and police procedure didn't suit him at all. He told me he'd managed almost a foot of his scarf, and I was due to give him another knitting lesson, but I'd been putting it off. Adelaide's information had given me too many questions I wasn't ready to ask our Gallant Herdsman. I needed to do more thinking and more research.

"Vincenzo said the guy from the zoo would be here this afternoon. He had to drive down from New England, and there was a bunch of paperwork to change the schedule of their trip across state lines and such."

Gavin looked at the herd, then looked at me. "They're worth it? All that fuss and expense?" To call his expression doubtful was an understatement.

"Come on in here," I said, leading him back to my office. We had to go in there to test my computer access to the camera feed anyway, and I had an idea.

Now, cramming a man of Gavin's size into my tiny office with me—even for security testing—was always a dicey proposition. We had too much history to be that close.

Making sure I kept the door open, I unlocked the filing

cabinet where I now reluctantly kept the remaining skeins of vicuña yarn. I pulled out a ball and handed it to him. "Touch this."

Gavin held the ball as if it were a hand grenade, wary and suspicious. Every person I knew who had touched the vicuña had an immediate reaction—a tactile bliss—but Gavin mostly looked baffled. "Okay, it's . . . soft," he said as if he were reaching for the right answer to an oral pop quiz.

"It's quite simply the softest thing there is. And light. And strong. The clothing they make from this is amazing. In Incan culture only royalty could wear it. Al Capone famously insisted on wearing vicuña overcoats, you know."

"The gangster? That's not an endorsement I'd promote. Especially given what's happened."

I didn't appreciate him drawing the connection. I was in no hurry to equate luxury with death. This past weekend was supposed to be about celebration, community, and beauty.

"Okay," he went on, "it's really soft and people are willing to pay a lot of money for it. Well, some people." His grunt roughly translated to "but not me." "Jillian's not going to be wanting some of this, is she?"

Teen girls can be impractical about a lot of things, but I was pretty sure Gavin's knitting enthusiast daughter would have enough sense not to ask for this. "I'd never do that to you. I'd steer her toward a good cashmere if she came in here looking for something high-end. Maybe vicuña as a wedding present, or if she was elected to Congress."

Gavin groaned and handed me back the yarn. "Please don't mention Jillian and weddings. She's *dating*." He gave the word a doomsday emphasis.

I knew Jillian had begun to think about boys—she'd let

her affections for a few young men slip into our occasional conversations together. She had just turned fifteen, and was a pretty girl. But she also had a very good head on her shoulders, so I wasn't nearly as fearful of the prospect as Gavin was. Then again, as Gavin had said more than once, "Nothing will make you fear teenage boys like having been one."

"Dating, huh? How are you holding up?" I asked, trying to hide my amusement. We were still quite close to each other, but I didn't want to force him to have this conversation out on the shop floor. And, truth be told, it was pleasant to be close to the man. If I were ever to go to pieces, I'd want it to be on his shoulders.

He made a tortured face. "I want to confiscate her phone and read every message."

I laughed. "No, you don't. It would be like reading her diary—she'd never forgive you. And you'd learn things you don't want to know."

"What if he's luring her someplace? Sweet-talking her?"

I knew from personal experience Gavin had a considerable gift for persuasion as a teenager. He made me feel like the center of his universe. That's a rare quality in a man. Still, I reassured him, "No one's going to talk Jillian into anything. You've raised her well. A Friday night date to the tree trimming and fireworks won't spell her doom."

Gavin's eyes widened. "You know about that?"

"She came in asking for help finishing the neckline on the sweater she plans to wear. Brent sounds like a nice boy."

Both of us stayed glaringly silent on the fact that we had done some rather spectacular kissing under summer fireworks our senior year. These were winter fireworks, after all. More layers between boy and girl, for starters.

"You should try to like him," I pressed. "You should try

and trust your daughter. If you come down too hard on something like this, you could regret it."

When he still looked forlorn, I teased, "If you end up hating him, tell her to make him a sweater."

Gavin reacted as if that was a terrible idea. "Why on earth would I do that?"

"It's an old knitting myth. Knitting a boyfriend a sweater is said to doom the relationship."

He raised one eyebrow. "You never knit me a sweater, and we broke up."

Yes, we did. And it was a catastrophic breakup, from my brokenhearted teenage viewpoint. But we were heading in different directions to different colleges and Gavin was trying to be practical. Perhaps it's what made my divorce to Sterling feel like such a blow—to be so sure and so wrong not once, but twice.

I returned the vicuña to the locked drawer and gestured for us to leave the office, ready to put a little space between us. "Like I said, it's a myth. Some people believe it, others don't. And it's not permanent. If you've decided he's 'the one' or you get married, it's supposedly okay."

I had, in fact, contemplated the fact that I never knit Gavin a sweater. How long a shelf life did our non-sweater-doomed relationship have? If we actually crossed the line and got back together, would it be because I never knit that fateful garment? I usually didn't place stock in such things, but I did wonder.

"So wait . . . do I worry if she starts knitting him one? Or should I be relieved?"

"Depends on if you like the boy, I suppose." Mom and Dad had both adored Gavin.

Gavin stopped. "What about the software? You need to check it out."

Getting back into that office with Gavin wasn't the smartest of ideas. "I'll figure it out."

"You sure? You want to be certain this works. There's no point in it if you can't review the recordings."

"If I can figure out our online sales platform, I can figure this out. I'm sure you need to get back to mayoral duties. The tree trimming is less than a week away." That felt like a decade from now, but I was trying to power through.

"It's okay, I can stay a bit longer." Bless him, he looked like he really wanted to.

Neither of us had the time. I was ready to admit that even if he wasn't. "I'm fine, Gavin. Really. Thanks for the help with the camera."

He ran his hands through his hair. "You want to grab some coffee later? You know, to talk over the holiday plans? The carol sing on Tuesday?"

I didn't like how all this had stolen the easy friendship I'd enjoyed with him. There was way too much of that going around—I actually caught people giving me wary looks in the supermarket yesterday. "I'd like that."

Gavin nodded. "Okay, good. I'll call you when I'm done with the budget meeting." He managed a small smile. "I'll need a friend after that battle."

I'd been to one of those budget meetings. He wasn't exaggerating.

It had been a long time since I'd seen Margo look as tired as she did when she walked into the shop an hour later.

"You okay?" I asked, concerned at the dark circles under her eyes.

"You should have warned me."

I reached up to the rack of mugs hanging above the shop

coffee maker. It was a small pleasure to be able to offer her coffee and refreshment after all the times she'd done so for me. "About what?"

She accepted the cheery candy cane mug I filled with gingerbread coffee. "Puppies."

I cast my memory back to those first chaotic weeks with Hank. He was such a well-behaved dog—well, until this week's pillow massacre, that is—that I'd forgotten how challenging he was at first. "Mocha turning out to be a handful?"

She sat down and took a large sip. "The beast never sleeps. Well, at night. He naps all day and then he's up half the night barking at . . . well, heaven knows what. He gets all rambunctious at ten p.m. You know what time I have to get up in the morning." She yawned. "Carl's ready to move into the inn for a few weeks."

"I'm sorry you're having such a rough go of it. He's a cutie, and it was a pretty impressive feat finding those clippers." I knew from experience that there were precious few ways to tamp down a puppy's relentless energy. It is rather how I imagine babies are at first—a whole lot of adorable aggravation you just have to power through.

"I'm in trouble." Margo sank her head into a hand after another enormous gulp of caffeine. "Libby, I'm cranky. I've got a ton of holiday stuff and the desserts for Frank's birthday party. I don't have time to be cranky."

I offered a commiserating smirk. "There's a lot of cranky going around these days. Not that it helps. I don't think any of us were planning on such an angsty holiday." I pointed up to the security camera. Linda, knowing how much I disliked the thing, had hung a pretty little knitted Christmas bell from it, complete with felted holly leaves. As far as I was concerned, you could have decked it out in Tiffany diamonds and I wouldn't have liked it any better.

Now it was Margo's turn to commiserate. "You swore you'd never put one of those up."

"That was before two grand of vicuña yarn went missing. Seems I have a serial yarn thief. Or an international vicuña activist, if you want to buy into Mom's theory." I indulged in one of the last of Mom's gingerbread vicuña and slid the plate in Margo's direction.

She took one, bit into it, and declared, "Not bad. But wow, that's a lot of stock to lose. It's probably the right thing to do. Maybe you can take it down after you find your culprit." She leaned in. "Speaking of shop problems, I came over for another reason, too."

I wasn't sure I could shoulder another shop problem at the moment. "What's up?"

"Your sister-in-law. Well, ex-sister-in-law—on several levels."

"Adelaide?" It wasn't much of a stretch to think of Adelaide causing trouble. "What did she do?"

Margo yawned again. "Well, it wasn't so much what she did. More of just a warning bell going off in my cranky head."

I trusted Margo's judgment on lots of things. If something was catching her attention, I wanted to hear it. "What kind of warning?"

She lowered her voice. "Sterling's family is well-off, right?"

Sterling's family was flat-out rich, but I appreciated her attempt at gracious wording. "The Jeffersons are loaded, yes." I won't say I didn't enjoy the privileges of that wealth, but I like to think I never wielded it the brutish way Sterling and Bitsy seemed to.

"Adelaide came into the shop yesterday and bought some of the most expensive goodies I've got."

"That sounds like Adelaide."

"And then proceeded to run through three different de-clined credit cards before she came up with one that went through. She tried to laugh it off. Then she tried to blame my credit card system. If you ask me, Adelaide is seriously strapped for cash."

Jeanette, who'd been sitting in one of the store's comfy seats finishing her Christmas tree socks, spoke up. "Oh, those credit card companies can be terrible, can't they? Per-haps we should give Adelaide the benefit of the doubt. She did just lose her brother. Grief does such strange things to the brain."

Most days I think the world would be a much nicer place if we all were as kind as Jeanette. "You could be right," I replied to her, remembering she was still coping with the loss of her husband. "But Sterling did say she'd gone off the radar for a while. It could be Bitsy finally cut her off. She's been threatening to for years. Self-sufficiency has never been one of Adelaide's strengths—it used to drive Sterling nuts."

Margo polished off her cookie. "I know it's a stretch, but I was wondering if I should tell Frank. I mean, would there be a financial reason why Adelaide might want to harm Sterling?"

"Of course there is," I had to admit. "She'd inherit all of it with Sterling gone. Only that's long-term—Bitsy would have to die for any of that to happen."

"And that woman looked in need of short-term funding," Margo remarked.

"Well, that's the thing. Other than her trust fund, I'm pretty sure Adelaide's main source of income is the divi-dends she gets from Sonesty stock. Harming Sterling would risk that income." In fact, Sonesty stock had taken an alarming nosedive since Sterling's death.

Margo's eyes narrowed. "Hmm. Not much there." They widened again. "Unless she's your yarn thief. You said that stuff was expensive. And she's got that connection to Vincenzo."

I added another dollop of peppermint whipped cream to my coffee, topping Margo's off as well. "I'd thought of that. Only she hasn't been in the shop. And as far as I know, Adelaide doesn't knit."

"But she wouldn't have to," Margo replied. "She could just swipe it to sell it under the table to some rich friends. If it's as hard to get as you say . . ."

It was more than plausible. Adelaide had a long history of making opportunistic choices. "Can you mention Adelaide's little financial struggle to Frank? I've filed a police report on the missing yarn, and I'd consider this a clue."

Margo glanced around the shop to make sure no one was close by before asking, "Speaking of clues, who do you think did kill Sterling? You must have a theory."

"I know it's possible, but I can't bring myself to believe it's Vincenzo. Only something fishy was definitely going on between those two. He's denying it, but he hasn't been straight with me about a lot of stuff. It's one of the reasons I'm teaching him to knit. I might get something out of him."

Margo smirked. "He's driving Gavin crazy. You know that. The man is downright territorial over your Gallant Herdsman."

I laughed. "I guess I've noticed." In truth, it was practically radiating off Gavin in waves. Under different circumstances, I'd find it an amusing kind of flattering. At the moment, it was just an unwelcome complication in an already complicated scenario.

"So, what are you going to do?"

"About Gavin?" I sighed. "Nothing. But I think I need to go talk to Bitsy."

"Bitsy?" Margo looked like she thought that was a terrible idea. "Bev says she's been a difficult guest at the inn. Bitsy hates you. And she thinks you did it. And didn't Frank ask you to steer clear of all this?"

I waved away Margo's list of discouragements. "I bet I can get her to tell me if she's cut Adelaide off." I leaned in. "And if I tick her off just enough, she might spill whatever it was Sterling was trying to convince her to do regarding the Sonesty stock."

Margo sat back. "Well, that won't be fun."

I gave a devious smirk. "Who's having any fun right now anyway?"

CHAPTER FIFTEEN

I knocked on my former mother-in-law's door at the inn half hoping she wasn't inside. Mothers-in-law as a rule can be formidable creatures, but Bitsy Jefferson took formidable to a whole new level.

Don't get me wrong—I had known that going into my marriage with Sterling. My mistake was believing that in the *us vs. her* battles that might ensue, Sterling would side with me. Mom once said that the true test of a marriage is how you argue. I thought it was a terrible way to look at things—until I realized the truth of it. When my parents fought—which wasn't often—it was always with respect. Sterling's arguments were winner take all . . . and he *always* won.

The click of the lock as Bitsy opened the door yanked me from my thoughts. Her face wore an expression of surprise and displeasure. "You." The woman's mastery of a one-word declaration was impressive.

I straightened my spine, determined to hold my ground against her. "Hello, Bitsy. I was wondering if you could spare a minute?"

"Is that Libby?" I felt my mouth fall open as Kevin Webster walked up behind her. Tie undone and a drink in his hand, he looked rather different than when I'd seen him last. Bitsy was entertaining? Him?

"You've met Kevin, I see." Her narrowed eyes seemed to warn me against making any issue about her choice of company. This looked like a decidedly cozy social visit. I never claimed to know Bitsy well, but this apparent May-December romance told me I didn't know her at all. Had I not had a long history of harsh judgment from the woman, I might have chided myself for my surprise. But Bitsy Jefferson ate judgment for breakfast. She gave me an annoyed sigh. "This isn't really a convenient time, Libby."

"No, no, Bitsy, let her in." Kevin put his hand on Bitsy's elbow. A decidedly socially cozy-like hand. "We have things to clear up with her."

"I wasn't aware . . ." I tried to find a safe way to finish that sentence, and found there wasn't one. I simply let my gaze bounce back and forth between the two of them.

Bitsy heard what I didn't say. "No need for that," she snapped. The woman's tone could weld iron.

Kevin gave a superior smile. "I'll admit we've had to be . . . discreet . . . for appearances' sake. But let's not get into that now. Come in, sit down."

Said the spider to the fly, my brain cautioned. I told myself to keep my wits about me and walked into the room to take a seat on the couch. Kevin refilled his drink and hoisted the bottle in offering to me.

I shook my head. "No thanks." Opting to go on the offensive, I asked, "Does Adelaide know?"

Bitsy arched a perfect eyebrow. "Do you really think Adelaide could handle something like this? I mean, after all that drama with Vincenzo? Please."

Why was I expecting a little more maternal loyalty from someone like her? She spoke about her own daughter as if she were a liability to be managed. I expect that wasn't far off from how she viewed Adelaide. Sterling's baby sister never quite had the aptitude for social strategy and sly civility that I associated with Sterling and Bitsy.

"You had questions?" Bitsy said as she accepted a refill from Kevin. Was the silky look she gave him real, or just a ploy to unnerve me?

I would not be unnerved. "It seems to me Adelaide isn't in the strongest financial position." I'd practiced the most gracious way to ask, "Did you cut your daughter off?"

"Teaching Adelaide responsibility has become a challenge," Bitsy said wearily. "I've had to get drastic."

"But she's staying in your suite."

"Her defiance isn't so strong that it won't swallow free room and board—although I think she was hoping to get that from Vincenzo rather than me." She tucked a lock of her precise blond bob behind one ear. "Principles were never her strong suit."

My mom says a lot of questionable things about me, but none of them ever make me think she doesn't love me. Sitting here, I wondered how Bitsy was adapting to the reality that what she thought of as a regrettable nuisance of a daughter was now the only hope for a Jefferson family heir.

"Was Sterling in favor of how you were handling things with Adelaide?" On the outs with her mother, Adelaide might have come here to try and get Sterling to side with her against Bitsy.

She set down her drink. "Is there a point to your questions?"

"Adelaide came to see me. I think she's been here longer than you realize. And I think she might have stolen the vicuña yarn from my shop. She's not going to be able to sell it anywhere, so if it is her plan, we need to rein that in. I won't press charges if you can talk to her and get her to return the yarn."

"Yarn?" Kevin clearly didn't see yarn as anything worth going to the trouble to steal.

"Vicuña retails at five hundred dollars a skein. If Adelaide is the one taking them, she's well into felony theft at this point. I think we'd all like to avoid that."

Bitsy put a perfectly manicured hand to her forehead. "Heavens, yes." She gave me the first direct look I'd had from her. "I'm sorry to say I wouldn't put it past her."

Kevin gave a grunt. "That girl doesn't have much sense when she isn't upset. And she's very upset."

I saw the first crack in Bitsy's veneer. "We all are. Dear God, Sterling. How?"

We knew how. In unnerving detail. "I'm afraid the real question is why? And by whom?" For the moment Bitsy appeared to be backing down off her theory that I'd done it, but I wasn't ready to discount the possibility that either she or Kevin might somehow have been involved. Or Adelaide. Or, yes, Vincenzo. Or someone we didn't even know yet—like whomever was stealing the vicuña.

Since Bitsy seemed in a talkative mood, I decided to do a little investigating. "How long has Sterling kept a loaded gun in his car?"

It annoyed me that neither Kevin nor Bitsy seemed surprised. Was I really the only person who hadn't known about this?

"He still did that, did he?" Kevin asked.

Bitsy settled wearily on the couch. "For all the good it did when it really mattered."

"I told him to," Kevin went on. "After that first South American trip. The one where he partnered up with Vincenzo. The whole snake business."

"Partnered up? In the snake business?" So those two were partnered in a full-blown reptile enterprise? The deluge of details coming to light was making me a bit dizzy. How exactly does one pair up adorable, priceless vicuña and snakes?

"Not the actual snake business," Kevin replied, sitting down on the couch cushion next to Bitsy. "More like business about snakes." He sat back and put his arm out as if he owned the room and could take up all the space he wanted. I watched the tip of one of his fingers rest on Bitsy's shoulder. "You'd be amazed how many pharmaceutical products contain snake venom." Kevin spouted it as if it were the most amazing of facts, while the concept made my skin crawl. "Wildly lucrative, but it can be a tricky thing. Hunting, importing, supply, all sorts of cross-border and conservational hurdles. Sterling had a habit of stepping on toes until he got a man on the inside."

"That would be Vincenzo." He'd told me funds were tight. Maybe all the funding for helping the locals preserve the vicuña herd wasn't coming from House of Marani. More and more, it seemed like Sonesty was involved. "But how?" I asked, not quite sure how the two animals fit together other than some sort of quid pro quo I could barely imagine.

"That I don't know. You'll have to ask Marani. I started to, but didn't get far. He seems rather taken with you, though—maybe you'll have better luck."

"Exactly how many of Sonesty's products are made with venom?" I don't know what made me ask.

"More than you'd think. You should remember from your days on the sales force that we have several very good ones for diabetes. But Sterling was working on a whole new application. Very promising, very lucrative. And you know Sterling—he never could quite keep things like that under wraps. Everyone at Sonesty knew he was working on something big, but only a handful of people knew what it was."

"Did you?" I pressed, annoyed by his casual tone. We were talking about a man's murder here.

"I can't confirm or deny that. And I wouldn't be much of an R and D man if I did, would I?" Every inch of his face told me he knew and wasn't ever going to tell the likes of me.

I turned to Bitsy. "Did you?"

"Please," she nearly moaned. "I get enough of that sort of drama from Adelaide. It was big, it was complicated, and we stood to make a great deal of money if it worked." She waved her hand in the air. "And now you know as much as I do."

I didn't believe that for a second. These two knew much more than they were telling.

Kevin rose, clearly done with this conversation. "I'm sure Bitsy and the family appreciate your condolences. And I'm sure we're all very busy."

I was being dismissed by the Jefferson family's new spokesperson. If I wanted to figure out the puzzle of Sterling's newest chemical scheme—dare I say "snake oil"—I was on my own.

I stood in the lobby amid the Riverside Inn's beautiful holiday decorations, utterly stumped. The layers of this situation kept building, like a tangled skein of yarn where

I didn't know where to start pulling first. There seemed to be a dozen ends, all leading nowhere.

If I wanted to play by the rules, I should have gone straight to Frank with this new information. At the moment, I was more miffed at Vincenzo and ready to stomp across the street to find out what that man was still keeping from me.

I pushed the inn lobby doors open and looked toward the shop. A large truck with zoo markings was parked in my driveway. This meant the herd was finally going home. I, however, wasn't about to let a quartet of wide-eyed vicuña and their travel plans keep me from a word with the Not-So-Gallant-Now Herdsman. For a man who strove to ooze integrity, he was losing it fast, in my view.

It took me a second, stewing as I was, to register the level of chaos around me as I got closer to the shop. Someone ran past me shouting. I heard the now-familiar sound of Vincenzo's high-speed Italian coming from behind the truck.

"Libby!" came Linda's panicked yelp from behind me. I whirled around just as a vicuña gave a spectacular jump across the shop's front sidewalk, knocking over a planter. "They escaped!"

I caught sight of the open gate of the vicuña pen and a flash of toffee-colored fur dashing across the backyard with Vincenzo in pursuit. The vicuña had indeed made a break for it.

From a distance, down toward the river from the sound of it, I heard the unmistakably earsplitting alarm cry. Given the flock of protest sheep herded in front of my shop last year, I would have thought it was hard to top such a thing in terms of main street chaos. Now, though, on top of a murder, I had a quartet of loud, highly stressed prized animals on the loose in Collinstown.

Vincenzo dashed up, breathless and supremely annoyed. "They scattered when we tried to load them into the trailer. I think they're all on the avenue. If one of them gets hurt . . ." Another vicuña screech sounded from across the street as if to finish Vincenzo's thought. "We need help. *Subito.*"

It came to me in a split second. We needed Collinstown's version of the Peruvian herding process I'd seen on the video. I grabbed Linda's arm. "Go down the far side of the street and get everyone out of their buildings and holding hands. I'll go down this side." I pointed at Vincenzo. "Go up that way to the top of the avenue. I'll call Paul at the coffee shop to block off the bottom."

Vincenzo looked at me as if I'd just earned the Nobel Peace Prize. "*Perfetto.* We'll close them in."

Relief filled me as I caught sight of all four vicuña in various positions up and down the avenue. One was poking a delicate nose into the garland around the bank window. Another—Zorro, I think—was peering into Margo's door, perhaps drawn by the mouthwatering scents within. A third was dashing down the middle of the street, sending cars veering for the curb. The fourth was way down at the bottom of the avenue, exploring the half tree awaiting all those decorations.

"Mommy," a child to my left asked his mother, "are those Santa's reindeer?" I thought of Mom's gingerbread vicuña. I'd probably never look at a Christmas reindeer the same way ever again.

Musings aside, I began pulling Collinstown shopkeepers out of their businesses, pleading for their help. If this worked the way it did in the Peruvian mountains, we stood a chance of getting this situation contained—or was that herded?—quickly.

"Hold hands!" I shouted as the vicuña in the middle of the street let out an alarm screech at a passing minivan. "Make a barrier and hem them in!"

Nancy from the insurance office next to the shop was confused for a moment, but took my outstretched hand regardless. Linda was frantically directing people on the other side of the street to do the same.

I heard the sound of a motor and looked behind me to see the zoo truck maneuvering the trailer into the street. If we could keep closing ranks, we could guide the vicuña in. Only it was a long street, the vicuña were scattered, and I didn't know how long we'd keep everyone's cooperation in this absurd effort.

"Make noise," Vincenzo shouted from his post up the street. "They'll gather in the center if we make noise."

I was just taking a breath to start shouting when Nancy started singing "Jingle Bells" at the top of her voice. I didn't have time to quibble as yet another screech echoed out across the downtown.

Had a stranger wandered into Collinstown at that exact moment, I'm sure they would have thought we had lost our collective minds. A hundred or so people, lining a small-town street, caroling and corralling a herd of adorable—but occasionally screeching—animals with their joined hands. I had the mixed sensation of being fascinated, somewhat charmed, and absolutely sure it would take decades for me to live this down.

The long circle became shorter and smaller, slowly closing in just like I'd seen in the video. Sometime around the second song, people began laughing at the absurdity of it all. After all, we were all holding hands with our neighbors in the middle of Collin Avenue while belting out holiday tunes to herd vicuña.

Nobody seemed put out or annoyed. Confused, or amused, maybe, but—no surprise here—only George scowled. He stood right next to the zoo truck looking like he would slam the gate shut behind the herd and drive it across the state line himself.

I could only laugh. The community carol sing-along wasn't until Tuesday, but what about this holiday had gone according to schedule?

"It's working," Vincenzo called as he went into the center of the diminishing circle, directing the motion and talking to the animals in soothing tones.

By the end of the third holiday tune, a small knot of about twelve pairs of clasped hands directed the last vicuña up into the trailer. Applause rose up from everyone else crowded around the final barrier, as Vincenzo—not George—latched the gate and fell against it in relief. The poor zoo employee looked as if he had no idea how he was going to explain this to the folks back home.

"*Grazie!*" Vincenzo called to the crowd. "They are safe. Thank you."

People seemed happy to have been part of such a crazy effort. They were adorable animals, after all—when they weren't screeching. I was still stunned something so cute could make such an earsplitting sound.

"They are too stressed to travel tonight," Vincenzo said as the zoo driver pulled the trailer back into my driveway. "They will spend the night in the trailer and leave first thing in the morning." Vincenzo looked longingly at his little herd. "I expect I will never be with them again after this."

As much as this was supposed to be a great victory for Y.A.R.N., I realized this represented a sizable failure for him, too.

That didn't stop me from addressing the serious bone I had to pick with him about his lies of omission. "Tell me about the snakes," I said to him. "All of it."

"Oh." His lips pressed tight.

"What else don't I know, Vincenzo? I'm sick and tired of people dropping bombs on me."

"I am sorry about that," he said, one hand on his chest in dramatic repentance that I wasn't buying. "I owe you an explanation."

"Yes, you do." Some small part of me wanted to grab his shoulder and shout, "You didn't kill my ex-husband, did you?" right there in the middle of the street.

"Libby," came Shannon's voice from behind me. I turned to see her walking out of the shop. In her hand she held one of the missing balls of vicuña yarn.

The remaining balls were locked up in a filing cabinet for which I had the only key. "You found one of the balls?"

"More like it found us," she replied, handing me the yarn. "I walked back into the store to find all of the missing balls piled up on the counter."

Bitsy couldn't have gotten to Adelaide that quickly, could she? "All of them?"

"I don't know how they got on the counter just now, but they were all there. No note or sign of anyone, just the balls lined up."

If it wasn't Adelaide—and I couldn't be at all sure that it was—someone had brought the vicuña yarn back to us. Not exactly a Christmas miracle, but I'd take it.

"Who brought them back?" Vincenzo asked, looking as baffled as I felt.

"I have no idea," Shannon said. "They must have slipped into the store during all the commotion."

"Or they slipped the latch on the pen to *create* the commotion," Vincenzo offered. "They couldn't have gotten out on their own."

Shannon's brows furrowed. "If they took them to sell them, why bring them back?"

I looked at Vincenzo. "I did just get done telling Bitsy that Adelaide wouldn't be able to sell these if she was the one who took them."

"You think Adelaide did this?" He didn't seem to find that possible.

"She's broke, she's mad at you, and let's face it—it's just the kind of thing she'd do."

Vincenzo seemed to realize just how much explaining he had to do. "I've got to get the herd settled. Come by tonight and I will tell you everything you want to know."

CHAPTER SIXTEEN

I was doing dinner dishes, getting ready to walk up to the shop and get my long-overdue explanation from the Gallant Herdsman, when I heard my mother's knock on my door. Mom always gives six knocks on my door. I laugh to myself that it's her way of saying "Why don't I have a key?" (six words), but she denies it.

I opened my door to see the unsettling sight of Mother standing on my threshold with a suitcase in hand and a particular look on her face. Every daughter knows that look: a narrow-eyed, head-cocked-to-one-side look that usually comes before something you don't want to hear. My store of coping mechanisms was near empty, and the wave of helpless panic nearly pushed me against the hallway wall.

"We have a problem," Mom pronounced. Funny how *she* had victories but *we* always had problems.

I gritted my teeth and opened the door wider so she could angle in with the luggage. "What's that?"

"Paint."

"Paint is not a problem," I replied. Murder, escaping vicuña, and missing expensive yarns are problems. Paint
comes in a can in lovely colors and is very boring to watch
dry. Boring sounded lovely right about now.

"Jesse says we need to paint my townhouse. Greige—it's
a thing now, something between beige and gray, and my
townhouse walls need to be it. I'm being staged."

It took me a full minute to catch up to Mom's whiplash
logic. "You hired a real estate broker?" I was glad, given
the problem Gavin and I had put on the back burner, but I
had hoped to have a little input on the decision. "You're
putting the townhouse on the market *now*? The week before
Christmas?" I didn't know much about real estate, but that
didn't seem like a solid strategy to me. Especially if it
meant "greige"—and meant Mom staying with me.

"Jesse says it's better if I'm not living in the unit while
they make it market-ready and show it. He swears it'll sell
in days. There's not much out there this time of year, you
know."

Probably for good reason, I thought. "Um . . . how did
you find this Jesse?"

Mom looked as if she'd just been waiting for me to ask.
"In the grocery store. We struck up a conversation. He had
the most amazing taste in tomatoes."

Mom is one of those gregarious souls who will strike up
a conversation with anyone, anywhere. That's not intrinsi-
cally bad, but I wasn't sure Mom should be trusting her
home sale to someone based on their produce selection
skills. Even George was sounding like a safer candidate
than this Jesse fellow.

She grinned. "I'll be his first home sale. Won't that
be fun?"

I did not have time for this. I did not have the mental clarity for this. But, as with most things about Mom, here it was. She set her suitcase down at the bottom of the stairs and reached into her handbag. She pulled out a paint chip and showed it to me, pointing to the *Greige* caption on the gray-beige square. "Is that the in color now? Do they make yarn in greige? I thought I might make him a scarf to say thanks when he sells it."

It looked like garden-variety taupe to me. "Mom, you don't have to make him a thank-you scarf when he sells it," I replied. "He makes money when he sells it. *He* thanks *you*."

Mom considered this for a moment, but it seemed to roll right off her like rain off the back of the ducks in the river. "I'll make him a scarf. Seems like such a nice young man."

I gave in to an absurd moment's gratitude that she did not add something about how I might want to consider dating him.

It's not that I have anything against knitting someone a thank-you gift—I do it all the time. But I couldn't shake the feeling that Mom's big heart was getting in the way of her common sense. She had a prime piece of real estate, and there was no reason to rush into this. Then again, when Mom gets an idea, patience rarely enters the picture.

I took the paint chip, tucked it into my pocket, and walked into the kitchen to find the calmest blend of tea in my cabinet. Dinner and murders would have to wait while I tried to keep my mom from squandering the largest financial asset she had. "Have you and Jesse settled on a listing price?"

Mom replied with a figure that at least told me Jesse knew what Mom's place ought to go for. She had only bought it three years ago, but still stood to make a respectable profit if the townhome went for that price. I made a mental note to find out Jesse's last name and do a little research.

"I'll be here a few days. At least through Frank's birthday party, and maybe through Christmas. That's okay, isn't it?"

Frank's birthday party. In all the frenzy, I had almost forgotten that Angie was throwing Frank a birthday party—at the Dockhouse, no less, the town's fanciest spot—tomorrow night. It was so sweet how Angie was going all out for her new beau. "I suppose so." It wasn't as if I had a choice, other than to book Mom a room at the inn, and that wouldn't go over well at all.

"Who are you going with? Other than me, I mean." She waggled her eyebrows with dramatic curiosity.

I had, in fact, been told I could bring a guest to the event, but given that everyone I might consider taking—meaning Gavin—was already invited, it seemed unnecessary. "No one," I replied. Hoping it wouldn't result in . . .

"Not Gavin?" Mom looked utterly disappointed. She clearly thought this could be the tipping point for Gavin and me, fulfilling her long-suffering hopes to match me off.

"He's already coming, Mom."

"Yes, but with who?" She sat down at the table, a sure sign this conversation wasn't ending anytime soon. There are days where I consider removing the second chair, but she'd probably just sit in the remaining one and expect me to stand.

"With *whom*?" I corrected. "And I don't know. I don't know that he's bringing anyone." In fact, I had not worked up the nerve to ask Gavin if he was bringing anyone to the party. How is it mothers can find the tiny speck of doubt in our lives and pounce on it like that?

"For a moment there I was wondering if you would bring Vincenzo. The Dockhouse has a dance floor, and I heard Angie's hiring a band. I bet he's a superb dancer." Mom's attempt to say this casually fell almost comically short of the mark.

"An out-of-town guest still here because he's under suspicion for murder is not the kind of person you bring to a good friend's birthday party." Drastic, I'll admit, but sometimes drastic is what you need with Mom.

"You're still under suspicion, and you're going."

I glared at her. "Whose side are you on here?"

"Oh, I'm Team Gavin, you know that," Mom replied.

Team Gavin? Mom was spending too much time around teenagers. Or watching television. Take your pick.

"But it goes without saying," she went on in supposedly sage tones, "that if you want to push a man into action, jealousy usually does the trick."

I planted my hands on the table and glared into her eyes. "I am not bringing Vincenzo to Frank's party to make Gavin jealous. This isn't the eighth grade. Grown-ups don't pull stunts like that." Yes, part of me was wondering how long it would take Gavin and me to take the next step in our relationship, but parading person of interest Vincenzo around at police chief Frank's birthday party tomorrow night was definitely not the way to make that happen.

"Grown-ups," Mom replied, wielding my own word against me, "wouldn't take this long to own up to love."

Love? I could describe my feelings for Gavin six different ways, but "love" wasn't one of them. Not yet, and probably not for a while, if ever. Dealing with the murder of the last man I loved tended to put a damper on romanticism, among other things.

"I am not in love with Gavin." I overpronounced the words—loudly—as if logic was a foreign language to her.

One side of her mouth turned up. "You were."

I fought the urge to dial Bev right now and ask her to book Mom a room. "Decades ago. A lot of water has gone under that bridge, if you hadn't noticed."

"I'm just saying—"

"If you are going to stay here," I cut in, "this conversation needs to stop. Now. I have enough on my plate with Sterling and snakes and . . . well, thank heavens the vicuña will be gone tomorrow." I looked down at Hank. "The store is yours again, sweetheart. You can come back to work tomorrow." I swear he smiled. I'd missed his sweet face around Y.A.R.N., and two more pillows had met a grisly end as Hank vented his frustrations. I was worried the couch upholstery was fated for the same demise if this kept up.

"Any clue who took the yarn?" Mom asked. "If they returned it like that, I'd think it would have to be someone local. You've looked at the camera footage, haven't you? That should—"

"Collinstowners," I cut her off, almost shouting, "are not stealing from Collinstowners! Knitters are not stealing from knitters!" Only I didn't know that for sure, and it made my heart ache.

I posed a theory instead as I tried to sit calmly down with the mugs of steaming tea. "My money is on Adelaide. Bitsy cut her off, so she needs cash."

Mom tsked. "That should have happened years ago. A mother's job is to raise self-reliant adults."

"I think she figured she could take the vicuña and make a quick buck while annoying Vincenzo and me at the same time. After all, the skeins reappeared right after I told Bitsy Adelaide wouldn't be able to sell them. No knitter committed enough to buy vicuña is going to go for black-market vicuña yarn. At least I hope not."

"True, but right after? Ten minutes after? Without anyone noticing?"

I pursed my lips. "Well, there is that."

"And the murderer? Are we any closer on that?"

I sighed. "Not at all."

Mom blinked. "Wait . . . did you just say snakes?"

"I did," I replied, and settled in to tell her what I'd learned.

After getting Mom updated, I decided Hank deserved to come back to the store with me, herd or no herd. Some part of me wanted the comfort of Hank's companionship as I grilled Vincenzo, and it wasn't as if we could stress the vicuña out any further than they'd already been traumatized. I told Hank to behave, gave a wide berth to the animal trailer, and walked up to knock on the Airstream door.

Vincenzo opened it, shirtless despite the December chill. What unjust law of nature makes the dubious guys always the most attractive? He had another think coming if he thought his impressive muscles could somehow divert me from my task.

"I'm here for my explanation."

Vincenzo hesitated, perhaps at my sharp tone, before saying, "Come in."

Hank clamored up the steps ahead of me, wildly sniffing around the mobile home at all the strange scents as Vincenzo eased himself onto the couch. I did not sit next to him this time, but took one of the swiveling chairs on the opposite side of the room. "I wonder if you wouldn't mind putting a shirt on."

He startled as if he'd forgotten he was bare-chested, but I very much doubt that. "Of course." With one fluid motion, he reached into a set of cupboards over his head and pulled out a black T-shirt, pulling it on. Only it wasn't a T-shirt— it was a very expensive-looking T-shirt-like garment, if that makes any sense. I doubt Vincenzo wore anything given away at a concert or shot out of a football game cannon. He managed to look exceedingly well groomed, even in jeans and a simple shirt.

"Snakes," I repeated, cuing him to begin his explanation. "And why I didn't hear about this from you, if you don't mind."

"You're angry."

"What I am is tired of finding out surprises and secrets about Sterling. You led me to believe you two hadn't kept in close touch."

He sat back. "Personally, yes. But he did come to me with a . . . business arrangement of sorts. Not the kind of arrangement you say a lot about, if you understand."

I'd done just enough poking around on the Internet to come up with my own theory. "Were you helping Sterling smuggle snakes out of Peru?"

His expression told me my theory was correct. "No, not Peru. Snakes are lowland, tropical creatures. He was after a handful of Amazon species. But it wasn't hard to convince my mountain friends to make the journey or use their contacts."

Hank came back from his initial exploration. Vincenzo looked at him, extending a hand for a pet or a sniff, but

Hank was having none of it. He looked at Vincenzo, then turned to sit at my feet. My dog was making his opinion clearly known.

Vincenzo pretended not to notice. He cleared his throat and continued. "Many of these men had honed their skills smuggling vicuña back before we made it worth their while to do it aboveboard. We simply tapped the skill set for a new purpose."

"And that new purpose was cash." Rather a lot of it, if I knew my ex-husband. Sterling would only have taken a big risk like this if there were big gains to be had.

"Yes, and no. It was quite the business, but I told myself it was really for the people. Living wages for the hunters, and life for the patients. Sterling's team was on the verge of a breakthrough. Lifesaving stuff. There was another company on his heels, so he had to bend a few rules in order to get the drug into formulation first. There's an insane amount of red tape in exporting exotic animals out of South America. It would have taken months, if not years, if we hadn't gone underground. I'm sure the other company was preparing to do the same thing. Sterling just had the contacts to get there first."

"And by 'contacts,' you mean you. You struck a deal to smuggle the snakes out to wherever Sterling needed them to go. Did you come out nicely in the deal as well?" Sterling often asked people to break rules for him—he truly felt as if rules were for other people, not industry giants like himself—but he got away with it because he paid his mercenaries well.

I will always be amazed by how little of this I knew before we were married. In that way he was like a snake himself, shedding one skin when he felt safe enough to do so only to grow another. He must have known on some level I'd find much of what he did objectionable. Our marriage was doomed from the start—I just didn't know it.

"It wasn't like that," Vincenzo said with imploring eyes. "This was a way to get enough funding to keep the vicuña project alive when I feared Father's interest was starting to wane. These people are too busy trying to survive, so they're not choosy about what keeps food on their tables and a roof over their heads. The minute selling the vicuña fiber elsewhere paid better than what we could offer them, they'd go right back to hunting them out of existence." Vincenzo pushed himself up off the couch and paced the small space, looking confined. "I'm not proud of it, but the ends justified the means in my book. Everybody won—the mountain community, the vicuña, the lives that were going to be saved. That seemed worth bending a few rules."

"What was this wonder drug supposed to do?"

"I'm not sure." He gave a vague wave of one hand as if reaching for the fact. "Something about a bleeding disorder, I think. Something genetic."

"Sterling had a blood thinner and another unknown drug in his system when he died. A lot of it. So I don't think he took it voluntarily. I think it was given to him. Part of how he was . . . killed."

"Killed by his own drug." Vincenzo shook his head. "Awfully dramatic."

"Someone wanted to make a point, staging him to bleed out on the shearing platform with a stab wound like that." I didn't want to think it had been the man in front of me, but I couldn't discount it, either, could I?

"You hate me." I found I didn't know whether to believe the wounded look he gave me.

"I make it a point not to hate anyone. But this seems like pretty shady dealings for the likes of you." I wondered if Vincenzo was promoting himself as the hero of the vicuña in order to avoid blame for such tactics. "Where's that integrity you claimed so proudly? And why did you lie to me? Why didn't you tell me all of this earlier?"

"Sterling committed to a full two years of paying the snake hunters. Only they were too good at their jobs. Once he got whatever it was he needed, he pulled out of the deal. Just when Father was growing weary of funding the vicuña herd. Like I said, I was furious. We didn't have enough yet to get by without House of Marani." His voice rose. "I needed Sterling to keep his word. I should have known better."

I decided I had to ask. "So you killed him?"

"I didn't kill him," he shot back. I felt Hank move a bit closer to my shins, getting protective at the rising tension in the room. "I was furious at him, but I didn't kill him. I certainly didn't inject him with whatever the killer put in his system."

I hadn't told him about the needle marks. "How did you know they were injectable drugs?"

He fumbled, and my suspicions rose. "Aren't they all? I didn't kill him, Libby," Vincenzo insisted.

"What I'm wondering is how nobody heard it."

"What do you mean?"

"Whatever happened to Sterling had to have happened in front of the vicuña. That alarm cry is loud and irritating. If two *strangers* were in a bloody fight right there in front of them, why didn't they make a sound?" I considered this possible evidence that Vincenzo had somehow been present to calm them.

He heard my doubts loud and clear. "I don't have an

explanation for that. I've been trying to work it out myself, honestly."

I stood up. "Have you told any of this to Frank?"

"Of course not."

"Well, you're going to have to now. Will you call him, or shall I?"

CHAPTER SEVENTEEN

I dearly hoped I had helped Frank move the case forward. I say "hoped" because Frank was keeping me at an infuriating distance regarding the murder. He thanked me for convincing Vincenzo to come forward with what he knew, but that was it. No hashing through the list of suspects—after all, technically I was still on that list—and no brainstorming of motives or opportunity. I found out through Vincenzo—not the chief—that Frank had insisted Vincenzo not leave town until given permission.

For all my griping about not wanting to be a detective, I missed the excitement of working through a case with Frank. Maybe I wasn't as good at it as Frank said. Maybe Frank had merely tolerated my presence on our two previous cases. My brain spun a wide range of unhelpful doubts and thoughts as I played reluctant spectator to Sterling's murder investigation. I have never been a very good sidelines sort of person, and the high stakes of this situation weren't helping.

In his defense, Frank had better things to do than deal with me. I tried to push all these thoughts from my head as I walked into the party room at the Dockhouse restaurant.

"Angie sure is going all out for Frank," Margo whispered as she and Carl walked in behind me. "Is this a big birthday for him or something? Oh, and look at the place."

Angie had unleashed her decorating skills on the room. Holly and pine dripped from every window. Candles with holly berries and red ribbons sat on all the tables, while a very elegant collection of candles in vases sat on the buffet table. The whole place glowed like Christmas Eve, even though it was only December 19.

"I'm always amazed at the wonders Angie does at the station with Frank's tiny decorating budget," I mused. "Looks like she took things to another level for this. They must be really serious."

"Of course they're really serious," Mom agreed, handing off her coat to the attendant. "You don't waste time on that sort of thing at our age."

She nudged my elbow as Gavin and Jillian came into the room. "Speaking of things that ought to get underway . . ." Jillian smiled and waved at Mom, while I tried to glance Gavin's way without being as obvious as Mom. The man looked amazing. Gavin didn't wear a dark suit often—he was mostly a sport jacket kind of guy—but when he did, he was stunning.

Back before all this murder business, I had thought that this event might very well be the occasion where we crossed *that* line. Who wouldn't be inspired to take a leap of faith surrounded by all of Frank and Angie's second-chance romance and holiday joy? But as it was, I sensed too much stress and suspicion floating in the air for any such thing.

I was pulled from my thoughts as Frank and Angie entered the room like the guests of honor they were. Frank looked so sheepishly happy that I couldn't help but smile. He looked dashing himself in a suit I had no doubt Angie picked out, sporting a small holly boutonniere that marked him as the Birthday Boy.

Angie radiated happiness beside him. I soaked up their mutual adoration as the perfect antidote to all that had gone wrong this month. "Frank finally got his girl," Mom said, then made a gasping sound. "No, wait . . . Frank really *did* get his girl. Look at Angie's hand!"

Sure enough, Frank stopped just inside the room to announce, "I made this more than a birthday party, if you all don't mind." Angie smiled broadly, kissed Frank on the cheek, and proceeded to wave her left hand—now adorned with a diamond.

The room broke into cheers and wild applause. It seemed like the perfect burst of joy to set the world back into balance. Sure, the murder hadn't been solved. We still didn't know who'd stolen—and then returned—the vicuña yarn. The vicuña had finally left town, but Vincenzo was still parked in my shop yard. Frank had commanded the Gallant Herdsman to stay until his name could be cleared—*if* his name could be cleared. Bitsy and Adelaide were still in town, making things difficult.

But this? Here was one gorgeously, perfectly right thing to warm the collective hearts of Collinstown. The announcement placed this event firmly in "party of the year" standings, and I couldn't be happier.

"I'd make their wedding cake for free," Margo whispered, nearly giggling. She and I had been the first people to get Frank to admit to his relationship with Angie. "Those two are downright adorable."

My heart lightened as I watched Frank and Angie make their way through the congratulating crowd. Happy marriages did still appear, despite the fallout I and Gavin had waded through in recent years. My own parents had a terrific marriage, and I confess I still hoped to achieve that one day. I wondered, as I felt Gavin's gaze on me from a small distance, if he was thinking the same overoptimistic *What if?* that currently hummed in the back of my mind.

Frank shocked us all by pulling his new fiancée into the center of the room and giving her a *showstopper* of a kiss to seal the deal.

Margo winked at her husband. "Why don't you kiss me like that?"

Carl pulled Margo to him. "Stick around, sweetheart, I'll see what I can do." Then he yawned. "As soon as I get a full night's sleep."

"Mocha still keeping you up nights?" I asked as we all accepted glasses of champagne to toast the blissful new couple.

Margo now yawned. "Why did I name that dog after a coffee drink? He's worse than six espressos."

"You wanted a puppy," Carl teased.

"I did try to warn you," I chimed in. "But I promise you, it'll get better. I wouldn't trade anything for Hank, even if he did eat my upholstery while the vicuña were here."

"What did I say about a man and jealousy?" Mom said.

I turned to give her a look. "How long 'til your paint dries?"

Mom replied by taking a healthy swig of bubbly. "Jesse says we got a nibble. I could be out of your hair by Tuesday."

I really didn't want Mom out of my hair. Just less all over my life.

I walked over toward Gavin, allowing myself a slip of a warm smile. I'd worn a dark green swingy dress, only half because it was his favorite color. It was my favorite dress, after all.

He noticed. "Hello, Libby."

Mercy, but that man can melt butter when he says my name.

Well into the party, Gavin caught up with me again at the bar. "I don't think I've ever seen Frank grin like he is tonight," he said, tipping his cocktail—his third by my count—in the direction of Frank and Angie, now taking a turn around the dance floor. "He's a goner."

I swatted Gavin's arm. "Don't say it like that. Like it's a bad thing." After a thoughtful pause, I added, "It's nice to think there'll be such a happy marriage coming into the world."

The unspoken "because our marriages surely weren't" hung between us for a moment before Gavin said, "Takes finding the right person, I suppose." He gave a small, gruff laugh before taking another swig of his drink. "Turns out I wasn't very good at that."

I took a sip of my own wine. "Me neither. But you got Jillian. She's such a lovely girl. You have every reason to be proud." She'd been having fun dancing with a pair of toddler twins who were Angie's niece's children.

"I don't think I'm very good at teenagers, either. I'm worried neither of us will survive her learner's permit. Every time I think this is as hard as it can get, it gets harder. Driver's ed. Driving. Dating." He gave me a helpless look. "Has she kissed him? Am I supposed to know if she's kissed him?"

I turned to him. "No, you are not supposed to know if she kissed Brent. I certainly wouldn't ask. Nor would I get all worked up and protective if she offers up that she has."

Gavin made a face that told me what a tall order that was. "I remember her toting around a stuffed bear. She wears makeup. I feel like she's going to start looking at colleges next week."

I pulled the drink from Gavin's hand. "I'm cutting you off."

He lowered his eyebrows at me. "I'm not drunk. I'm not even tipsy."

"No, but you're moping, and that's just as bad."

"Has he tried anything? Marani?"

I balked at Gavin. "What's that supposed to mean?"

"He's been hitting on you from the moment he arrived. Don't think I haven't noticed. Don't think everyone hasn't noticed."

"Well, you're just full of inappropriate questions tonight."

"I was half afraid you'd bring him tonight."

I wanted to roll my eyes. "I would not bring Vincenzo to this. Even if he wasn't a murder suspect."

"Which he is," Gavin reminded me. "I think he did it. Do you?"

I did not want to get into this tonight. "I think the question of the hour is, who does Frank think did it? He has all the information. And I'm sorry to say he's not sharing."

"It's Marani," Gavin declared in muttering tones.

Did Gavin have any idea how jealous he was acting at the moment? "Because there's evidence, or because you don't like him?"

"Both."

"I have doubts it was Vincenzo. Then again, I can't rule

out Adelaide and Bitsy. And the wild card here is Kevin Webster. He's seeing Bitsy, did you know that?"

That gave Gavin a shock. "Those two? He's . . ."

"Sterling's age," I finished for him. "Never underestimate a Jefferson."

Gavin's look warmed a little. "Don't I know that. I would never underestimate you."

"I never was a Jefferson," I sighed. "And that is probably the root of it all."

CHAPTER EIGHTEEN

With Christmas fast on our heels, Hank and I tried to settle into something close to normalcy at Y.A.R.N. It wasn't easy—I was still earning suspicious looks around town, and the shop traffic was unnervingly slow. This morning I battled the urge to write "Yuletide Attacks Render Nonprofit" on the chalkboard. Rather than give in to that notion, I swapped out my too-close-to-bloodred knitting project earlier for a green and white brioche stitch cowl dotted with bright red baubles. All the holiday cheer without any of the murderous undertones. Complex enough to occupy my tumbling thoughts, but not so difficult that I couldn't put it easily down to help a customer who walked into the shop.

If only a customer *would* walk into the shop. Sunday was Shannon's day off, so Linda was due to come in this afternoon, but I called and told her to take the day off. I didn't need her. My wisely planned-for holiday rush wasn't happening, and I knew Linda needed some time and space to sort things out. As such, Hank and I held down the fort while I tried to tell myself I was enjoying the Sunday solitude.

About a half an hour after opening, someone walked in. Not really a customer, mind you. I hadn't expected Kevin Webster to come in, and would wager one of my returned vicuña skeins he wasn't here to make a purchase.

"Hello, Kevin."

Kevin nodded, looking around the shop like a secret service detail. "Are we alone?" he asked after a lengthy scan of what I considered to be obvious.

"Seems that way," I sighed. "Recent events haven't been especially good for business. Would you like a cup of coffee?"

He waved it off. "No thanks. I just wanted to do a quick check-in with you." He shifted his weight. "Bitsy and I . . ." He circled a hand rather than get into details.

"Are two grown adults capable of making whatever decisions you want," I finished for him. His expression from the moment he had walked in told me this "check-in" was more about "How will you handle Bitsy and me?" than "How are you holding up through the murder investigation?"

"I'll admit I was surprised," I added as graciously as I could.

"It's complicated."

"I imagine it is." And especially now. I voiced something that had been on my mind for days. "Sterling's passing makes Bitsy the major shareholder, doesn't it?"

Kevin's agitation grew. "Well, now, that depends."

Things were getting interesting. "On what?"

"Well, you know Sterling was making changes to his holdings and estate plans. Switching things up quite a bit."

"Or trying to," I corrected him. "I doubt you are surprised I wasn't in favor of some of those changes. Where I come from, you stick by your agreements, even when you think you've come up with something more profitable." I was talking about Sterling and me, but it seemed to me the same virtue had been lacking in his dealings with Vincenzo and the snakes.

"Yes, trying to. He had all the papers drawn up. Signed them. No countersignatures yet, but very close."

"Not in my case," I replied. "Oh, I'd seen those papers. He sent them to me and my attorney. More than once."

Kevin stepped closer. "It's come to my attention that there were also papers shifting shares away from Bitsy. They'd been fighting. Sterling didn't care for some of Bitsy's choices of late."

Like you? I thought to myself. Sterling and Kevin were close colleagues, but I doubt close enough for Sterling to easily stomach the thought of his mother dating the man. If Kevin were to actually marry Bitsy, could that give Kevin control over Bitsy's large chunk of Sonesty stock? If you ask me, Kevin was wielding some major influence right now.

"You can see where it might look . . . difficult . . ." he began, and I thought he was talking personally, but when he went on to say, ". . . if it came to light how Bitsy might benefit from those papers never being signed."

Bitsy had motive. "Why are you telling me this?"

"I'm hoping we can count on your discretion."

That struck me as a rather bold request from a pair of people who'd been so cold to me mere days ago. "Your relationship with Bitsy is your business. But should it come up, I won't lie for you. Or anyone, for that matter."

I decided now might be a good time to play my advantage on a hunch I was exploring. "I'm sure you have already gone over this with Frank, but I know Sonesty had its share of disgruntled employees." Sterling could be hard-nosed as a CEO—maybe even ruthless at times—and I expect he made his share of enemies among the rank and file, if not the executives. "Can you think of anyone angry enough to do Sterling harm?"

Kevin looked a bit put out by my direct question. I suppose he came here hoping to get a pledge of loyalty to the Jeffersons and Sonesty. I wasn't giving one.

"You know Sterling's personality," he hedged. "Probably better than most. He wasn't the type to go easy on someone if they weren't performing up to expectations."

"Has there been anyone recent? A particularly sour exit?"

Kevin eyed me. "Anyone I think could have killed Sterling for revenge?"

"I was trying not to put it quite so bluntly, but yes."

He picked up a skein of hand-dyed worsted wool, hefting the green and blue fibers with a judgmental air, as if the weight would tell him something. "There was someone last year. He was a lead chemist on a major development of ours."

"The new breakthrough drug. What was it supposed to do?" I already knew, but I wanted to see if he'd tell me.

I was surprised when Kevin answered, "A clotting agent."

"I know Sonesty made blood thinners, among other things. That's what they found in Sterling's system when he died. But a clotting agent?" Wouldn't a clotting agent have saved him from a stabbing, rather than kill him?

Kevin put his hands in his pockets. "Hemophilia, mostly. And that was the issue with Ingalls. As a hemophiliac, he had too personal a relationship with the project. It got in the way. We managed to keep his termination quiet, but the man was 'sour,' as you put it. He did actually threaten Sterling on his way out the door."

This seemed like important information. "Did you tell Frank this?"

"No."

Now it was my turn to eye Kevin. "Well, why on earth not?"

He gave me a dismissive glance, as if I was being as overly dramatic as Adelaide. "Because there is no chance Thomas Ingalls did any harm to Sterling."

He seemed certain. "How can you be so sure?"

Kevin put down the skein. "Because Thom Ingalls is dead. He was a rather unstable fellow. Brilliant, but like I said, with a lot of issues. Who spells 'Thom' with an h like that? His personal stake in the project was affecting his decisions. He and Sterling locked horns one too many times, and it became necessary to cut him loose. So while he might have had motive, unless you believe in ghosts, Ingalls couldn't have done it."

"Any others?" While we had several other personal suspects, I still thought it was entirely possible someone had killed Sterling for professional reasons. Perhaps it had to do with this venom-derived drug and the unethical way it seems Sterling might have been developing it.

"I hardly think it's appropriate for me to be analyzing Sonesty's list of employees for you. I've shared what's necessary with Chief Reynolds. We ought to leave such matters to him."

It was an elegant little "butt out" speech, but the message was the same. And Kevin's reaction told me I wasn't that far off base in my thinking. There evidently were a few Sonesty employees angry enough to seek revenge on Sterling. But all I was going to get was the name of a dead man, which meant I had nothing at all.

I changed the subject. "Have Bitsy and Adelaide made

any plans for services yet? I'd like to be there." Cleared of my "person of interest" status and with the murder solved, I hoped.

"Of course. We're waiting for the coroner's office to release"—he stumbled a bit on the words—"the body. Astoundingly complicated business, this."

Murder rarely seemed simple in my experience. "Seems to be. If there's anything I can do to help, I hope you'll feel you can call on me." I would never reach my goal now of getting things to a civil level with Sterling, but maybe I could manage it with his family and colleagues. Unless, of course, one of them was his killer. That tends to put a strain on a person's manners.

I caught Kevin's eyes straying to the ball of vicuña. I had returned it to display, but this time in a little glass case the antique shop around the corner had lent me. This case, while pretty, had a little loop in back that allowed for a padlock. It bothered me to use it, but it seemed the best compromise between leaving the yarn out and locking it away. I'd placed the soft round ball of yarn in a silver candy dish, and it looked rather refined and museum-like in its glass enclosure.

He nodded toward the display. "So this is what all the fuss is about?"

I'd heard some version of that question several times a day since this whole thing started. "It is."

"You really think Adelaide took them? And brought them back?"

Where was this sudden chattiness coming from? "I think it's quite possible, yes. Seems like something she would do. Impulsive and then backing down."

"Well, Bitsy laid into her after your visit. If she did it, she isn't admitting it." He paused. "Would you need her to?

I mean, would you press charges if she confessed and apologized?"

Did he know something? "Honestly, I haven't thought that far. But yes, I suppose I would only need an apology. She caused an awful lot of trouble. And it certainly didn't solve her financial problems." I decided to ask. "Do you think she did it?"

He pinched the bridge of his nose. "The yarn or the murder?"

I took just a second to recognize the absurdity of even having to ask that question. "I suppose both."

"I hope not."

His noncommittal answer left a lot of room for doubt. While I fully believed Adelaide capable of swiping the yarn and then losing her nerve, I wasn't sure she had the nerve to kill Sterling in the rather brutal way in which he had died. Adelaide was a champion pouter, but the kind of rage fueling that murder? It seemed unlikely, but not impossible. I found I couldn't ignore the medically informed nature of how Sterling was killed. And Kevin seemed no more able to discount the possibility than I was.

And then there was Bitsy. Of the two of them, I could far more easily believe Bitsy capable of that kind of fury than Adelaide—especially if there was a lot of money involved. Kevin himself could have provided the brute strength needed to hoist Sterling up onto that shearing platform. I found I still couldn't rule anyone out.

Kevin kept looking at the yarn, so I finally asked, "Would you like to feel it? That is, after all, what all the fuss is about."

He looked nearly squeamish. "Oh, no. I mean, *why*?"

It seemed that this month I could easily divide the world into two camps: those who understood what a high-quality yarn was worth, and those who found it absurd. I mean, a vicuña scarf lasts far longer than a fabulous meal, but I know many people who would drop $200 on a gourmet meal without blinking. And dozens who probably spent that much on coffee in six weeks.

If he had shown any kind of interest in it at all, I would have unlocked the vicuña and let him experience it. But this looked like a instance of "pearls before swine"—or, in this case, camelids before executives.

We paused, neither one of us ready with an exit to this awkward conversation. "Yes, well, I should probably get back to Bitsy. Things are tense over there."

Things were tense everywhere. "Yes, well . . ." I was going to say, "Thanks for stopping in," like I do to many customers, but it didn't really apply in this case. "Keep me posted."

"Will do." With a last look around the shop, Kevin turned on his well-polished heels and headed out the door.

"That was weird," I said to Hank, who stared after Kevin as if he couldn't figure the guy out, either. "But we know some new information."

CHAPTER NINETEEN

Mid-morning on Monday, Hank bounded to the shop door to woof a friendly hello to Jillian.

There was no friendly hello in the look on her face. In fact, she looked furious and on the verge of tears. Throwing her backpack down on the floor, she flopped dramatically into a chair and growled, "I hate him." I stared into the sad anger of Jillian's face and wondered if this was what it was like to be the coffee shop owner—or even the bartender at the tavern a few blocks over.

"Hate who?" I asked, even though I was pretty sure of the answer.

"He doesn't get it," she snarled, wounded. "I shouldn't have to wait. It is a big deal. I don't care what he says."

I remember everything in high school being a big deal. "What?" I tried to ask innocently.

Jillian looked up at me. "I can get my learner's permit when I'm fifteen and nine months. I was sure that meant I could sign up for driver's ed during summer school. But no, Dad says I have to wait until I'm sixteen. I'll be a *sophomore*." She groaned the last word. Jillian wasn't even halfway through her freshman year—this dilemma was months away. Still, that wasn't the thing to say to her right now. I could easily imagine Gavin being stumped by the drama of this.

I tried to think of something age-appropriate to say. "Well, that rots."

The look she gave me in return was half "Nice try, older lady" patronizing and half "At least you get it" gratitude. "I told my friends I was signing up for a parking space for next year. I'm humiliated."

Just as I was wondering why she wasn't nursing her wounds with friends—school was on holiday break, after all—she added, "I'll be the last of my friends to get my license. They'll all be driving to school in the fall," she moaned in end-of-the-world tones. "How pathetic is that?"

I sat down, hesitating only a moment or two before sliding the plate of gingerbread vicuña—Mom was still making them—toward her. I didn't want to model eating your feelings, but this looked fresh enough to require immediate intervention. "I'd be disappointed, too."

She looked at the cookies, laughing for just a moment as she worked out what they were. That tiny, damp laugh was worth any caloric intake.

When she gave me an inquiring look, I said, "Grandma Rhonda's new project. They're actually pretty good."

Jillian picked one up, turned it this way and that, and then took a bite. "Not bad."

"I'm sorry about the rules," I offered. "Maybe it won't be hard to get rides to school with friends."

"Brent said he'd give me rides to school. You can imagine how Dad reacted to that."

Did kids still make out in the backs of cars? Did they even call it making out? I didn't dare ask—no matter what they call it now, Jillian didn't need to know I was well acquainted with steaming up Gavin's car windows back in the day.

"I think your dad's having trouble getting used to the idea of you having a boyfriend."

She gave me a look. "You think? It's like he forgets I'm fifteen now."

Oh, I didn't think there was any chance of Gavin forgetting *for one second* that Jillian was fifteen now. "What did your dad say?" I was almost afraid to ask.

"All the stupid Dad things." She made air quotes with her fingers. "'It's better to wait.' 'Driving is a big responsibility.' 'It's just a few months.' 'You're making too much of it.'"

I could suddenly see why she was here rather than with her dad. I felt the little surge of pride that she'd felt welcome enough to come here. I wasn't ready for Y.A.R.N. to become the teen hangout the Corner Stone coffee shop down the street was—heaven knows how Paul handled that crowd every day—but I was glad Jillian came here.

"Part of Dad's job is to make a lot of people live by rules they don't like," I consoled.

Jillian merely grunted and reached for another cookie.

"He's so good about all those rules that, well, sometimes he doesn't remember how they can feel unfair."

Her eyes welled up as if I'd just said exactly the word she was looking for. "Yeah. You get it."

There was no need for me to feel so pleased that she thought I "got it," but I was.

I folded my hands on the table. "So you won't be able to drive to school next year—at least at first." I borrowed one of Mom's favorite phrases. "What do you think you want to do about it?"

Jillian slid down in her chair. "Sulk."

I was glad she wasn't offended by my laugh. "That's an option, definitely. And this is a good place to do it. You can stay here as long as you like. Did you bring any knitting with you?"

"No," she said.

I take knitting with me everywhere, but I didn't say that to Jillian. "What are you working on right now?"

Oops, that was the wrong question. "Nothing special enough," she grumbled. Sometimes, like a really luscious slice of chocolate cake, you need a really indulgent knitting project to pull you out of a slump. The yarn equivalent of buying yourself a nice piece of jewelry or a new handbag.

I don't know what came over me. It made very little sense, but I suppose Kevin's dismissal of the vicuña as not worth the price fueled my certainty of how much Jillian would appreciate it. I wouldn't advise her to buy it, nor could I give her the yarn outright. But I could do something almost as good.

"How would you like to be the test knitter for the cowl pattern. *With the vicuña?*"

Jillian's whole body reacted as if I'd given her one of the keys to the city on her father's office wall. "No way," she gasped, astounded.

I'd already started knitting the pattern, but that suddenly didn't seem nearly as important as giving Jillian the chance to do it. "You'd have to do it here in the shop or at home— no taking it out and around. It's expensive stuff. And you wouldn't get to keep the cowl; it would stay here in the shop as a sample."

"That's totally okay. Really. You can trust me," she said. I realized feeling special was exactly what Jillian needed at this moment. So many people think knitting is just about making things, but really it's about so much more.

"I know I can." I had, in fact, trusted Jillian with some important yarn before. Jillian had made a beautiful sweater out of the last yarn ever created by yarn dyer Julie Wilson. The last work of a brilliant artist isn't yarn you can sell to just anyone—I was glad to know it went to someone with Jillian's enthusiasm and talent. The same was true now.

Just because it felt like more of a treasure than fetching one of the hanks from out of the locked cabinet in my storage room, I opened the small lock on the glass case and pulled out the display ball of vicuña. It may have been a little over the top, but I presented it to Jillian like a trophy.

One of the great pleasures of this whole event had been watching people touch the vicuña for the first time. I had no words to do the thing justice. It is, quite simply, exquisite. Luxurious and indulgent. Jillian's reaction was blissful, her mouth making a stunned little "oh" while her eyes fluttered closed in a rapture no non-knitter might ever understand. It's the whole point of what I do, really. And after the days I'd been having and the murder that hung unsolved over my head, it felt wonderful to do this one little happy thing.

Jillian stroked the soft ball of yarn as if it were a kitten. All that softness was remarkably soothing. "This is amazing," she nearly whispered. Almost all of the sour dejection had left her features. "Can I . . . could I start like now?"

I'd had the same reaction with the first ball Vincenzo sent. I wanted to drop everything and start knitting with it.

The thought of Jillian being eager to hang out in my shop and knit the vicuña warmed me. "I don't see why not." I'd commissioned a beautiful cowl pattern from a favorite designer of mine, and I pulled out a copy of the pattern draft from my desk and handed it to her. "Grab some size eight circular needles from the box over there and I'll make us some hot chocolate while you cast on."

"Totally." Jillian's shoulders straightened with the confidence of a young person entrusted with an important task. She'd still have to wait a year before the independence of driving came within reach, but just for today I'd soothed the sting.

Sure enough, Jillian had scanned the pattern and begun casting on the first row by the time I was finished topping two mugs of hot chocolate with whipped cream. I stuck a peppermint stick in each one. It felt like a tiny little impromptu Christmas party in the shop. I stopped at the blackboard and scribbled "Yarn Always Returns Niceness" before setting the mugs down between us. I picked up my green and white project. We both were a little more soothed.

Jillian slid the mug farther away from her on the table. "Don't want to risk a spill," she said. She was taking this "commission" very seriously. I made a mental note to ask Vincenzo to stop by and compliment her next time he was in the store. What would be the next time? We'd kept a distance between us since our last conversation, even though he couldn't leave. The vicuña were gone, but I was still hoping I'd be welcoming the new year without a motor home in my shop's backyard.

"Isn't it adorable about Chief Reynolds and Ms. Goldman?" Jillian asked as she finished casting on the first row and deftly joined the first and last stitches to make the start of the circular cowl. More of the young woman I'd known returned, leaving the grumpy teen behind.

"Absolutely adorable," I agreed. "I'm happy for both of them."

"You and Dad danced a lot at the party," she teased.

"Your father was always a good dancer."

Jillian snickered. "He's not totally awful, I suppose." I didn't have to wait long for where she steered the conversation next. "What about him?" She nodded toward Vincenzo's motor home. "Dad was totally freaked you'd bring him to the party. Are you making Dad jealous on purpose? Hailey Connors told me that's the way to get boys."

I set down my own needles. "That is *not* the way to get boys. At least it's not a good way. And no, I am not trying to make your father jealous. I'm not trying to make your father anything. Playing games in things like this never works, in my opinion."

"I don't know," she said, "it seems to be working pretty good on Dad."

Gavin was right—teenagers really were impossible.

The townhouse is under contract!" Mom pronounced as we sat down for dinner that night. I had to admit I was enjoying having her cooking meals for me—she'd taken to feeding me as compensation for launching her stay in my guest bedroom.

"Mom, that's great!" Jesse's first sale seemed to be well underway—and as fast as he'd predicted. I felt guilty for underestimating the guy. In fact, I owed him. Mom needed to be on her way to her next residence, and he was making it happen. "Now you can really look for a new place without worrying." I wanted her close, but not this close.

Mom set down a pot roast big enough for six. "I'm not buying a new house."

My stomach dropped, and not from the whopping poundage of meat in front of me. My reply of "Really?" was closer to a gulp than a question.

"Yes. I've been talking it over with Jesse. I don't think a new house is the right place for me."

This did not sound like promising news. "So where will you live?" *Not here, not here, please don't say here.*

Mom began doling out slices of pot roast, carrots, and potatoes. "Jesse took me out to lunch to celebrate the contract, and he had a long talk with me. What a compassionate young man he is. He'll make some girl a wonderful husband. I'll have to think of who."

"You two talked about where you should live?" I cued, hoping to drag the conversation off matching up Jesse and back onto the essential topic of where Mom would live.

"After lunch he took me over to the loveliest little apartment at The Moorings."

I almost tumbled off my chair. "You went to look at The Moorings?" I had dropped dozens of hints for her to look at that independent living facility, and she'd ignored every single one of them. I didn't know whether to be thrilled or annoyed that Jesse had finally managed it.

"I put a deposit down this afternoon."

I am certain my jaw hit the table. "Huh?"

"It makes so much sense. I won't be this spry forever, you know. They have a bus that goes from there to church every Sunday and a ton of activities I can either do or ignore. If there isn't a knitters group, I plan to start one." She cocked her head to one side. "Why didn't you ever suggest I look at that place?"

I ground my teeth together. "Silly me. But you put a

deposit down? Already?" I knew better than to say "Without me?" even though every inch of me was silently yelling it.

"I didn't want to let that adorable corner unit go to someone else. Sometimes you just have to act. I hope I've taught you that, Elizabeth."

"Good for you," I managed to sputter out. I hoped I didn't sound too shocked or relieved when I asked, "When's moving day?"

"I move in New Year's Day. Poetic, isn't it?"

Good news, but wow. "That's awfully fast."

"Like I said, sometimes life asks for quick action. I don't see any point in waiting. Do you?"

"Um, I suppose not." I was still reeling from this near-instant solution to a worry that had been bugging me for most of the year. Jesse was looking like my very own Christmas miracle. I think. Now that it was coming so fast, some weird part of me was panicked she was leaving. Proof, perhaps, that stress really can play with your sensibilities.

"Relax," Mom said, cutting her pot roast as if she'd just announced something mundane, like that we were out of paper towels. "I'll still be here for Christmas dinner. In fact, I invited Gavin and Jillian."

Okay, maybe there were parts of Mom-in-Residence I wouldn't miss. But I also knew that this sort of meddling would happen no matter where Mom laid her head.

"Of course Gavin and Jillian are welcome to have Christmas dinner here. But isn't Tasha coming in?" Gavin had been bemoaning the arrival of his ex for the holidays and the flurry of drama that followed Tasha's every visit.

Mom grimaced. "Not anymore. Evidently Tasha got a better offer. In Mexico."

Much as I hate to say it, this wasn't out of character for Tasha. It didn't take a genius to realize that one of the reasons Jillian had become so attached to both Mom and me was the total lack of quality attention she got from her own mother. Gavin was an exceptional father, and I knew this wounded him deeply. Part of the reason he tried so hard—and perhaps paid so much laser-focused attention to Jillian—was Tasha.

"They're absolutely welcome here," I repeated, immediately beginning to catalogue all the things I'd need to do to make that happen on four days' notice. Christmas with Mom and me was easy. Christmas with Gavin and Jillian took things to another level—although a pleasant one.

"You didn't go and invite the Italian, did you?"

It took me a second to realize what she was asking. "You mean did I invite Vincenzo to Christmas?"

"Well, yes, but he also looks like the sort who would invite himself."

"I hadn't even thought about that. I don't think any of us expected Vincenzo to still be in town by now. He is still technically my guest. I might have to do something if he's still here." The thought of us having to go all the way through Christmas without having Sterling's murder solved made my temples throb.

"I don't think you want to put him and Gavin in the same room," Mom advised. "'Peace on Earth, good will to all' only goes so far."

I heartily agreed. Justice aside, this murder needed to be solved so I didn't have to host Vincenzo and Gavin at the same table. That had no hope of being anything close to merry.

"Maybe we can get him back together with Adelaide. They were a thing once, weren't they?" Mom's matchmaking urges were evidently still in full bloom. "Wouldn't that be the solution to a hundred problems?"

"I don't think so. I'm pretty sure each one thinks the other might have killed Sterling." And both were still on my list of possible suspects—and hopefully Frank's. That's a list I wanted to get myself off of as quickly as possible.

"Either one of them could have done it in my book," Mom pronounced, digging into her meal. "Adelaide gets more money if Sterling's gone, after all."

"But not until Bitsy's gone, and if Bitsy is dating Kevin, she's got a lot of life left in her."

Mom choked on a carrot. "Bitsy's dating that Sonesty man? That horrid, slimy, *much younger* Sonesty man?"

"Hush. You're not supposed to know." That request was about as effective as asking the Chester River to flow backward. "I caught the two of them together at the Riverside Inn."

Her features pinched. "I thought she had more sense than that."

"Kevin also told me that Sterling intended to change her allotment of Sonesty stock in his estate planning. He had papers drawn up, just like he had changed papers drawn up for me." I took a bite of my own meal. Mom could always do a mean pot roast, and evidently mystery did great things for my appetite. "He was shaking up a lot of things in his financial position. There has to be something behind that."

"Sounds like he knew this new drug was about to make him a whole lot of money." Mom pointed at me with her fork. "So you have to ask yourself, if the drug still goes to market, who gets all that money now? Do you know who's in line to become Sonesty's new CEO?"

A jolt hit me as I came up with the likely answer. "Kevin, maybe?"

If Kevin and Bitsy were together, and both knew Sterling was planning to reduce Bitsy's holdings, then each of them had twice the reason to ensure those papers never got signed.

"The Italian" was not the only one with a motive.

CHAPTER TWENTY

I had just finished updating Margo on all the latest Mom reasonable-ness on Tuesday when Frank walked into the shop. This made me happy—I had new thoughts about the case, but was pretty sure I was no longer welcome to barge into Frank's office with my theories.

"Congratulations, Chief!" Shannon called, hoisting her coffee mug from behind the sales counter. Given how tense Linda was these days, I appreciated Shannon's cheerful disposition. We still had a few inter-employee rough edges to work out, but I was glad I'd made the choice to hire her. Now that the vicuña had been returned—even though we didn't yet know by whom—Shannon had returned to her upbeat self, even if Linda hadn't.

Margo joined in the celebration. "Cheers to the groom-to-be! How are you, Frank? Set the big date yet?"

Frank's sheepish look and flushed cheeks told me he was very much enjoying being a fiancé. It warmed my heart to see him so happy. His surprise proposal had been the most sweetly romantic thing I'd seen in a long time—it was just like Frank to give Angie such a gift on his own birthday.

"Do you have a minute, Libby?" Evidently this was an official visit. Our chief was back on the beat.

"Sure, Frank. Coffee?"

He waved away the offer, but sat down at the table in the center of the shop just as Margo rose to head back to the Perfect Slice.

"Angie says no one can do our wedding cake but you," Frank called before she was out the door. "I expect you'll be hearing from her."

Margo beamed. "Music to my ears." As she opened the shop door, she called, "Don't you two kids wait too long, now."

Frank chuckled. "This is taking a little getting used to."

I felt a smile warm my face. "How's Angie?"

"Floating around the station like she's on a cloud." He was trying to sound annoyed and completely failing. It was just so sweet. "It's only three days 'til Christmas, but she bought more decorations for the station," he mock-grumbled. "We're going to look like one of those china villages if she keeps this up. How are you supposed to give an air of authority when there's a giant light-up snowman on our reception desk?"

"She'll settle in," I reassured him. "Besides, I think we could all use a giant dose of your happiness right about now."

He flushed a bit more at the remark, then cleared his throat and adopted a more serious tone. "I came for two reasons. One, to thank you for pushing Marani our way. That backstory between him and Sterling casts a lot of shade on him. I'm certain he wouldn't have come forward with that information if you hadn't forced his hand."

Now, here was the thanks I'd been waiting for. And a bit of a return to the partnership with the chief I'd been missing. "You would have worked it out eventually."

"Maybe not in time. I was running out of probable cause to keep him here, and I expect someone with his resources would be long gone the minute he was able. But now he'll be camping out in your backyard until we solve this thing—unless you want me to order him vacated to somewhere else."

"No," I replied. "He can stay. I'd rather him be here where I can keep an eye on him." Since Frank was feeling indebted to me, I dared to ask, "Are you thinking he did it?"

"He could have."

Much as my gut was telling me he hadn't done it, there were still plenty of reasons to doubt Vincenzo—chief of which was my theory about the missing vicuña alarm cry. I shared with Frank how its absence could mean Vincenzo had been present when Sterling was murdered.

"Libby, I can't discuss the particulars of this case with you. I came to say thank you, but that doesn't mean I can treat you like you're in the clear. Yet."

My earlier relief deflated like a balloon. So we weren't past that. "Come on, Frank, you can't tell me you really believe I did it." I hadn't realized how much his ongoing suspicion had wounded me.

Frank pinched the bridge of his nose. "You know I can't answer that. Or you ought to. I'm trying to keep this as congenial as possible—don't make this difficult."

For the hundredth time, I wished this was over and behind us. If I told him what I'd learned about Kevin and

Bitsy, would it be welcome information or just perceived as diverting suspicion? "What was the other reason?" I asked, opting to play it safe. After all, it would look better if I could do what I'd done earlier and convince Kevin to go to Frank on his own.

"Do you want us to pursue the yarn thing? You did make a report on the theft. But now that it's been returned, it's up to you how much we continue to investigate."

How keen was I to know who'd stolen from us? In all the murder chaos, I'd forgotten we still were the victim of a theft. And if it really was Adelaide, I'd be sending my former sister-in-law to jail. Then again, if she'd stolen from me, didn't she need to bear the consequences?

I told Frank the truth. "I don't know. I'm glad whoever it is brought it back, but it's upsetting that it was taken in the first place."

Frank looked up to the little white camera still mounted in the corner of the ceiling. "So what did you learn from looking at the security camera footage?"

Now it was my turn to look sheepish. "Well, there's a little problem with that."

Frank gave me his best grandfather scowl. "You didn't turn it on, did you?" It was almost comical how disappointed he looked—as if I'd been a misbehaving child who hadn't done her chores.

"I did," I admitted. "The first day, at least. But Frank, I couldn't stand the thought of spying on my customers. A lot of very personal stuff gets said in this store. It's supposed to be a safe space, not a reality television show."

"No one needs to see the recordings but you," Frank argued, clearly frustrated. "You don't even have to look at it unless there's an issue. In fact, it's proven that just the camera's presence—running or not—reduces theft."

I felt my chin jut out in defiance. "You can spout all the security data you want, but I know how I felt the minute we turned that thing on. And it wasn't good. I'm going to take it down just as soon as I can find a free minute." The way things were going, that might be after New Year's, but I'd made my decision and I was sticking to it.

"I'd advise against it," he pressed. Him and Gavin both, I'm sure.

"And you know my track record for heeding your advice," I pressed right back. I had, in fact, ignored if not gone directly against his advice on more than one occasion. I was rather proud that our friendship had stood against that friction, even if I had new doubts it would make it past this current case. I didn't kill Sterling, and I didn't want to lose my friendship with Frank over who did.

The chief replied with the only remark that could have smoothed things over. "You're as stubborn as your mother."

That was Frank. Always incredibly deft at walking the line between professional and personal. "I'll take that as a compliment," I said, not bothering to soften my pouty tone.

He grunted at the stalemate we'd reached. "I should point out, however, that if you had one of those running on your backyard, we wouldn't be where we are now. We'd have footage of Sterling's murder."

He had a point—and then not. "We thought we had footage of Nolan Huton cutting the yarn bombing off of the Collin Avenue trees last fall, but it turned out to be staged. I'll admit it *might* have helped, but it still isn't worth the downside in my view."

Since Frank was already peeved at me, I decided it was okay to risk asking something I had been wondering about the case. "So we know the other drug in Sterling's system might be a clotting agent. Like something a hemophiliac would use, right? Do you know for sure yet?"

"Libby, you know I can't—"

I'd been up half the night forming my theory. "'Cause here's what I'm thinking. You know I can't figure out why the vicuña never sounded an alarm. To me, that means either Vincenzo was there when it happened or there wasn't much of a struggle."

"Libby . . ."

I wasn't going to be deterred. "What if Sterling's wounds were given elsewhere—like the other side of the yard where we found the clippers—but he had this blood thickener in his system then? What if whoever did this could have injured him, prevented him from bleeding out where the struggle would have been, moved him quietly, then given him the thinner once he was on the platform? He wasn't murdered on the shearing platform, just staged to bleed there."

Frank blew out an exasperated breath. "You realize how ridiculous that sounds. I know you want to find the killer and clear your name, but you're grasping at straws here."

I didn't think so. "According to Kevin, Sonesty was on the verge of introducing a new blood drug. A real game changer of some kind that would make the company a lot of money. I think that's the second drug in Sterling's system. I think someone used the extraordinary properties of Sonesty's new drug to kill Sterling."

"That's far-fetched at best. How would they get their hands on it if it hasn't been released? Why go to all that trouble and drama if no one would understand the point they're making? And I'm not even sure your theory is chemically possible." Frank glared at me as much as I've ever seen him glare at anyone. "I'm telling you, Libby, you need to stay hands-off on this one. You're too close to it personally to be objective, and I was trying not to remind you that you're still officially a person of interest in this case. I mean it, Libby," he said darkly. "Stop."

If I couldn't count on Frank's help, I had to look elsewhere for assistance. Which is why I walked into the Perfect Slice an hour later to ask, "Can I borrow Mocha?"

Margo looked up from a batch of cookie dough. "Huh?"

"More precisely, can I borrow Mocha's nose?" I continued, "He found the clippers. I want to see if there's something else over in that part of the yard that we missed."

She wiped her hands on the dish towel beside her. "Didn't Frank and his team go all over that place?"

My pout returned. "Frank's told me to keep out of this."

I watched Margo put on her "Do as you're told" face. "But you're not going to, are you?"

"No. We're missing something about what happened that night."

"No," Margo countered, "Frank is missing a piece of what happened." She looked at me, resignation filling her eyes. "But you've got a hunch, and you're going to follow it. I know better than to try and stop you when you get this way. So I suppose I'd better just give up and help. What's up?"

I told her my theory about the blood drugs. "It makes so much sense. Sterling was stabbed away from the shearing platform and moved onto it later. Maybe the mystery drug made him drowsy, or confused, or whatever so that he didn't struggle. But it's the only way I can think of that he could have been killed without anyone noticing."

"True," Margo agreed. "It's not like there was a gunshot

for anyone to hear. Bleeding to death makes no sound at all." She grimaced and put her hand to her chest. "That's a grisly thing to say, isn't it?"

"It was a grisly murder. But I don't think it happened on that platform. After all, the clippers were what stabbed him, and we found them back under the bushes. What else haven't we found yet?"

"What else is there?" Margo asked.

"I don't know. However those drugs got into Sterling's system. A syringe, a vial, a tourniquet, something. I'm hoping Mocha can sniff it out."

She sighed as she put the bowl back in her refrigerator. "I hate to say this, but Libby, is it possible you're letting your emotions run away with your imagination? I don't think Mocha can really help. He's a rambunctious puppy, not a trained police evidence dog. It was only luck that he found the clippers. Hank would probably be as much help as Mocha would."

Hank has many gifts, and loads of intuition, but not Mocha's nose. It was a long shot, I knew, but I was in the mood for long shots. "Even so, can I borrow Mocha? I've got to do something, and this is the only thing I can think of to do. So just indulge me and my crazy theory, okay?"

Margo picked up her cell phone. "You're as stubborn as your mother, you know that?"

I fought the urge to roll my eyes. "I've been hearing that a lot lately."

Margo replied as she dialed the phone. "He's at doggy day care down on Maple Street. I'll tell them you're picking him up for a walk in ten minutes. And yes, I *am* indulging you, because I don't think this is going to get you anywhere."

"Think of it as a playdate with Hank . . . with a side of

crime-fighting agenda." Hank and Mocha should learn to be good friends, because I knew they would be spending a lot of time together. What better time to start than now?

"I'm giving you fair warning," Margo said. "You saw how he digs. My yard looks like a gopher hill."

"Well, mine looks like a herd of vicuña trampled it, so it can't get much worse."

I'll admit, Hank gave me a very confused dog stare as I walked by the store window with Mocha bounding happily at my feet a few minutes later. He darted out of his usual spot in the window to scramble to the side door. I let the two of them play in the backyard for a few minutes, glad for the easy canine friendship they seemed to strike up.

I was surprised to see Vincenzo come out of his trailer at the ruckus. We'd been avoiding each other.

While I felt awkward, he didn't seem to feel the friction. "I have mastered the purl stitch, thanks to you. And I'm halfway through the pattern, thanks to all my free time."

I'd sent him a video to review after giving him a quick and awkward-feeling lesson on purls, knit-two-togethers, and yarn-overs Monday. "Good for you. The rest of it is just versions of those stitches, so you're off and running."

Vincenzo nodded toward the dogs. "So are they. Amazing how easy their life is, isn't it? Just the basics of existence, the happiness of just chasing around?"

Hank enjoyed much more than the "basics of existence" if you ask me, and I suspect Mocha was in for a pampered lifestyle as well. I tried to keep the conversation short and light. "Puppies are a lot of work, but they sure are entertaining."

Just as he had tried to do multiple times during our Monday lesson, Vincenzo kept pushing our conversation toward more serious matters. He walked up closer to me than I would have liked. "Libby, stop trying to keep me at a distance. I did have my reasons for wishing harm to Sterling. But I didn't kill him. I have to know you believe that."

I opted for the truth. "I wish I knew what to believe." Mocha and Hank began playing a spirited game of tug-of-war with one of Hank's rope dog toys.

Vincenzo touched my elbow, and I nearly flinched. He sought to draw my gaze away from the dogs with those mesmerizing eyes, but it was getting harder to find them mesmerizing. "You should know what to believe," he said. "You should know you can believe me. I had no love for the man, but I did not kill him."

"You lied to me about other things—why not this?"

Vincenzo pulled back a bit. "I omitted certain truths, yes."

I wasn't going to let him off that easy. "You lied. About Adelaide. And about your relationship with Sterling. Where was all that famous House of Marani honor when it counted?"

"You should know Adelaide came to see me last night. She threw herself at me like a . . . like a lovesick schoolgirl. Told me her life was falling apart and that I could help her put it back together. There was a lot of weeping about how she is alone now, without Sterling or Bitsy to lean on."

I imagined Vincenzo had endured a fair amount of women throwing themselves on him. "What did you do?" Hank and Mocha began a game of chase and keep-away across the back lawn, barking and jumping. I didn't really want to stand here listening to some kind of confessional declaration from Vincenzo.

"I told her the truth. That although my life was unraveling as well, her place was not with me. I told her to go back to Bitsy. She's coming apart at the seams, Adelaide is. It makes me wonder if she really has done something drastic."

"Did you know Bitsy has taken up with Kevin? Maybe that's why Adelaide is feeling abandoned—not that Bitsy ever really gave her much attention in the first place."

"Kevin?" Vincenzo looked as shocked as I had been on the discovery. I know Kevin had asked for discretion, but I didn't see how I owed him anything at the moment. Vincenzo shook his head. "Bitsy was always one to surprise." He looked at me. "She'd gain a lot from Sterling's passing. You know that. Actually, they both would. Kevin is next in line for CEO, you know."

For someone who claimed not to be keeping in touch with Sterling, Vincenzo knew a lot about Sonesty and its dealings. "I thought he might be. But how do you know this?"

"Sterling mentioned he was growing wary of Kevin. It had something to do with the drug. I got the impression they were at odds over it somehow. I think Sterling thought Kevin might try and oust him. Sterling thought he was trying to maneuver control over shares of the company." He cast his gaze in the direction of the inn. "Which also might explain the unlikely liaison with Bitsy."

"Unlikely" was one way to put it. The Jefferson family seemed to have a hefty appetite for office politics and intrigue.

"Webster knows more than he's saying," Vincenzo accused.

I gave the Gallant Herdsman a narrow-eyed glance. Him, Frank, Bitsy, Adelaide—everyone seemed to know more than they were telling me these days. "There's an awful lot of that going around."

Out of the corner of my eye I saw Mocha digging at the base of my stone wall. "Mocha, stop that!" I had to add "Hank, you too!" as my dear pooch gave in to the corrupting influence of Mocha's digging frenzy. My hope for a canine sniffing-out of clues was going down the drain . . . or was that down the hole?

Suddenly Hank gave a whimper of pain and pulled back, pawing at his face. Had Mocha nipped him in his exuberance? I cursed my long-shot theory as Vincenzo and I rushed over to a whimpering Hank.

"*Guarda!*" Vincenzo called out, pulling Mocha back from a freshly dug hole. "Libby, check his nose."

I pulled Hank's face to me, concerned to find a drop of blood oozing from his nose.

"Call your vet. Now!" Vincenzo said, scooping up Mocha before the puppy could return to his digging.

"It's okay, I think it's just a cut," I said, examining the small wound and the bead of blood coming from it.

"No, it's not." Vincenzo pointed to the hole. Ice ran down my spine as I leaned over to see four uncapped medical syringes freshly buried in the dirt.

I somehow found the strength to scoop up Hank with one hand while dialing my phone with the other. "Take Mocha back to the pie shop. Then tell Shannon to call Frank to get over here right away."

CHAPTER TWENTY-ONE

I felt like I hadn't taken a deep breath in twenty minutes when Dr. Vickers put a reassuring hand on my shoulder. "Relax. Hank is fine as far as I can tell. Still, I'd like to keep him here for the next twenty-four hours for observation just to be careful. There may have been a trace amount of whatever was in those syringes, but if they were in the dirt and used days ago, I think you've got more to worry about from the dirt than from the needle."

"I've seen Hank eat dead fish—and pillows—and he's okay, so I'm going to take that as good news."

Dr. Vickers laughed. "Those deer in his backyard stress him out?"

I couldn't yet manage a laugh in return. "Actually, I think it was more that I felt I had to keep him away from the shop and the vicuña. He felt left out, and he took it out on a few of my throw pillows. Maybe more than a few."

He handed the vials of blood he'd just taken from Hank

to his assistant. "We'll run a full set of tests just to be sure. You really think those syringes were used in the murder?"

My voice shook as I said, "I think so. Why else would you bury a set of syringes near where we found the clippers that were used to stab Sterling?" The sheer absurdity of that sentence made me lean against the examining table and hug Hank more tightly. I wasn't at all looking forward to a night without him, given the current state of my blood pressure.

Dr. Vickers must have seen my expression. "You can come back and check on him after dinner, if you like. I'll tell the overnight tech to let you in. But it might make it harder on Hank if you do."

I bit my lower lip, suddenly feeling the threat of tears. "I'll muddle through."

From behind me in the front of the office I heard Vincenzo's voice. "Is he okay? Is the dog unharmed?"

"Just give me a minute with him," I asked the kind vet, feeling a bit silly for how much I needed to hug Hank very tightly.

I was so grateful that he understood. "Absolutely. Just lead him over to Gina's desk when you're done. I'll make sure she has a few treats ready."

"I need to know if he is okay," Vincenzo's voice—even louder—echoed behind Dr. Vickers as he opened the door.

"I'll take care of your guest," Dr. Vickers assured me. "Take all the time you need."

Hank has been my rock, my companion, my advisor, my just about everything. I could not bear the thought of him coming to any harm. Suddenly all my frustration over shredded pillows seemed trivial. "Oh, Hank baby, I'm so glad you're okay," I sniffled, hugging him tight as he buried his wonderful chubby face into my neck like the precious child he was to me. I smoothed his dear little ears and his wrinkly haunches, not minding a bit the slobber now soaking my shoulder. I pulled back to look at his loving brown eyes, the dark pink prick on his nose shooting a pang through me.

"It's just for tonight, just so we can be extra sure you're okay." I failed at sounding confident and reassuring. Hank cocked his head as if he could hear my efforts to be brave, then gave me a lick I would have sworn meant, "I'll be okay."

Certain Dr. Vickers would never endorse it, I swallowed the urge to have a steak from Lilly's bistro sent over for his dinner. "Let's go get a nice big treat from Gina, and then I'll see you in the morning."

I opened the door to see Gavin coming through the office entry. "What happened? Is Libby okay? Is Hank?" and then, upon seeing Vincenzo, "What are you doing here?"

Hank barked and bounded out of my grasp over to Gavin. Vincenzo seemed to take great offense at that. "I was with them when he was injured."

"You've been with her a lot lately." Gavin almost seemed pleased with the bristle that produced from Vincenzo. He hunched down and examined Hank. "You okay, boy? We don't want anything to happen to you."

"I told Libby she needed to come here right away," Vincenzo declared as if it gave him hero points.

"It's what anyone would do," Gavin countered, still clearly irritated. For all I knew, Gavin blamed Vincenzo for Hank's mishap. That wasn't out of the realm of possibility, I suppose, but then again, Gavin would be quick to blame Vincenzo for just about anything. Gavin angled himself between Vincenzo and me, taking my arm with a very possessive air. "Come on, Libby, I'll walk you back to the shop."

Frank walked in at that moment, looking supremely annoyed. I wondered what sort of standoff was about to unfold in poor Dr. Vickers' tiny waiting room.

"*I'll* escort her back to the shop, if you don't mind," Vincenzo shot back, puffing up like a rooster.

"No, you won't," Frank said. "You're going to have another long talk with me."

Gavin looked very pleased at that.

"I told you everything." Vincenzo balled his fists.

"Well, I want to know why I found an empty hole in Libby's backyard. I'm betting you can tell me."

"What?" I asked.

"There were no syringes. Shannon took me straight to the hole where they were, but it was empty when I arrived."

"How can that be?" I nearly shouted. How had my newly discovered and quite possibly very important evidence vanished into thin air?

Frank looked as if he had some theories on that. He squared off at Vincenzo. "Since you were alone at that hole after Libby was headed here, I think you have some explaining to do."

"Why didn't I think to gather them up and take them with me?" After all, it would have been useful for Dr. Vickers to be able to test them. It would have been very useful for Frank to be able to test them, but now we weren't going to get that chance. Maybe Frank was right—I was too close to the case to be of any use.

"Someone moved those syringes." Frank continued to glare at Vincenzo.

The Italian put a hand out. "It was not me. I swear it."

Gavin pulled me back a bit from those two. "Libby, are you okay? You weren't pricked or anything by those needles?"

"No, I'm fine. I never touched them."

Relief filled his features. "And Hank?"

"Dr. Vickers says he'll be fine," I replied. "They're keeping him overnight just to be sure."

"That sounds wise," Vincenzo offered, earning a "Who cares what you think?" look from Gavin.

"I promise you, Hank will get our full attention," Dr. Vickers assured me. "You have my word, I'll be in touch if there's any change in his condition. I expect the test results will be in by noon, and you can pick him up then."

"Okay." My voice still wobbled at the thought of him spending the night at the animal hospital, even though I knew keeping him there was the right thing to do. I found myself glad Mom was still at the house and I wouldn't be alone.

"Let's take a walk down to the station, Marani." Frank gave it as a command more than an invitation.

"I did *not* move those needles," Vincenzo insisted as Frank led him out the door. "You believe me, Libby, don't you?"

"I . . . I have to get back to the shop." I couldn't—wouldn't—give Vincenzo the answer he wanted. Too many facts were lining up against his innocence. And I could say that about more than one person lately—which wasn't a comforting thought.

"Are you ready?" Gavin's voice was steady and reassuring. He would wait until I was ready, I knew that.

"He'll be fine," Dr. Vickers encouraged. "Go on now."

Gavin and I left the animal hospital and headed down the sidewalk. Neither one of us could appreciate the crisp, bright morning, a perfect December day in Collinstown. Gavin put his arm around my shoulders when I shivered—more from worry than from cold. "He's gonna be okay."

I swiped a tear from my cheek. "I couldn't bear it if anything happened to him."

". . . And nothing will. It was a scare, but nothing more. At least you've got the concert tonight to keep your mind off Hank."

I stopped in my tracks. I'd forgotten all about the Collinstown Community Carol Sing that was taking place tonight. "I can't go to that now."

"No," Gavin countered, "I think you should. You'll just worry if you sit at home, you know that. And Jillian is singing in the second half—she'll be disappointed if you and Rhonda aren't there."

"But those needles are out there somewhere. We have to find where Vincenzo's hidden them—if he's hidden them."

Gavin's exhale puffed a cloud of white into the air. "There's no 'if' in my book. Frank is right—Vincenzo's the only one who had the chance to move them. Which has to mean they incriminate him."

"I'll admit, things are lining up against Vincenzo. The lack of warning cry from the animals, the proximity to his motor home, the murder weapon—"

"It has to be him," Gavin pronounced with a certainty I didn't yet feel. "I knew it. I haven't liked him from the start."

I'm not sure all of that dislike was murder-based, but I wasn't going to get into that now. "There are still a handful of people with plenty of motive to want Sterling dead. Vincenzo had opportunity, definitely, but I still can't work out how he might have gotten access to the Sonesty drug. Kevin's the only one who could have that. And since he's taken up with Bitsy—"

Gavin stopped walking. "Wait . . . Kevin and Bitsy? *Bitsy?*"

"Yeah," I agreed. "Didn't see that one coming."

He shook his head. "Just how messed up is this family you used to be part of?"

"That's the thing," I replied. "I'm not sure I was ever really part of it."

G avin was right—unsolved murder or not, Christmas was still coming to Collinstown. And so I found myself donning my gay apparel—in this case a favorite sparkly red holiday shawl—for the Collinstown Community Carol Sing.

"This is always my favorite holiday thing," Mom bubbled as we walked to the Community Theater, just up the street from my shop. "Everybody comes." She was trying to keep up a steady stream of upbeat conversation to distract me. It wasn't working, but I did appreciate the effort.

Indeed, almost everyone in town was there. Margo and Carl were there, as were George Barker and his wife, Vera. Even newcomers like Shannon were in attendance. I invited Shannon to sit with us, but she declined, taking a seat toward the back once she saw Linda and Jason just a few seats away.

"Let her be," Mom said. "This night will brighten your spirits for less calories than that quart of peppermint ice cream I saw in your fridge."

"Don't you always say holiday calories don't count?" I refuted. "Not until January?"

"What do you know?" Mom said with a grin. "You *were* listening." She spied Gavin and Jillian coming down the theater aisle. "Gavin and Jillian, honey, come sit with us. I want to hear that sweet voice of Jillian's."

I won't say I wasn't grateful Gavin took the seat next to

me. While I was a bit miffed at his protective posturing earlier today, there was a part of me that welcomed his continually steady presence. "Are you stopping by to see Hank afterward?" he leaned in to ask quietly.

"I've already been by. He looks like himself. I wish he were home with me, but I know it's best they keep an eye on him."

Gavin gave my hand a quick squeeze. "He'll be fine. It'll all be fine." Then he straightened up, catching something across the aisle. "You've got to be kidding me. Why are *they* here?"

I turned in the direction of Gavin's glare to see Bitsy, Kevin, Adelaide, and Vincenzo taking seats—in a row near the front, no less.

"Well, that's a bold move," Mom muttered.

That was one word for it. The four of them had to know what people were thinking when they showed up. Was this some act of defiance? A declaration of non-guilt? With a wince I realized there might still be Collinstown residents who thought the same of me. "Well," I admitted, "it is a public event. There were flyers up everywhere."

"What do you suppose Frank thinks of that appearance?" Gavin wondered, sounding as baffled as I was.

Mom nudged my shoulder. "I don't think our chief is pondering murderers at the moment. There are the love-birds. Don't they look so happy?" Mom pointed to where Frank and Angie—wearing matching red plaid scarves—walked down the opposite theater aisle hand in hand. "Practicing coming down aisles, are they?" Mom teased. "Just look at them, oblivious to the whole world around them." She waggled her eyebrows. "You could light a dozen Advent candles off the sparks between those two. I've always said the right person can have a sizzling romance at any age."

"Mom," I moaned, nodding my head toward Jillian. What little filter Mom ever had seemed to be disappearing on a regular basis lately.

I received a hefty dose of maternal side-eye for my censorship. "You kids think you invented fun," she muttered. "I'm tickled pink for them. Angie's fairly glowing, bless her heart."

Out of the corner of my eye I caught Gavin pinching the bridge of his nose. "Maybe you could be tickled pink in the privacy of your own mind?" I whispered to Mom, nodding toward Jillian again.

I was saved—or backed up—by a woman in front of us turning to offer a sharp "Shh!" as the lights went down.

While Mom can be wrong about a lot of things, she was right about this evening. As the familiar songs wafted into the rafters on the raised voices of my friends and neighbors, a sense of holiday joy snuck into my spirit. Sure, a large portion of the season hadn't gone nearly according to my plans, but much of it had. It was beyond odd to have Bitsy, Collin, Adelaide, and Vincenzo sitting a few rows away, but I refused to let it destroy the evening. I had Gavin's familiar presence and Jillian's lovely voice beside me. Mom had found the ideal place to live with the help of the totally unexpected Jesse, and tomorrow night my Christmas tree decorating celebration might actually come off exactly as planned. Sterling would have liked to think that even in death, the whole world would revolve around him, but it wasn't the case.

After intermission, Jillian and the madrigal singers from the high school gave a lovely performance of three songs.

After two more numbers where everyone sang, the choir director walked to the front of the stage for the traditional finale of "O Holy Night."

"Now, I know all of you were waiting for Marge's solo," he said, "but I'm afraid she's come down with the flu."

A gasp went through the audience alongside a ripple of sympathetic comments, like "How awful" and "That's terrible."

Mom gave me a thankfully silent look. In my opinion—and Mom's—this wasn't the travesty people made it out to be. Marge Burtow was a sweet woman who considered her voice to be a gift to the world. She sang loud and long. And, as Mom so aptly put it once, she was prone to overestimating her octave range. Marge seemed to be of the opinion that if you hit a high note hard enough, you could reach it. I confess that on many occasions I didn't agree. Her annual "O Holy Night" solo was a prime example, and while it may have been Scroogey of me to admit it, I wouldn't miss its absence tonight.

"We wish Marge a speedy recovery in time for Christmas Eve services, and we'll just muddle along without her, shall we?"

For a brief moment I thought the choir director could encourage Jillian to step forward—she was a beautiful soprano, after all, and I knew her to be quite capable of the notes that continued to . . . elude . . . Marge.

Something else—a totally unexpected something else—knocked that thought from my mind. Vincenzo rose from his seat near the front. "I will sing for you," he stated in grand tones.

Astounded looks darted back and forth between Gavin, Mom, and me. Throughout the entire audience, for that matter. Some of them, I'm sure, recognized him from the shearing events, but I couldn't help thinking the rest of the audience members were asking themselves, "What's with the handsome, overly confident murder suspect declaring he'll sing for us?"

Vincenzo began walking toward the stage looking like this had always been the plan, smiling amiably and saying "*Buona sera*" to a few women on the aisle. What on earth was happening? I'd never heard Vincenzo even mention singing, much less any talent for it. He'd not sung during the spontaneous "Jingle Bells" that had herded the vicuña, either. Hadn't we just spent the afternoon discussing his guilt? Does one let the murderer take the solo?

I caught Frank's eye, knowing he read the wild question in my expression. He shrugged a "Search me" in return, but I could see him shifting to the edge of his seat to rush the stage should anything go awry. Gavin was doing the same thing right beside me.

"Can he sing?" Mom asked me.

"I have no idea," I whispered back. "Why would he do this?"

"Either way, this ought to be memorable," Mom snickered, squinting at the stage.

Bitsy looked shocked but smug. Adelaide looked transfixed. Kevin looked mortified. Vincenzo, on the other hand, looked as if he was about to grace this audience with the gift of the century. The church choir director looked—rightfully so—as if he'd lost control of the entire situation. I waited for him to stop Vincenzo, but he never did.

Vincenzo looked at the terrorized piano player and said, "You may begin." The poor woman looked wide-eyed at the choir director, but what else could she do? Short of someone taking a hook to pull Vincenzo from the stage, it was clear to everyone in the room that our event had a new soloist whether we'd agreed to it or not.

I'd asked for a distraction, and I was getting one in spades. The piano began the soft, rolling opening of "O Holy Night," and I held my breath.

"Did you know?" came Gavin's exasperated whisper as Vincenzo's shockingly brilliant tenor voice sailed out over the astonished audience.

"No," I said, absolutely stunned. All that swagger made perfect sense in light of the talent Vincenzo was now displaying. How had I not known this about the man? Why had he not joined in the singing that herded in the vicuña? That seemed exactly the kind of thing the Gallant Herdsman ought to do.

"How are we going to nail him for murder now?" Mom asked, entirely too loudly. I admit, I was having the same thought, but I knew not to say it out loud. Every head in a ten-foot radius seem to turn in our direction.

Oblivious to our shock, Vincenzo continued his performance. The choir had little choice but to come in on the chorus, backing Vincenzo up as he sailed effortlessly up into the high notes—up and over the high notes in a way no Collinstown Community Carol Sing had ever heard. For a moment my heart went out to our poor Marge, who was sure to hear dozens of accounts of how she was so spectacularly shown up by the Gallant Herdsman. This would be the talk of the town for weeks, leaving every future version of "O Holy Night" paling in comparison.

The crowd leapt to its feet at the end, cheering wildly. Vincenzo put his hand to his chest and bowed. I realized that Mom, Gavin, Jillian, and I were the only ones not standing—even Angie was standing at this point, while

Frank sat steaming. Reluctantly, I rose to my feet and clapped. Vincenzo, for all else he might be, was an extraordinary tenor. I suppose I had to give him that.

Much to Gavin's aggravation, Vincenzo made straight for me after the concert.

"What was I just saying about people not telling me things, Mr. Marani?" I said to his pleased smile.

He seemed to get an enormous kick out of surprising me. "You have never heard me sing? Sterling never mentioned it?"

"I'm sure I would have remembered," I replied.

"You've got some pipes there," Mom said. "We don't get to hear a voice like that here often."

Vincenzo took Mom's hand and gave it a theatrical kiss. "Consider it my holiday gift to Collinstown."

I was sure I heard Gavin's teeth grind from behind me.

"What gave you the idea to just stand up like that and offer to sing?" Jillian asked. "It's not like you live here."

"Maybe it was easier because I don't live here," Vincenzo explained to her. "I always find it easier to perform for strangers. It was Adelaide and Bitsy's idea to come to the concert, actually."

That seemed out of character for the Jeffersons. Fraternizing with the commoners for something as homespun as a carol sing? Perhaps the loss of Sterling made them nostalgic for community—who knew? "Where's Kevin?" I asked.

"He had to leave at intermission," Bitsy answered. "Things have been a bit chaotic at Sonesty. He's been getting calls and emails at all hours."

All hours. I really didn't want any details about the "all hours" Bitsy and Kevin were keeping. By the look on Adelaide's face, she shared my "TMI" reaction.

I was pleased to see Shannon come up and join the conversation. She moved closer to extend a hand to Vincenzo. "That was a remarkable performance. It's always been—" Shannon yelped as she tripped on the aisle carpet edge and went careening to the floor. Gavin tried to catch her, but she slipped beyond his grasp and twisted to send her head whacking against the wooden chair armrest with a sickening thud. Her wrap and handbag went flying in all directions while she slumped still against the carpet.

"Shannon!" I cried out as I hunched down. She'd hit her head hard, and a worrying amount of blood oozed over her face when I turned her over. My poor employee had knocked herself out cold.

By the time I looked up to Gavin, he was already on the phone to the paramedics. Frank appeared at my side moments later, offering a stack of napkins from the refreshment table to hold against the wound. The last thing I wanted to see was more blood—it seemed to instantly push all the holiday joy out of the room.

I shook her gently. "Shannon?"

"Miss Kingston," Frank said, squeezing one of her hands. Shannon's eyes fluttered open for a second, and she moaned, trying to sit up.

"Best not try that," Frank said, easing her back down. "You took quite a fall."

"I'm fine," she attempted, even though her words came out with a woozy slur.

"You most certainly are not. Let's let the paramedics have a look at you, okay? I want my star employee well and healthy." The compliment was for Shannon's sake, and I suddenly hoped Linda wasn't in earshot.

"No," Shannon offered a weak protest.

"I'm afraid I'll insist," Frank said, looking over his shoulder as the paramedic team made their way down the aisle. "I think Santa may be bringing you a shiner for Christmas. Hopefully no stitches."

The quick inspection from the paramedics indicated that Shannon might very well be getting stitches for Christmas. She was loaded—still offering woozy resistance—onto a gurney headed for the ambulance and the county medical center.

I found her spilled handbag under one of the seats and collected its contents. "Here," I said, starting to tuck it onto the gurney with her. "I'll follow in a few minutes and stay with you until everything is all settled."

Out of nowhere, I saw Linda's hand shoot out to take the handbag. "I'll do that," she said.

I looked at Linda, frankly a bit shocked at this display of care.

"You sure?" I questioned. They hadn't been fighting, but it was more of an "I can tolerate being in the room with you" kind of détente than an "I'll follow you to the ER" friendship.

"I . . . I owe her," Linda admitted.

"Okay then." I put the bag and wrap in Linda's hands. "Keep me updated." I hoped what passed between our gazes told me things were feeling better for Linda. She deserved a nice Christmas. We all did.

All of us stood staring for a moment at the spectacle of the paramedics making their way up the aisle and out the theater's back door.

Mom turned to me. "Tonight has been the most exciting carol sing I can remember. But I'm getting a little weary of all the drama, aren't you?"

"Yes," Gavin and I answered in unison.

I could literally watch Gavin steel himself to take the high road. He extended a hand to Vincenzo. "Thank you for that performance."

After a surprised moment, Vincenzo shook Gavin's hand. I said a tiny prayer that this would, indeed, herald a bit less drama in my life. "*Prego*," Vincenzo replied.

"Spaghetti sauce?" Jillian asked, eyebrows furrowed in puzzlement.

Vincenzo laughed. "It means 'you're welcome' in Italian."

She eyed him. "Who names a spaghetti sauce 'you're welcome'?"

"It's also what we say when we present someone with a delicious dish," he replied. "Sort of a 'there you go.'"

"Well, that makes a little more sense."

"What makes the most sense," Mom said, "is for us to all head on home and bring this wild evening to a close."

"I've got to pick something up at the shop, but after that I'm ready for bed. It has been a long day and I am tired," I agreed.

"Good night, everyone," Angie said, coming up to the group to take Frank's hand. Lovebirds, indeed.

Frank wasn't thrilled to know I'd be walking in the same direction as Vincenzo. He caught my elbow with his free hand. "Check in with me in the morning to let me know how Miss Kingston is doing?"

"Sure thing."

Jillian stooped down to fetch something from under a seat a row down. "Oh, look, here's a bit more from Miss Kingston's purse." She handed me a few items—an old photograph in a plastic sleeve, a compact mirror, and what looked like a gentleman's handkerchief.

"Thanks, Jillian," I said, looking down at the items. "These look like sentimental things she'd be sorry to lose." I tucked them into my own handbag. "I'll keep them at the store for her."

I felt Gavin touch my shoulder. "Good night, Libby."

"Good night, Gavin. Good night, Jillian. See you tomorrow night, if not sooner."

"You bet." Jillian gave Mom a quick peck on the cheek. "G'night, Grandma Rhonda. You be good—no coal in your stocking."

Mom giggled while Gavin and I traded tolerant looks. Everything turned to wonder, however, as we all headed out into the night air. Much to our happy astonishment, big, fat, perfect-for-Christmas snowflakes fell gracefully from the sky. Maybe there was hope for a good Christmas after all.

CHAPTER TWENTY-TWO

Collin Avenue did indeed look like a Christmas card. Holiday greetings and cheery cries burst forth as people spilled out of the theater. This, right here, was the Christmas I had hoped to have in Collinstown. I felt as if I was able to catch my breath for the first time in days.

"Look at that, Dad," Jillian marveled, face turned toward the starry sky. "You couldn't have planned it better."

"It's like it was meant to be," Mom chimed in. I felt a welcome surge of "comfort and joy" as I took in the scene. While there was a tiny moment of friction as Gavin and Jillian headed one way down the street while Mom, Vincenzo, and I headed the other, even that couldn't dampen the wonder of the night.

"*Bellissimo*," Vincenzo exclaimed as we made our way toward Y.A.R.N. and the motor home. "I have been frustrated not to be going home, but it would have been a shame to miss this." He had been forced to extend his stay in Collinstown far longer than planned. Part of me wondered if he would be trying to make it back to Italy, or to Peru, for Christmas, but I had no intention of asking.

"We do have lovely holidays here," I admitted instead, smiling at how the snowflakes danced in the light of the streetlamps.

"I do love our springs, but there is something about Collinstown at Christmas," Mom shared. Her face drew into a frown. "It doesn't seem right without Hanky Boy sitting in the window, does it?"

My momentary joy melted like the snowflakes on my mittens. The cozy bed tucked beside the mock fireplace and hearth we'd built in the Y.A.R.N. window looked unbearably empty. I thought of the red and white snowflake sweater I'd had to take off him for his overnight stay. The thought of his usual goofy grin behind a crate door in the animal hospital rose a lump in my throat. "Oh, Hank," I sighed.

"He will be fine," Vincenzo consoled with such genuine tenderness that I wondered if he really was innocent. After all, just because he was stingy with the truth didn't make him a murderer. "Good night, Libby, Rhonda," he said, giving a debonair bow. "I enjoyed myself so much tonight."

I ventured one of his own phrases in return. "*Prego*." Feeling generous with my good cheer upon his grin, I asked, "How do you say 'Merry Christmas' in Italian?"

"*Buon Natale*," he replied.

"Well then, *Buon Natale*, Vincenzo."

"*Buon Natale*, Isabella." What I assumed to be the Italian version of Elizabeth certainly had its charm, the way he said it.

"That was a nice evening," Mom said as I put my key in the shop door. I only needed to collect a file and a box of stitch markers I was wrapping up as a holiday gift, and then I could enjoy the picturesque walk home in the gentle snowfall and tuck myself into bed.

That plan evaporated the minute Vincenzo burst in, looking nothing like his former suave self. "Libby!" he nearly shouted. "The Airstream. It's been broken into."

Mom and I followed him out the door and around to the side of the shop. The motor home door was wide open, swinging in the slight wind. Items were strewn on the grass in front of the door, and even from here I could see that the inside of the Airstream was a mess of items tossed everywhere.

"Did you lock it?" Mom asked.

"Of course I did. There are pry marks on the door where they broke it open. It looks like they've gone through everything."

Despite knowing I'd be ruining his evening, I pulled out my phone to call Frank. "Can you tell if anything is missing?"

Vincenzo picked up an expensive-looking sweater from where it had been tossed on the ground. "It will take me hours to figure that in this mess."

"Who would know you wouldn't be home?" Mom asked, gathering a trio of books from next to one of the trailer's tires.

"Everyone," I said. "He was onstage for the last twenty minutes of the concert. If someone was looking for a sure opportunity, they had one." I caught Vincenzo's eye. "And didn't Kevin leave at intermission?"

Vincenzo's eyes narrowed as he followed my thinking. "And now I am wondering if Bitsy and Adelaide's insistence that I come to the concert wasn't as cordial as it seemed."

"You've been set up?" Mom asked.

"I wouldn't put it past any of them," I answered her. And I wouldn't. But none of those suspicions answered what it was they might have been looking for.

It only took Frank a matter of minutes to show up on the scene. "What's a man have to do for a night off in this town?" he grumbled. Frank was known to be a bit of a workaholic, and part of me was slightly glad to see him have other places to put his attention now.

He scanned the scene. "Someone decide to go through your things while you were onstage?" he asked, quickly coming to the same conclusions we had.

"Looks that way."

"And remember, Kevin left the concert early," I informed the chief, now reasonably sure there was more to Adelaide and Bitsy's attendance than met the eye.

"They were insistent I come," Vincenzo added. He looked ready to march down the street and accuse the three of them right this minute.

Frank dialed his phone, since he was technically off duty and wasn't carrying his radio. "Send an officer over to the inn," Frank said once someone from the department picked up the call. "Confirm the whereabouts of Bitsy Jefferson, Adelaide Jefferson, and Kevin Webster. If they're in their rooms, keep them there." He looked at Vincenzo. "I want to go through this place with a fine-tooth comb. Where else can you stay tonight?"

"With us," Mom answered without even a nanosecond of hesitation. Count on Mom to totally ignore that it was both my house and a terrible idea.

"I'm sure I can get you a room at the inn," I backpedaled.

Mom gaped. "And put him under the same roof as Kevin and those evil Jefferson women? You can't do that."

"I don't want to put you out," Vincenzo said, looking like he thought Mom's idea a superb solution.

I was cornered. "No, it's no trouble." As a last-ditch attempt to save myself, I added, "But you'll have to sleep on the couch."

"Nonsense," Mom countered. "He can have my room."

"Where will you sleep?" I challenged.

"With you, of course. It's a queen. We'll have plenty of room."

I had completely lost control of the evening. My peaceful, joy-inducing concert now left me sitting in my living room with Vincenzo. Mom had waltzed upstairs earlier and was now likely to be blissfuly snoring in my bed. As Vincenzo produced an occasional yawn, I knew I would be the only one struggling for sleep tonight. My brain was too tangled with thoughts and theories to quiet down for slumber. The only positive was that I would probably get a lot of knitting done here by the fire I'd lit.

"I am sorry to impose," Vincenzo said with another yawn. "I'm not sure why the chief needs hours to inspect my trailer."

"He wouldn't if you told him what he was looking for." I let a bit of my current crankiness show. "You can't tell me you don't know what whoever was in there was trying to find."

Vincenzo steepled his hands. "I have theories. Especially if it was Webster."

I didn't feel like wasting time. "Was it the syringes? Did you take them? Evidence of Sterling's snake-related importing crimes?" I nearly rolled my eyes. "Snake-related importing crimes" shouldn't even be a phrase, much less one I'd just used in conversation.

"I didn't hide the syringes. And I wouldn't be foolish enough to hide them right next to the shop if I did, so that should prove my point."

I didn't think that proved anything. "Okay, then what was Kevin looking for?"

"If he thinks I have the syringes, he might be looking for those. Or a dose of whatever was in them."

Why would Kevin need the drug if Sonesty is already making it? There had to be something else. "I'm not even sure Kevin knows the syringes are missing. So what else is he looking for?"

Vincenzo pushed out a long breath. "I expect he is looking for what Sterling was trying to get me to give him."

Now we were getting somewhere. "And what was that?"

"I have known Sterling long enough to know he is not always a man who keeps his word. You need leverage with someone like him."

"And you have leverage?" For a disturbing moment, I reminded myself the sneaky character we were discussing was my ex-husband.

"I have papers and other things that document Sterling's"—he circled his hand in the air, searching for the right word—"disregard for import regulations."

The firelight and the twinkling holiday village on my mantel clashed with a dark idea that came to mind. "You said you feared your father was going to pull back on his support of the vicuña. Were you planning on blackmailing Sterling?"

Vincenzo's laugh was dark. "I'd not play that game with a man like Sterling. It was more like a stalemate. He had something on me, I had something on him." He cupped both hands upward and moved them up and down like an antique scale. "We kept each other in balance."

"Okay then, what did Sterling have on you?"

He laughed again, a touch more sinister this time. "You don't really expect me to tell you that, do you?"

I rather thought he owed me the truth, but I wasn't going to get it out of him tonight. "Was it enough to kill him for?"

The man fixed me with an intense glare. "I did not kill Sterling." He said the words slowly, purposefully, as if his inflection would help me believe him. "I think you know that, or I wouldn't be under your roof tonight."

If it weren't for Mom, you wouldn't be, I thought sourly. But then again, I wouldn't have learned what I just had. What is it they say about keeping your enemies close?

He yawned again. "I believe I will turn in. Will you as well?"

"No," I replied. "Not just yet."

I watched him head up the creaky stairs to the extra bedroom—I refused to call it "Mom's," even though she'd begun to refer to it with the word "mine." The room felt empty without Hank at my feet, as if no amount of knitting could turn tonight cozy without his companionship. "Sleep tight, boy," I whispered to the firelight, trusting he could somehow hear me. I'd give every one of those shredded pillows right now to know he was safe and sound.

Speaking of safe and sound, it occurred to me I'd not yet heard how Shannon was. Should I text her? Linda had texted me that Shannon had been sent home, but I felt like I ought to check in. If she'd turned off her phone for the night, she'd at least know I cared enough to make the effort. And if she was awake, maybe she would appreciate the outreach. At the very least I could tell her that I had the other items she might be missing from her handbag.

I decided to text her a photo of the old Polaroid, the

compact, and the handkerchief, and fished in my handbag for the items and my phone.

I stared at the grainy black-and-white image. It was a sweet, sentimental shot of a man and a young woman. The man had his hand protectively on the woman's shoulder, and it wasn't hard to make out that the woman was a younger Shannon. She had the same quiet smile, the tentative eyes. Eyes that matched the man in the photo, so I guessed this was a shot of Shannon and her father. The protective gesture certainly looked fatherly.

"She'll surely want this back," I said to Hank before I remembered he wasn't here. I swallowed hard—again—and placed the photo beside the mirror on my kitchen table. I unfolded the handkerchief with the crisp monogram of *S-I-K* on one corner. Shannon told me she'd divorced a few years back, so I wondered if the middle initial was her middle name or her maiden name. We'd talked briefly about the different choices she'd made—mine never to take Sterling's name and hers to keep her husband's name even after they'd split.

Even after I snapped the shot and sent it, my eye kept wandering back to the photo. The man's face and very distinctive handlebar mustache struck me as familiar—which was impossible. Then again, she'd grown up around here, so I supposed it wasn't that unlikely that I'd met him. We'd never talked about her family. And I was tired. My imagination was surely running haywire.

. . . Until I realized that maybe it wasn't. After all, how many handlebar mustaches does a woman encounter in a lifetime? I had seen that face before. I just had to figure out where. So I did what any knitter would do when needing to figure something out: I knit. I settled myself back in front of the fire, bolstered with curiosity and a cup of good tea. I picked up my own version of the luxurious vicuña cowl and let the texture and stitches lead my mind through a maze of people, places, and events.

For an hour, I came up short, with nothing but several rows of knitting done. I'd need to go to bed soon or I'd be no use to anyone tomorrow—and Y.A.R.N. would already be short a staff member, thanks to Shannon's accident. I was just tucking my knitting back into my bag when it came to me. I'd seen that face in another photo. A holiday photo—I remembered making a remark about the handlebar mustache looking perfect under the fur trim of a Santa hat.

Thankfully, I was of a certain age where not every photo I ever snapped ended up only on social media. Instead, I had a handy stack of photo albums to flick through. I started on the most recent year and worked my way back through several Christmases, focusing on group shots, since I had an inkling that's where a less-than-familiar face would hide.

Five years back, I found him. The mustache man showed himself in the last place I'd ever expect: the Sonesty Christmas party.

CHAPTER TWENTY-THREE

S onesty?" I said aloud to the empty room, wide awake with the shock of it. I dashed to the kitchen table, bringing the Polaroid back to line it up next to the Sonesty holiday party shot. There was little doubt. Unless I was sorely mistaken—and I was sure I wasn't—Shannon's father had been at that party. And since Sterling only threw on-site holiday parties for employees—glamorous off-site parties were only for clients and customers—the appearance meant Shannon's father had been a Sonesty employee.

What? Why had she never mentioned such a connection? The only logical answer was that she didn't want me to know. Why?

I stared at the three objects, somehow thinking they would yield a clue to the strange connections showing themselves tonight. Well, this morning. The monogram kept drawing my eye. Or, rather, kept drawing my "I." Like handlebar mustaches, there aren't that many I surnames around. I'd heard one in recent conversations, though.

I stared at the monogram for another ten minutes before I remembered Kevin Webster mentioning Thom Ingalls. Like the mustache and the name, the "Th" spelling of Thom wasn't something you saw often. A shiver that had nothing to do with the dying fire ran down my spine.

Shannon Kingston was the daughter of Thom Ingalls. And Thom Ingalls had a whopping bitterness against Sonesty. Could Shannon have told her father where to find Sterling? Had he taken his revenge? The man looked big enough to carry out the gruesome killing. But then I remembered Kevin telling me Thom Ingalls had passed away. So we might only be looking at an eerie coincidence.

. . . Until I remembered a detail Kevin had mentioned about Thom Ingalls: He was a hemophiliac. Not only was Thom Ingalls Shannon's father, he was a hemophiliac. And who needs a wonder drug clotting agent more than a hemophiliac? This could not be a coincidence. I began to pace around the kitchen, my thoughts racing in a dozen directions. I stopped and felt my breath hitch as I realized the only other person with a chance to hide the syringes—or who might know how to use them—was Shannon. After all, she had called Frank as Vincenzo rushed Mocha to the pie shop and then followed Hank and me to the vet.

Shannon? Sweet, soft-spoken, so-grateful-to-be-hired Shannon? My chest squeezed tight at the level of long-range planning that must have gone into this if my hunch was right. But there was still a host of details I couldn't quite work out.

My phone dinged with an incoming text just then, making me jump. It was from Shannon. Thanks. Those are important to me.

I was glad it wasn't a phone call—I'm sure my voice would have been squeaky and tight had I tried to talk to Shannon just then. How are you? I texted, my fingers shaking. Stitches?

You're up? came the reply. Fourteen. I look like a boxer.

You look like more than that to me right now, I thought. Then, feeling brave and unreasonably impatient, I typed, Can't sleep. I could bring them to you now if you like. Better than insomnia.

When the answer of OK, as long as you're sure came, I reached for my coat. I wasn't at all sure, but that was exactly why I was headed out the door.

I scribbled "Going to see Shannon" on a note for Mom. Or Vincenzo. Or the police, if I was about to make a reckless mistake. *If Shannon meant to do me harm,* I told myself, *she's had plenty of opportunities for it before now.* Besides, I didn't even know if my far-fetched theory held any water. But I was hoping I was about to find out.

I'd never been to Shannon's home, but I had her address from my employee records. A middle-of-the-night visit was unconventional to be sure, but these were far from normal circumstances. I didn't want Shannon coming into the shop one more day if what I suspected might be true.

She was right—she did look like she'd come out on the wrong side of a boxing match when she answered her door. A thick white bandage covered her brow and most of her puffy eye, the purple beginnings of a shiner appearing. Her lip was split in one place, and there was a scrape on her jaw.

"Fetching, huh?" she remarked as she let me into the

small, tidy home. Her friendly greeting made my skin crawl, given the suspicions I was harboring.

"I'm just glad you weren't seriously hurt," I managed to say with equal friendliness. "You could have given yourself a concussion. Those theater seats are sturdy and heavy."

She led me to the kitchen—*where the knives are*, my crazed imagination chimed in—and gestured for us to sit down at a small table crowded with bandages, alcohol, pain medicine, and those disposable ice packs they give out at the ER. "I've always been a bit of a klutz. I'm afraid I'll scare away your customers like this."

I'm afraid you'll scare away my customers for other reasons, I thought. "Let's not worry about that just yet." I reached into my handbag and produced the trio of items, laying them out on the table. Realizing they might be important, I'd taken detailed photographs of both the Polaroid and the handkerchief before coming over.

"Oh," she said, touching the black-and-white image with tattered edges. "I would have been so upset to have lost this."

I decided to get straight to it. "Thom Ingalls was your father, wasn't he?"

Shannon's whole body changed. She stiffened straight up in her chair, gave a sharp little intake of breath, and pulled the Polaroid to her. Her eyes gave as much of a flash as they could under the bandage.

"I worked it out about an hour ago," I continued, wanting to keep control of the conversation for as long as I could. "That mustache makes an impression."

"He's gone now." A sudden anger clipped her words short. "He used to work for Sonesty. Did you know that?" It was more accusation than question.

"Yes."

"He was important there. He was brilliant. He had sixteen patents to his name. Did you know that?"

"No, I didn't." But Sterling rarely wasted his time with anything less than exceptional people. If he'd risen that far in Sonesty's research staff, he must have been a gifted man.

"Dad discovered a groundbreaking drug. I mean something that would change the world. Would change his life. And mine. My nieces' and nephews' lives, too." Her words became eerily precise and cold. "Do you know what your ex-husband did when Dad demanded the credit he was due? How he rewarded my father's brilliance?"

I knew from Kevin. "Not well," I admitted. "I'm sorry about that." I thought it needed saying, even though I had nothing to do with the wrongs done by Sterling.

That turned out to be the wrong thing to say. It lit a blaze in Shannon's eyes. "He fired him. Found some stupid reason to let him go and threw him out like trash."

I didn't think it was safe to say anything. I was watching years of bitterness suddenly erupt out from behind Shannon's mild-mannered exterior.

"He was a hemophiliac. From birth. So is my nephew. It's genetic. It's why I don't have children. But this drug was going to change everything. There was no known cure before Dad's work, you know. 'Something so amazing from something scary like snakes,' he would tell me."

I'd had a similar thought myself. Snakes seemed such an unlikely source for such a big medical breakthrough. "What happened?"

"Sterling had him sign security papers because they weren't getting the snakes legally. Dad was breaking the rules even by telling me. But Dad believed in loyal he *believed*"—she gave the word a sarcastic edge—"that when it all went to market, Sterling would reward him for what he'd discovered."

It wasn't hard to guess that Sterling had planned to grab all the glory for himself. For a man who always wanted to change the world, this must have lured him like a siren. My pulse rose when Shannon got up from the table and began to pace the kitchen. I'd been up for almost twenty hours, and it was starting to fray my nerves. Maybe coming here alone in the middle of the night hadn't been the smartest move. Frank would understand if I roused him in the middle of the night to stop me from being stabbed by a steak knife, right?

Shannon turned to fix me with a glare I felt down to the pit of my stomach. "He took his own life. The thing about hemophilia is that it makes it *so very easy* to bleed to death."

I gulped, any reply choked by my growing sense of fear.

"You don't even have to know the best place to cut. Everywhere works when you can't stop bleeding."

I started calculating how many steps there were to the door. If I threw something to hit the wound on her forehead, I might stun her long enough to get out of here with all my blood on the inside where it belonged.

"He did it in his Sonesty lab coat," she explained as she reached into a top cabinet and pulled out a small lockbox. "All that blood. Sometimes visual statements can say so much, don't you think?" Shannon used a tiny key already in the lock to open the box.

I decided I didn't want to see whatever was inside, and I grabbed the pottery from the table and hurled it at her head.

"No!" she shouted, deflecting the crockery so that it shattered into pieces on the floor. "You *have* to see this.

Someone else has to know this exists." She stood between me and the door out of the kitchen as she pulled out a handful of syringes exactly like the ones Mocha had unearthed behind the shop. "I found these in Dad's freezer. Prototypes of the clotting drug. Oh, they're expired, I know, but I discovered they still work quite well. As for dosage—who cares? Sterling was startled when I told him who I was. I kept talking, and it let me get just close enough to give him the first injection. When it started to kick in—it's fast—I just kept injecting them until he started to pass out. Rich, powerful Sterling Jefferson fumbling to his knees, confused and frightened. All because I could turn his blood to pudding with this."

I was almost ill from the terrible image and the frightening calm of her words.

"He had to crawl the last few feet to the platform, but I needed a strong visual. The vicuña only needed a little Benadryl in some apples to keep them quiet. And the Italian really should be more careful with his sharp tools."

"The clippers," I said. It turns out you didn't need Adelaide's nursing training to know where a carotid artery is—and what it can do when pierced.

"It was all too easy, really. By the time I strapped him into the harness he couldn't put up any kind of fight. Then I just started injecting a whole bunch of the Sonesty blood thinners. Pretty soon he became just like my dad. A hemophiliac out of luck—for the little bitty rest of his lifetime, that is." She laughed, sounding like a witch over a cauldron.

Linda, you were right, my panicked brain pulled up out of nowhere. *And I may not live to tell you.*

"You made sure Sterling's own wonder drug was part of what killed him. You hid the syringes when we them."

She puffed up with an eerie pride. "*My dad's* wonder drug. Brilliance runs in the family." Then she deflated a bit. "You know, I thought it would feel better. Victorious. But Dad's still gone." Her voice shook on the last word.

Maybe if I could just keep her talking, I could come up with a way out of here. "You came to work at Y.A.R.N. to do this? Why?"

Her one good eye went wide. "Oh, I was going to do it to you at first. You know, make Sterling lose someone he loved just like I did. And by needles—it really was poetic, wasn't it? But he didn't really love you anymore, so it wouldn't count the way I needed it to."

What I saw in her eyes made my heart jump. She'd come to town, learned to knit, to kill me? I couldn't fathom it.

"It would be easy if I hated you. But you were so . . . nice. I didn't think I'd like working there so much. I didn't know what I was going to do until *he* came to town." She said "he" with so much menace I had trouble breathing. "It was like it all fell together perfectly. What is it Rhonda always says—'It's like it was meant to be'?"

None of this was *ever* meant to be. Any scary, long-fanged snake I could imagine paled in comparison to what I saw in Shannon's features. I was in danger, and I'd better think fast.

"Did you steal the vicuña yarn?" I edged my hand toward a squeeze bottle of rubbing alcohol I spied on the table next to the bandages. If I could grab it fast enough, and aim for her face, maybe I stood a chance.

"I don't steal," she asserted. "Too much has been stolen from me." *But murder is okay?* She wavered a bit, putting her hand to the side of her face that had been injured.

"Do you want the ice?" I tried to make my shaking voice

sound kind and concerned. "That must hurt." I picked up the ice pack with one hand while I grabbed the alcohol bottle with the other. As we moved close enough to hand off the pack, I mustered my nerve and splashed her face with the alcohol. She screamed as the liquid burned her cuts and eyes, and I scrambled for the door with my purse in my hands. I ignored her yelps of pain as I dashed to the car and threw it into gear while I locked the doors. Heart pounding, I drove it straight to the police station. I barreled past the decorated pine boughs out front to bang on the door like a wild woman. Irrational as it sounded, I was convinced Shannon was running up behind me, ready to stick me with syringes like a dartboard.

An officer opened up the door—it was nearly two in the morning, after all—astonished at my near-collapse inside. "Shannon Kingston," I gasped, head down, light-headed from my narrow escape. "She killed Sterling. I just left her. She did it."

The man blinked at me, trying to connect the crazy collection of facts I'd just thrown at him. "Isn't she . . . Doesn't she work for you?"

I leaned against the wall, telling myself I was safe even though my pulse rammed against my eardrums. "Her father worked for Sterling. He fired him, and there was a drug . . ." It was too complex for right now. "Just go get her, she's at her house and she was getting ready to stab me with the lethal drugs that killed Sterling."

I told him the address and then proceeded to dial Vincenzo multiple times until he picked up. "Libby?" How did he manage to sound as if I'd woken him from a peaceful sleep?

"Go wake Mom and come to the police station. It was

Shannon who did it. I just confronted her and I don't want her coming to the house thinking I'm there."

"You what?"

"Shannon killed Sterling," I repeated, feeling time tick away and imagining Shannon's capacity for vengeance. "With the new drug. And an old drug. I'll explain later, just *get out of there*. She's crazy."

CHAPTER TWENTY-FOUR

I was standing in Frank's office with a regrettably medio-cre cup of coffee when Gavin came bursting through the department doors. The sun was just coming up and it felt like years had gone by since we sat in the concert hall en-joying the songs of the season.

He barreled straight into Frank's office looking as fran-tic as I've ever seen him. "What am I going to do with you?" he shouted. "Why do you keep doing that? Putting yourself in danger?"

"I didn't think she'd be so . . . unhinged." I'd been wired for so many hours I suddenly felt as if I could fall asleep on top of Frank's desk.

"She killed Sterling like that and you didn't think she was dangerous?"

"She had me fooled. She had everybody fooled. Well, everybody except Linda." The events of the night caught up with me. "She told me she was planning to kill me, Gavin.

Before Sterling showed up." I felt my voice waver. "I was so ticked when Sterling showed up, and it turns out that saved my life."

Gavin's face paled at that revelation. "I never thought I'd say this, but thank God for Sterling." He walked over and put his arms around me before I could gather the strength to stop him. "Libby," he said as he pulled me tight, breathing out my name in the way that always undid me back in the day. "We could have lost you. *I* could have lost you."

Clinging tight, I managed to mutter a damp "You didn't" into the solidness of his shoulder.

He pulled back to look at me. "I'm so very glad for that."

I sniffed, and he wiped my wet cheek with his thumb. I knew, at that moment, that the line between us no longer existed.

"Libby," he said again just before he leaned in and kissed me. It was sweet and tender and urgent and everything a second-chance-at-love kiss ought to be. The stuff of gushy movies and valentines, only solid and sure between two people who weren't kids anymore. If I'd ever needed reminding what a stellar kisser Gavin Maddock could be—which I didn't—I sure got it just then.

Emboldened by my brush with lethal needles, I kissed him back. Enough to make his breath catch and the room spin around us. And then we just stood there in the wonder of it all, some crazy combination of stunned and exhausted and exhilarated. A magical moment, if you will.

. . . Until we heard someone clearing his voice very loudly, and turned to find Vincenzo leaning against the doorway.

"Your mother wants to know when we can go home," he said, barely containing his amusement. His expression was half surprise, half gracious loser. I felt my face go as red as the ribbons garlanding the department's trees.

"In a minute," I stammered. I tried to pull away a bit, but Gavin's arm was *not* leaving its place around my shoulders. Mr. Mayor was staking his claim loud and clear. Unnecessary and annoying as it was, it still warmed a corner of my heart.

"No," Vincenzo replied, "I think perhaps you should take your time."

Mom's voice came down the hallway. "Why are you telling Elizabeth to . . ." She pushed past Vincenzo to see Gavin still holding me. We must have looked like teenagers caught necking on the front porch. I certainly felt like it, despite the fact that I had every right to kiss the man without apology. "Oh." Mom's mouth fell open. I can count on one hand the number of times I have rendered that woman speechless. "Well it's about time," she finally pronounced, stepping into the office to swat at Gavin with the mittens in her hands. "I was running out of patience with you two."

"Mom," I moaned.

"Don't you 'Mom' me," she warned. "Jillian and I were getting ready to shove you two under the mistletoe. Why don't you and her come over for Christmas dinner?"

"You already invited them, Mom. The other day."

"Did I?" She shrugged. "Well, it's just as good an idea today as it was the other day, then."

"Maybe we should go see if the pie shop is open," Vincenzo said, yanking on Mom's elbow. "I need better coffee."

We all did, but I wasn't sure I was ready to face Margo's whopping smirk over my relationship status.

Mom planted her hands on her hips. "Well, who'd have thought it would take a murder?"

I suppose it was more accurate to say it had taken som̶ one threatening my life. Still, since I hadn't shared Shann̶ original plan with Mom yet—and maybe shouldn't ever—I kept my mouth shut. Some part of me was still worried she'd yank her deposit back from The Moorings and move in forever if she learned Shannon had duped all of us and plotted my demise right under my nose. I could still barely believe it myself. Would my firm belief that all knitters are nice people survive an episode like this?

"*Buon giorno*, Libby," Vincenzo said as he tugged on Mom's arm again. And then, looking at Gavin, he added, "*Bravo, signore*."

It felt as if Gavin and I needed a three-hour conversation, and not the kind you can have in Frank Reynolds' office. I knew—as I had always known—that things would change dramatically from here. The complications were staggering, but also exhilarating. Falling for Sterling had been like jumping onto some wild exotic ride. Returning to my feelings for Gavin felt like . . . well, like finally settling into something I should have done long ago. But maybe that was the fatigue—and that rather spectacular kiss—talking.

Gavin turned to look at me, his gray eyes as warm as I'd ever seen them. The panic that had been there earlier was replaced by a glow of affection and relief. He slid his hands around my waist—a gesture that melted me now just as quickly as it had way back then—and gave me a lopsided grin. "How do we do this?"

I shrugged, returning his grin with one of my own. "I have no idea." Somehow, that didn't seem as daunting as I'd expected. After all, once you've solved a murder or three, how hard can a little interpersonal complexity be?

"I bet Rhonda and Jillian have ideas," he joked quietly, still not moving his hands from my waist, despite the fact that Frank could walk in at any moment. As I knew he would be, Gavin was all-in now that he'd declared _his_ feelings.

". . . Which we absolutely should *not* take to heart," I warned. Despite the early hour, Mom was likely considering who it was okay to call with such earth-shattering gossip. One thing was certain—there was no way Mom would walk into Margo's without shouting the news. Instead of calculating the number of seconds until my phone started beeping with incoming smug-but-happy texts from Margo, I decided to kiss Gavin again. Because I really wanted to, and because I knew exactly how to melt him the way he'd melted me. History had its advantages.

"Well, good morning and Merry Christmas to you, too," came Frank's voice a tiny bit later. The twinkle in his eye would have given Santa a run for his money. In fact, I'd convinced him and Angie to play Santa and Mrs. Claus at the tree lighting. With a small jolt of alarm I remembered that was tonight. Tonight? Exactly how much can one yarn shop owner pack into forty-eight hours?

"Good morning, Frank." Gavin gave an awkward cough but still managed to keep his voice steady and ordinary. I, on the other hand, still felt as if anything I said would come out as a breathy, swoony sigh.

"Shannon gave a full confession. And I'm glad of that, but Libby, you and I are going to have a *long* conversation about taking unnecessary risks without the support of law enforcement."

I nodded, remembering what it felt like to recognize how easily Shannon could have jabbed me with one of those syringes. I, who make my living with yarn and needles, could all too easily have died by one. It would take a while for the ice of that to leave my spine.

"Just because you seem to have a knack for this does not mean I endorse what you've done."

"Yes, sir," I managed to gulp out in reply to my lecture.

"Did she break into the motor home?" Gavin asked.

"She couldn't have," I said, finding my voice. "She was in the theater the whole time. It had to be someone else."

"I'm heading over to the inn in a bit to have that conversation with Kevin. He left the concert early, and I'm betting he worked with Bitsy or Adelaide to arrange the distraction of Vincenzo's impromptu appearance." He pointed a finger at me. "You will *not* be coming with me. Am I clear?"

I was going to have to step very carefully around the chief for a while. Shannon had probably revealed her original plan to do me in, and I doubt Frank took kindly to that one bit.

Frank turned to Gavin. "Take her home and make sure she stays there. Lock the blasted door behind her if you have to."

I had no intention of being corralled like some misbehaving toddler. "Now wait just a minute, you two—"

Gavin silenced me by kissing me, right there in front of Frank. All-in indeed. I wiggled out from underneath his romantic declaration. "I'm going home to take a nap, pick up Hank, and then Y.A.R.N. is opening on schedule today. And we have the tree decorating tonight. One homicidal maniac is not taking down my Christmas."

Gavin raised his hands in defeat. "You heard the lady."

Now it was my turn to point a finger at Frank. "Get your Santa suit ready, Chief, you're on at seven."

Frank gave me a friendly salute. "Yes, ma'am." He then bounced a gaze back and forth between Gavin and me, wagging a finger at each of us. "Took you long enough."

"I might say the same of you," I teased in return, then gave in to a massive yawn.

Gavin handed me my coat while Frank started humming "Deck the Halls." This would be a Christmas none of us would forget anytime soon.

I grabbed a two-hour nap and a double-shot peppermint mocha from the Corner Stone, picked up an exuberant Hank from the animal hospital, and joined Linda at the shop just after lunch.

"Wow," Linda said the minute I walked into the shop. "I mean, just wow. I've never been so sad to be right in all my life. I had a bunch of reasons why I didn't like her or trust her, but murder wasn't anywhere on my list."

"I've always trusted your judgment—maybe I should have in this, too." I hugged her. "I'm so sorry about all this. It's been so stressful for both of us."

"Vincenzo's been packing up most of the morning," Linda said, looking out the window.

"Well, I guess he can leave now that he—and I—aren't suspects for murder." I took Hank off his leash and tucked our things into the office, glad to be doing something ordinary-feeling on this wild ride of a day.

"But we still don't know who ransacked his motor home, do we?"

I sighed. "Not yet. And maybe not soon, since Frank has banned me from all investigative activities until further notice."

Linda gave me one of her reprimanding looks. "You took a huge risk going over there alone in the middle of the night." I expected I'd be getting a lot of those looks for a while—from Frank, Gavin, Linda, and probably even Mom. "We need you," she said, sounding a bit emotional. "Don't go pulling stunts like that."

Margo chimed in as she pushed through the door. "I heartily agree, even though I've been right beside you on some of those stunts."

I held up my hand in a scout's-honor salute. "No more reckless sleuthing." I tried to laugh as I added, "At least not until New Year's," but it didn't quite come off as a joke. In truth, knowing how close Shannon had come to sticking those drugs in me scared me off any feats of derring-do for quite a while.

Margo's tone turned to a teasing one. "Speaking of stunts, Gavin? As in you and Gavin? Finally? In Frank's office, no less?"

Linda's gaze whipped over to Margo. "What?"

Margo, who clearly had been waiting for the minute I set foot in the shop to race over here, looked all too happy to be able to break the news to my employee. "Our mayor and our chamber president finally got together." She smirked. "And I don't mean in a civic way."

"I'm amazed it isn't all over town already," I bemoaned. "Mom's acting all victorious and I bet Jillian isn't far behind."

Margo smirked. "Angie called me. And yes, it is all over town already."

"I thought Paul was looking at me funny as he handed me my coffee." Part of me was relieved. Another part of me wanted to hide in the stockroom for the next week.

"Murder, surprise tenors, romance—it's a Christmas extravaganza of town gossip out there." Margo's smile of pure and genuine happiness helped settle down my feeling of being so exposed.

"Lucky me," I murmured, trying to hide in my enormous to-go cup from the Corner Stone. Suddenly I totally identified with Frank's blustering shyness once word about him and Angie finally got out. Shocking good news is still a bit shocking.

Margo walked over to pull me into a tight hug. "You know I'm totally happy for you. And I'm *really* happy the murder is solved."

Linda came over to us. "Me too. And guess what? I also get to be happy because Jason and I aren't going anywhere anytime soon."

"Really?" I replied, filled with relief. "That's wonderful news."

"They cut some other guy in Ohio."

"They fired someone this close to Christmas?" Margo said. "Who is Jason's new boss? Scrooge?"

Linda shrugged. "He could be the ghost of eleven different Christmases past and I'd be okay with it if Jason's job is safe and we don't have to move." She teared up a bit as she delivered the news, reminding me again how much that had weighed on her.

"I'm so glad, Linda. Especially since it seems I need you now more than ever." I looked at both women. "I fired the homicidal maniac, just in case you were wondering. Well, I haven't actually formally terminated her, but I think it's rather implied."

Linda managed a grin. "Hard to run the cash register from jail." Now it was her turn to fix us with an amazed look. "We were working alongside someone capable of that kind of killing. Sort of makes your skin crawl, doesn't it?"

I had tried unsuccessfully to squelch the same thought. "She'd been plotting this for months. I think she knew exactly what she was doing when she took that knitting class and looked like such a star student. I feel like I'll be looking over my shoulder for a long time."

"It's wrong on so many levels, what she did. I get that

her dad was treated terribly, but that doesn't ever give her the right to murder someone as revenge." Linda hugged me again. "Not even Sterling. And especially not you."

I sighed. "I always said I wanted to get to the place where I could think of Sterling kindly. I suppose I'm there, but it's more pity and sadness than kindness."

"Have you seen Adelaide or Bitsy?" Margo asked. "Or Kevin, for that matter? After all, we still don't know if they were involved. Or who broke into the motor home and what they were looking for."

"Frank swore me off all case-related conversations—especially with those three—and for once I don't mind doing as I'm told."

"Well," Margo commented with a smirk, "that's a first." She looked out the window at the gleaming coach. "What about him?"

That was a good question. "I don't know. I'm glad to know he didn't kill Sterling. But there's a lot of mystery still circling around our Gallant Herdsman. Sterling had something on him, he admitted to that much, but I might not ever know what it was."

"Still," Linda added, "that yarn. I was going to say 'It's to die for,' but I don't think I'll ever say that about vicuña again." She looked at the glass case. "We still don't know who took it—or brought it back—do we? It could still be Adelaide, like you thought."

"I'm not sure it matters. I mean, given everything else that's happened, it seems a tiny detail by comparison." I touched the glass case, struck by a craving to touch the ball and be soothed again by its extraordinary softness. While I could never hope to afford it, to be wrapped up in a whole blanket of this stuff would be more calming than any sedative.

That's the thing about knitters—we're tactile people. How things feel matters to us. We're deeply affected by color and texture. While I was still bone-tired, I was glad to be in the shop today, surrounded by color and fiber and good friends.

"Don't you want to know who robbed you?" Linda asked.

"After knowing someone plotted to kill me, not really." I looked up at the device still perched in an upper corner of the shop. Part of me wanted to find a ladder and yank it down this instant, crocheted holly and all. "I never did turn on the camera after that first day, you know," I admitted to them. "Call me foolish, but I don't want to spend my time and attention on things like that. I opened Y.A.R.N. to celebrate what's good in the world."

"And tonight," Margo reminded me, "you get to do just that. I can't think of a better day to decorate the tree than today. I'm more than ready to put all this miserable business behind us."

I couldn't have agreed more.

CHAPTER TWENTY-FIVE

By the middle of the afternoon, Vincenzo had taken all the decorations off his motor home, had secured the broken door with duct tape, and was ready to leave.

"Goodbye, Libby," he said grandly when I came to see him off. "Will I see you again?"

"Maybe in three years?" Vicuña were shorn every three years, but I doubt the zoo would ever allow a repeat of our event. "Or Y.A.R.N. could sponsor a trip to Peru."

He took my hand. "You are always welcome there."

"Will you ever tell me whatever it was Sterling held over your head? What Kevin went through your trailer looking for?" Nosy as it was, I wanted all the secrets from this sorry affair out in the open so we could put it all behind us.

Frank had found enough fingerprints in Vincenzo's trailer to charge the Sonesty executive with breaking and entering. But our chief remained close-mouthed about what it was Kevin sought. I wanted to try this one last time to see if Vincenzo would trust me enough to tell me.

I expected another refusal, but was surprised when Vincenzo sat down on the steps and motioned for me to do the same. "You know Adelaide and I were together. It was a brief, dramatic thing. We didn't belong together, and never have." He took a deep breath, bracing his hands on his knees. "The truth is that our relationship was not without . . . consequence."

It was an odd choice of words. "Consequence?"

"Adelaide became pregnant."

The weight of that statement nearly knocked me off the steps. Adelaide and Vincenzo having a child together? I couldn't have been more surprised.

"She was in an absolute panic. We weren't at all meant to be together, and neither of us was ready to be a parent. So we arranged for Adelaide to do one of her disappearing acts until the child was born, and placed him up for adoption. In Peru, as a matter of fact. Away from Marani and Jefferson family meddling. Neither of us wanted what we knew our families would do."

Vincenzo and Adelaide had a son. Sterling had had a nephew. Bitsy had a grandson. I felt the world tip off balance at the shock of that. "Who discovered it . . . him?"

"I expect Bitsy knows now, or will soon. Sterling didn't know until a while ago, just before our . . . partnership."

"Was he judgmental? Bitter, even?" After all, here was the Jefferson heir I couldn't give him.

"It was more that he knew leverage when he saw it. He knew I would agree to just about anything to protect my child from becoming exactly what he couldn't give Bitsy." No wonder he was desperate to make a legacy for himself. "And Kevin?"

"I'm not really sure. Maybe Adelaide sent him looking for the documentation. Maybe Kevin felt he could keep me quiet about Sterling's activities if he had the leverage Sterling had. But no matter. Everything is in a safe-deposit box in Milan, not here. And he would never have found this." Vincenzo pulled his wallet out and showed me a photo of a dark-eyed baby wrapped in what looked like a Peruvian blanket. "His name is Javier. I don't go back to Peru just for the vicuña."

I looked at the sweet, tiny face. "Does the boy know?"

"Not even the parents know. That's best. And is why we hoped Bitsy and my parents would never know." He sighed. "I don't know what will happen now. I doubt Bitsy will leave it alone, especially now."

That was true. Bitsy would never leave it alone. I found myself again grateful I had extracted myself from that dysfunctional family.

"I'm sorry." It wasn't exactly the right thing to say, but I didn't know what else to offer.

"It is what it is. Secrets never do stay in the dark, do they?"

"What will you do now?"

Vincenzo rose. "Fly back to Milan for a while and make it up from there. Keep going back to Peru, find a way to help keep the community and the herd thriving. I am thinking maybe it's time to take part in Javier's life. Somehow. Find new ways to be gallant." He said the last word with such a sardonic smile I felt a pang in my heart.

I rose to hug him with an ease that surprised me. "I hope you find what you're looking for. What you need."

He shrugged. "I'll have to figure out what it is first. But at least now I can knit while I'm working it out."

"I find I do my best thinking while I'm knitting."

Hugging me back one last time, Vincenzo said, "Goodbye, Libby. I would like very much to see you again someday."

I would welcome the chance, but I had a feeling it wouldn't ever happen. "Goodbye, Vincenzo. *Buon Natale*."

"*Buon Natale*," he said, returning my greeting before getting into his vehicle.

I watched it pull out of my drive—most likely out of my life—and pushed out a long, sad breath. I hadn't seen that coming. I hadn't seen any of this coming. I dearly hoped tonight launched the start of a peaceful Christmas and a pleasantly boring new year.

I was just locking the door to close up shop and get ready for the night's festivities when I found Jeanette standing outside. She's normally one of those eternally happy people, but she'd seemed stressed of late. News of Shannon's murderous intent had spread like lightning, and several customers had stopped in during the afternoon to express their shock and surprise.

She hugged me tight the minute I pulled open the door. "Are you okay?" she asked. "You sure you're okay?"

"Shocked," I admitted. "But okay. Why were you standing outside? Why didn't you just come in?"

Jeannette ignored my question and stepped inside. "Shannon. Never in a million years would I have guessed it would be Shannon." She gave me an uneasy look. "Seems you never know what someone is capable of, do you?"

She wasn't herself, I could see that. I couldn't remember if this was Jeanette's first holiday season without her late husband, but did that really matter? All of the first few m̶ be hard. Maybe *all* of them were hard. It had been n̶ years since Dad passed, and to this day I miss his New Year's Day brunch pancakes.

"Need something?" I ventured. Lots of people dash in at closing time for a set of needles or some other last-minute necessity.

She glanced around the shop. "Is it okay if I come in for a minute?"

She was already inside. "Of course you can." Her eyes were wide, almost fearful. "Jeanette, are you okay?"

She pulled off her mittens—beautiful, hand-knit color-work ones from the patterns we'd featured last year. "Yes. Well, no. I hate to bother you with this after everything that's happened, but . . ." She stuffed the mittens in her coat pocket with an anxious thrust. "Can we sit down?"

This visit clearly wasn't about yarn. But I consider Jeanette a friend as well as a customer, and I'd make time for anyone coming into my shop looking so distraught. I took my coat off and put my bag back on the counter. "Do you want me to put some coffee on?" This didn't look like a short conversation.

She shook her head. Hank walked up to Jeanette, leash still on, immediately ready to offer his sweet gaze and loyal company.

Jeanette smiled down at him. "Hello, Hank. You're such a sweetheart." She sighed. "Maybe I should get a dog."

"Don't you already have a cat?"

"Well, yes," she replied. "But she isn't much company. She mostly hides. And it's not the same."

So she was lonely. Who wouldn't fall prey to a bit of that this time of year? "Well, you might want to talk to Margo. She's finding Mocha a bit more than she bargained for. But I'll tell you, Hank is worth every bit of the trouble he was as a puppy. Every bit of the trouble he's been lately. He missed the shop more than I realized and misbehaved at home."

But I shouldn't have been talking about me. I sat down as she cautiously perched herself in another of the chairs. All the comfort I'd seen from her in the shop—most of the Gals considered Y.A.R.N. a second home—was gone. Her edginess worried me. "Jeanette, you seem upset. What's wrong? How can I help?"

"I don't know that you can."

The hopelessness in that statement pulled at me. "I hope that's not true. What's going on?"

Her hands were on the table, clasped tightly. She wore a deep red sweater with the most wonderful cable work, reminding me again what a skilled knitter she was. Instead of offering the compliment I normally would have, I stayed silent. It seemed best to let her work up the nerve to say whatever it was she came here to say.

"It's been hard," she said after a long pause. "With Jim gone. I hadn't counted on it being this hard."

"I think it's the hardest thing there is," I offered. "You and Jim were really happy together."

"We were. Jim took care of everything. My daughter tries to help with some of the more complicated things, but everything is so . . . overwhelming."

"I've seen you tackle some of the most complicated patterns we sell. You'll get the hang of it. And you have a lot of friends to help you."

"All this Medicare stuff, plans and endless waits on the telephone for someone who can't answer the simplest of questions. And the bills." She looked up at me. "Did you know I'm still paying bills for Jim's final days?"

That seemed cruel. "I'm so sorry. Really, I'll do anything I can to help you."

"We don't have enough." It burst out of her like a flash flood. "The insurance . . . it wasn't enough. I'm . . . I'm not getting by."

Was she coming in here to tell me she couldn't buy yarn anymore? Was she asking for Shannon's job? Did she just need to speak it out loud to someone? I couldn't make out where this was going.

"Maybe there's something we can do if we put our heads together." The church had a food pantry, but pride can keep someone away even if they could use the help. The Gals would close ranks around Jeanette in a heartbeat if she could bring herself to ask. I said a quick prayer that maybe today was the first step in her asking. I have always thought that Y.A.R.N. gave me the privilege of knitting people together as well as yarn.

"And now I have to take this new expensive heart medicine," Jeanette went on, her voice rising in tension. "How can they charge so much for those things if we need them that badly?"

That question was one that had always bothered me as a sales rep, even though I knew the costs of research and development. I could give the speech about how it takes developing ten drugs to find the one that works. And heaven knows I had heard a similar lament from Mom—she always insisted Sterling could personally do something about that if he just had the moral fiber to put people over profits. He didn't.

"I wish I had an answer for that," I replied. "But we want you sticking around for a long time, so let's figure out a way to keep you in that medicine."

She flinched at my words, then started to cry.

I grabbed her hand. "Jeanette, there's got to be a way to work this out. Please let us help."

"I'm sorry. I'm so sorry," she moaned. "It was such a horrible, evil idea. I don't know what came over me. I'm so ashamed."

For a heart-stopping, dark second I considered the notion that Jeanette had somehow helped Shannon hurt Sterling. It made no sense at all, but her words had such an air of confession about them.

And then it came to me. Honestly, it seemed almost as impossible an idea. Jeanette. It *couldn't* be. I put my hand over hers, feeling her cold fingers shaking under my palm. "The vicuña?" I said as gently as I could. "You took the vicuña yarn?"

She shut her eyes for a moment, new tears seeping out from her gray lashes. "Just the one at first. The price was so close to the cost of that drug. I've never done . . ." Her expression was fragile, pleading. Heartbreaking. "I'm not that kind of person. At least I thought I wasn't that kind of person."

My brain would not hold the image of Jeanette stealing from Y.A.R.N. What level of desperation would drive her to something like that? I couldn't come up with a response.

"I can't come here anymore. I know that." She looked around. "I'll miss this place so much."

That knocked me out of my shock. "Don't say that. I . . . well, I admit, I don't really know quite what to do. But I'm pretty sure it's not ban you from the store. You brought it back, after all."

"I didn't sleep a single night with that yarn in my house. I couldn't do that to you. I'd rather let my heart go bad than live with doing that to you."

Jeanette buried her face in her hands. I rushed around the table to hug her, momentarily stung by how she pulled away until she melted onto my shoulder and sobbed. To fe that trapped, to be driven to what I knew was a bone-deep betrayal for her? It made my heart twist in pity. Never in my wildest imagination would I have considered this a possibility.

I said the one thing I knew to be true. "I'm glad you told me. I had no idea things were so bad."

"You don't hate me?" she cried into my shoulder.

"No," I replied with surprising ease. "I'm worried to death about you, but I don't hate you." I pulled away so that she could see the truth of that in my eyes. "And you are absolutely not banned from the store. Do you hear me?"

"I'd understand," she insisted. "I'd deserve it."

"Stop that," I gently scolded. Then I realized why she was really here. "I forgive you, Jeanette. I'm not sure how we fix this for you, but I do know that we will. You're forgiven. Do you hear that?"

She nodded, fresh tears wetting her cheeks along with the relief that fell off her shoulders.

"Nobody has to know. I'm glad—really glad—you told me, but no one else has to know."

"Not even Frank? I'm not going to be arrested?"

"No." Actually, I had no idea. A police report had been filed. What was the proper protocol in a grief-stricken rescinded fiber theft? Restitution had been made. I didn't have to press charges, did I? I couldn't bear that. "But we might want to think of a few people we can pull in to help you figure out the money stuff. Linda's really good at that. Could you see your way clear to letting her help?"

She wiped her eyes. Her whole face and body had changed, lightened, with the confession. It must have been eating her alive, poor thing. "I'll think about it." Her gaze darted up to meet mine. "You won't tell Rhonda, will you?"

Mom was the last person who should ever know about

this. She'd swoop in with a dozen invasive ways to help, not to mention she is one of the worst secret keepers around. "Absolutely not."

With a second wave of anxiety, Jeanette looked up at the security camera. "Oh no," she wailed. "You've got it on record now. I'm finished."

"It's not turned on."

"But . . ."

"I know, I know, there were a million sensible reasons why I should have the thing running. I guess I just learned the one very important reason why it shouldn't. If you can't come into Y.A.R.N. and safely spill your guts, where else can you?"

The tiniest of laughs bubbled up from her, and I saw a hint of the old Jeanette return. "Don't let Pastor hear you say that."

CHAPTER TWENTY-SIX

I couldn't tell you if the Collin Avenue decorations were extra beautiful this year, but it certainly seemed that way to me. Gavin and I were standing at the top of the avenue beside a box overflowing with donated decorations. From here I could see every store lit up and decorated. I could hear the carols being played by the high school band down by the riverbank and the fountain that now housed our lopped-off town tree.

And, in all honesty, the tree didn't look lopped-off. The Gals had managed to make it look not short, but somehow lush and fat, surrounded by the boughs on the bottom around the fountain. I could just make out Arlene, Jeanette, and the other "decorators" who had been commissioned to oversee how the ornaments made their way onto the tree. They weren't upset that it was shorter than last year's. Instead, they were determined to make it Collinstown's best tree ever. And while the giant lighted star wasn't as far up into the inky night sky as in past years, I would bet you it shone brighter than ever.

The sidewalks down either side of Collin Avenue bustled with shop owners and townspeople. A long and jolly "bucket brigade" of merchants and onlookers stood looking up at Gavin and me in anticipation, ready to pass the collection of donated ornaments hand to hand down the avenue to the tree.

The whole scene shone with hope and joy—just the way you want Christmas to feel. I swear even the moon shone brighter and the stars twinkled with extra effort. Mom kept saying tonight was sweeter for all the stress that came before it. While I would have gladly done without all the darkness of Sterling's death, I suppose Mom was right. I did treasure my loved ones more than usual tonight. I have always loved Christmas, but this Christmas was more splendid than any I could remember.

At seven o'clock, exactly as planned, every church with a bell—and that was most of them in town—rang out. A soft snowfall had begun half an hour ago, a perfect, picturesque dusting that made everything look new and wondrous. The town glowed. I glowed. It felt like the whole world glowed.

Gavin grabbed my mittened hand and gave it a squeeze. "This is perfect. Your best idea ever."

I smiled in return, squeezing his hand as well. "Ready?"

"Ready."

With that, we both reached into the box and pulled out an ornament. Gavin simply grabbed the nearest one, but I had chosen which ornament to send down the line first. It was a miniature striped stocking, knit by Jeanette. I saw her down with the other Gals, her shoulders no longer slumped in the way I was sorry I hadn't caught sooner. She was bac amongst us in more ways than one, and I was grateful. I said a small prayer that she would let us help her more as I passed the decoration off to Margo. No one would ever know what Jeanette had done, but if I knew my YARNies, they wouldn't need to know anything to enthusiastically lend a hand. They'd help because it was Jeanette, and because Y.A.R.N. was a community.

Margo held it up for a moment, admiring the needlework before handing it off with a smile to the clerk from the bank standing next to her. And so it went. Ornament after ornament went down the line—beautiful hand-crafted ones, silly ones from the preschool, clever ones from the coffee shop and the hardware store, elegant ones from the boutique up the street, and even George's salesy signs—I admired them all. And why not? They were us, in all our differences, our quirks, our connectedness. I generally leave the symbolism and metaphors to the writerly types, but I couldn't escape the power this moment held for me.

It only took about an hour, but I would have stood there for three. No one minded the cold. My throat kept tightening, near-tears of gratitude and wonder threatening as I watched shop owners pass each ornament down. They would talk and laugh, point out how the plastic reindeer with the light-up nose was just as much fun as the cotton-ball snowman, wonder who made what (except, of course, for George's donations), and generally enjoy each other's company and what we were doing together.

The tree wasn't just being decorated; it was being decorated by *all of us*. It was our version of the community-wide effort to bring in the vicuña herd, just like I'd seen. I was bursting with pride that we'd recreated our own little version of that town-wide bond.

Even from my distance at the top of the line, I could

watch the tree and boughs grow bright and colorful as they filled with the decorations. To call it lovely, or touching, was a gross understatement. It felt important. Necessary. Healing. I felt as if years from now I would still view this event as one of the most significant things I had ever done.

Even as the wind picked up and the snow began to swirl harder, every face I saw was still smiling. Finally, I watched Gavin reach into the box and hand me one of the last two ornaments. With a bit of ceremony, we passed the decorations off to the line on either side as I quietly wondered if there was still space anywhere on the branches below.

Of course there was. While I don't think there was a bare inch on any of the branches, it still looked gorgeous. One of Mom's "meant to be" moments if ever there was one. The crowd slowly followed the last ornament, the two sidewalk lines merging into one moving crowd heading toward the tree behind the final ornaments. By the time they'd made it onto the tree, most of the town was gathered around our half tree, which didn't look half at all.

Gavin and I walked over to the oversized lever the theater tech crew had set up. Frank and Angie stood there as Mr. and Mrs. Claus—ready to throw the switch.

"Three, two, one . . ." Collinstown's newest couple—well, maybe second-newest couple—pulled the lever, and the tree glowed with a stunning array of brilliant, twinkling lights. Everyone cheered—even George. Christmas Eve was tomorrow night, but I found myself stumped for how we'd ever top this. This felt like Christmas, New Year's, Valentine's Day, the Fourth of July, and every other holiday wrapped into one.

As the glow of the tree lit the faces of everyone around, I caught sight of Jillian. She stood with Brent just a few steps away, the boy's arm around her shoulders in a cautious test of teenage public affection. I knew the minute Gavin must have noticed the hold Brent had on her, for our mayor straightened and gripped my hand a bit tighter, but didn't say a word. Few things in this world are more endearing than a protective father trying hard to "be cool about it."

I caught Jillian's eye long enough to send a knowing wink, with the tiniest of nods toward both her father and Brent's arm around her.

To my amusement, Jillian returned an equally knowing wink with a similar nod at my hand in Gavin's. Her approval was so over-the-top I almost laughed. Without missing a beat, she lifted her beautiful voice and began singing, "We Wish You a Merry Christmas."

Within seconds everyone else joined in. I found myself standing in a real-life Christmas movie, catching Gavin's eye just enough to see the moment had touched him in the same way.

"Merry Christmas, Mr. Mayor."

"Merry Christmas, Libby." Gavin put his arm around me. All around the circle of Collinstowners, people hugged and smiled and sang. Angie winked and snuggled up under Frank's arm. Mom beamed, and I'd swear Hank did as well.

Two nights later, Gavin leaned back in his chair and put his hands on his stomach as we polished off the last of Christmas dinner. "I won't be able to eat for a week after this."

"Nonsense," Mom countered. "I'll be back for coffee and pie in a couple of hours. So will you."

"There's always pie for breakfast," Jillian suggested.

"Grandma Rhonda says that's practically the law the day after Christmas."

I laughed. "It is in our house. Actually, we just bring all the goodies to the shop and have a second party there."

"Are you really going to come in your pajamas, Grandma Rhonda?" Jillian asked. Mom had been threatening to show up at Y.A.R.N. in her pajamas on December 26 for years.

I ate the last of my pecan pie. "Given the wild holiday we've had, I could almost go for it. A Y.A.R.N. pj party sounds just wild enough to work."

Gavin sought to put an instant stop to such madness. "You wouldn't."

"No, I won't." Then, when he looked all too relieved, I added, "You'd have to send out an advance email for that kind of thing. Otherwise we'd be the only people in jammies. Well, us and Hank." Mom had even bought an absurd set of holiday jammies for Hank last year in an effort to convince me.

"Hank is people," Jillian declared, reaching down to pet him. "He's totally one of us."

"Who needs advance notice? It wouldn't stop me," Mom announced. "But then again, there's always New Year's Eve. Is next week enough time to pull something like that together?"

Gavin groaned. "I thought you were moving into your new place on New Year's Day."

"I most certainly can do both. No one said I had to be all unpacked the same day I move in." She sat back. "It'll be pleasantly hectic. Just my speed."

More like chaotic, if you ask me. "No thanks," I argued. "I'd like a quiet new year." I slipped my hand into Gavin's under the table. "I'm thinking we'll really get into socks next at the store." That might be the perfect way to pull

Jeanette in, and the knitting world had a whole host of great sock designers to tap into for events and classes. I may or may not have envisioned Gavin relaxing in a really stunning pair of hand-knit socks. By the fire. Next to me.

"Socks?" Jillian smirked. Perhaps my thoughts showed a bit too much in my expression.

"Yes, socks," I covered. "Nice, low-key, absolutely-not-dangerous socks. I want as uneventful a year as I can possibly manage."

"I concur," chimed in our mayor. "Efficient, quiet, productive, maybe even downright boring." I felt him squeeze my hand. "Except for maybe a few pleasant surprises."

"Nobody wants boring," Jillian said, balking.

"There's Frank and Angie's wedding," Mom offered, then added a loaded, "At least," wildly hinting that maybe theirs shouldn't be Collinstown's only big nuptial in the coming year. "Besides, where's the fun in boring?"

"I'll have to let you know," I replied, yawning. "It's been so long since I've seen boring I can't remember if it *is* any fun."

"It's not," offered Jillian. "And not that you all aren't loads of fun, but Brent should be here any minute."

As if on cue, my doorbell rang. Gavin had agreed—with no small amount of effort—to let Jillian have dessert with Brent at his parents' house. "Be home . . ."

". . . by eleven thirty. I know, Dad," Jillian said with a teasing moan as she stood up to get the door. Brent walked in with a cheery greeting to everyone, taking care to give Hank a good scratch and Gavin's hand a firm shake while addressing him as "sir."

Jillian planted a kiss on everyone's cheek—including mine—and skipped out the door to spend Christmas night with her new boyfriend.

Gavin and I walked to my front windows to watch Jillian and Brent walk down the street, arm in smitten arm. "I'm not gonna make it through this next year," he muttered.

I put my head on his solid shoulder, feeling him exhale at the contact. We were good at holding each other up, Gavin and I. "Oh yes, you are," I consoled him. "*We* are."

"How?" he moaned, sounding all too much like Jillian.

"The same way even the biggest afghan gets knit," I replied. "One stitch at a time."

ACKNOWLEDGMENTS

As it turns out, inventing fictional pharmaceuticals is a rather tricky business. I could argue that plotting mysteries is always a complicated endeavor, and certainly a great deal of fun. But I feel compelled to remind you, dear reader, that all the companies and chemicals in this novel are purely fiction. I was able to base my fictional drugs, however, in the realm of good science with the help of pharmacist Yanna Varonstova. She was a delightful brainstorming partner as I dreamed up the hows, whens, and whys of Sterling's untimely and dramatic demise. While "wonder drugs" exist to address a host of medical issues, Sonesty and its products do not exist anywhere except in my imagination.

Vicuña, thankfully, is *very* real. And loads of fun to research. Have no doubt that it is just as exquisite as I describe in the book (yes, I did spring for some—research and all). I owe many thanks to Shelley Brander and her fine team at Knit Stars for giving me access, information, and guidance in showcasing the luxurious fiber and the charming animals from which it comes. The pattern in this book is the talented work of Mitzi Thomas. As always, should you knit it (with vicuña or any of the other suggested fibers), please don't hesitate to share a photo with me.

I do love to hear from readers. You can find me at alliepleiter.com or email me at allie@alliepleiter.com. If social media is your thing, you can find me on Instagram (@alliepleiterauthor), my Facebook page (Facebook.com /alliepleiter), Twitter (@alliepleiter), Goodreads (Allie Pleiter), and BookBub (Allie Pleiter). If you're a knitter, you can also find me on Ravelry (@alliewriter).

Thanks as always to the team that keeps me up and writing: my steadfast husband, Jeff; my savvy agents, Karen Solem and Sandy Harding, at Spencerhill Associates; my capable assistant, Michelle Prima; my encouraging editor, Michelle Vega; and my trusty proofreader/fact-checker, Judy DeVries.

And, of course, to you. Thank you so very much for joining Libby and her Collinstown friends on another adventure. Stay tuned to see what Libby casts on next!

CHACU

By Mitzi Thomas

MATERIALS:

- Suggested yarn: 1 ball each of Natural and Black Amano Vicuña yarn
- *Or* approximately 164 yards each (328 total yards) of 2 contrasting fingering weight colorways (Alpaca or Alpaca blend is preferable to get a similar feel and drape, but any fiber content can work for this project)
- US 4, 24" or 32" circular needle
- 1 stitch marker for BOR (beginning of round)
- Tapestry needle for weaving in ends

GAUGE: 6 STITCHES PER INCH IN STOCKINETTE

You'll be using the helical method of knitting to create a one-row stripe with no cutting, joining, or jogging. This continuous spiral method will allow you to use all of the precious vicuña yarn and to preserve the yarn with only the beginning and end tails to weave in. The cowl looks great from either side.

Cast on 138 stitches in color A (Natural).

Join to work in the round, place BOR marker.

Continue using color A, knit 6 rounds in 1x1 rib. (K1, P1), slip marker (sm) at end of round throughout pattern. Be careful throughout the pattern not to twist the yarns as you change colors. TIP: Adjust the tension of the slipped stitches as you come to them. They may loosen as they rest.

1. With color A, knit 1 round.
2. Drop color A and pick up color B (Black), knit until 3 stitches of color A remain on the left needle.
3. Slip those 3 stitches to the right needle. Drop color B and pick up color A. Knit until 3 stitches of color B remain on the left needle.
4. Slip those 3 stitches to the right needle. Drop color A and pick up color B. Knit until 3 stitches of color A remain on the left needle.

Continue the last 2 rounds until you have used almost all of color A and can complete the round and end with color A. At the BOR marker, drop color A and pick up color B; knit one round. At BOR, knit 6 rounds of 1x1 rib in color B; bind off loosely. Lightly block and weave in ends.

Ready to find
your next great read?

Let us help.

Visit prh.com/nextread

Penguin
Random
House